Bright Lights
and
White Nights

Andrew Carter

BRIGHT LIGHTS AND WHITE NIGHTS — Struggling with the daily torture of call-centre work, Troy's mid-twenties disillusion hits its lowest ebb when his girlfriend reveals that she has been sleeping with her driving instructor. Something has to change. Troy exchanges Leeds for the bright lights of Hong Kong where he finds a flat in the infamous Wan Chai district and hopes to rekindle his dwindling enthusiasm for life. After finding a job teaching English to adults and befriending some colourful characters, it seems that moving east was an inspired decision. However, following a chance meeting with Sophie, a beautiful girl from his past, things take a disastrous turn and Troy inadvertently becomes embroiled in a debauched adventure involving the players and oddballs of Hong Kong's cocaine underworld.

ANDREW CARTER was born in Leeds in 1986. After graduating from Lancaster University in 2009, he spent two years working as a care worker for young people with disabilities. In 2011, he moved to Chengdu, China where he taught English in a secondary school. After a few months of struggling with the language barrier and the spicy food, Andrew relocated to Hong Kong where, despite a frightening lack of business knowledge, he attempted to teach corporate English to adults. Andrew is passionate about football, which is not ideal as he is not particularly good at it and suffers from the trauma of being a Leeds United fan. He also plays the guitar averagely, falls over frequently and has not yet grown out of playing computer games. Fast approaching thirty, Andrew is trying to make the transition from cheap lager to fine ale. He currently lives in Leeds.

You can email Andrew Carter at andyc1421@hotmail.co.uk or follow him on Twitter @andyc1421.

Bright Lights
and
White Nights

Andrew Carter

Proverse Hong Kong

Bright Lights and White Nights
by Andrew Carter.
Published by Proverse Hong Kong,
October 2015.
Copyright © Proverse Hong Kong, October 2015.
ISBN: 978-988-8228-03-4
Printed by Create Space.

1st published in pbk in Hong Kong by Proverse Hong Kong,
9 April 2015.
Copyright © Proverse Hong Kong, 9 April 2015.
ISBN: 978-988-8227-79-2

Enquiries to:
Proverse Hong Kong, P.O. Box 259, Tung Chung Post Office,
Tung Chung, Lantau Island, NT, Hong Kong SAR, China.
E-mail: proverse@netvigator.com; Web: www.proversepublishing.com

The right of Andrew Carter to be identified as the author of this work
has been asserted by him
in accordance with the Copyright, Designs and Patents Act 1988.

Page design by Proverse Hong Kong.
Cover design by Marcus Fox.
Cover image by and courtesy of Lee Butcher.

British Library Cataloguing in Publication Data.
A catalogue record for this book is available
from the British Library.

For Louise

Author's Acknowledgements

I'd like to thank Louise for her encouragement and advice. I'm also thankful to my brother, John, for first suggesting that I 'had a book in me' a few years ago. Also, thank you to my mum and dad.

Thanks to Gillian Bickley and Proverse Hong Kong for agreeing to publish my book and being extremely supportive with editing and marketing.

I'm grateful to Luke Menzer, Marcus Fox and Lee Butcher for their help and ideas with my cover design and Steven Dawson for his honest and insightful feedback.

Finally a big thanks to the following for giving me some great memories and providing me with the inspiration to write a story; everyone in my family, all of my pals in Leeds, Lancaster and Hong Kong, staff and students at Wall Street English school and everyone at Corinthians Football Club.

CHAPTER ONE

Forty-three days after Imogen told me that she'd been sleeping with her driving instructor, I was on a one-way flight to Hong Kong. Although the cuckolding was undeniably the catalyst for my move, there were other, not-quite-as-heartbreaking, contributing factors. Since arriving in my mid-twenties, my growing sense of directionlessness had become overbearing and I had no idea what the hell I was doing. Until I'd graduated from university with crippling debts and a barely (maybe even less-than?) worthwhile, third in Sociology, the middle-class expectation of school, college, university, job had been mapped out for me. When it dawned on me that university is the last stop on the expensive, heavily subsidized train, I wasn't quite ready to be on my own and was surprised at just how bad I was at fending for myself. I tried to drift along until I discovered what I wanted to do but in hindsight, I was living in a fantasy world where I assumed that at some point in the near future, I would drift into a well-paid job that I enjoyed. Unfortunately I had, and still have, no idea what this dream job is.

After university, Imogen had reluctantly agreed to move to Leeds, my hometown. Her preferred choice was London where she would have been closer to her family in Reading and quite rightly argued that there were more opportunities in her designated career, which had something to do with marketing I think. Prone to making rash decisions, Imogen insisted that we move into the first house that we looked at; a damp box-room in a shared terrace house which had a living-room without heating and a kitchen that attracted slugs. Our housemates were a bearded Bulgarian man who owned a Samurai sword, a wild-haired evangelical Christian girl who was six foot one and looked at me with a smile that said, "I'm nice and don't judge anyone because of my faith. . . but you are destined for hell," and a man from Bradford who didn't turn the volume down when he was watching PornHub videos and smoked too much weed.

After moving in together, Imogen and I landed similarly crap jobs from the same temping agency. Like all fresh graduates, we were both unjustly arrogant in regard to employability and believed ourselves to be better than the menial, low-paid work that we landed following a typing test and an interview with a fidgety recruitment consultant called Leo, who unashamedly wore foundation. Instead of excitement at starting our adult lives together, there was an overwhelming feeling of, "Is this it?"

The monotony of work and paying bills with earned cash rather than the free money that student loan companies chuck at you isn't much fun. (I am fully aware that this complaint doesn't warrant sympathy.) We had spent nearly a year treading water – in the vicious circle of blasting most of our wages on alcohol to forget about the drudging hours spent earning them – when the atmosphere in our house became increasingly hostile. All of a sudden, (or more realistically, after months of slandering us behind our backs) the other occupants grew spiteful that we were paying less rent than them because we were sharing a room. Somewhat unfairly, they didn't broach the subject with Imogen and seemed to blame me entirely for an arrangement that everyone had shook hands on, and smilingly agreed to, when we'd first moved in. The culmination was a disastrous "house meeting" (whenever these things are given names, they are destined to be awful) where the Bulgarian added to the general feeling of disdain towards me by publicly – wrongly – accusing me of stealing his expensive sausages.

One week after the house meeting, at five thirty-six on a Tuesday evening, my recent struggles escalated into a depressing, yet probably predictable, crescendo as Imogen told me, with an agonizing nonchalance, that I'd been usurped by an overweight, thirty-four-year-old BSM employee who'd cheerily waved at me when he'd picked her up the previous weekend. Although suitably devastated, I actually felt a small measure of euphoric relief that the grim chapter of my life was over.

With nowhere else to go, I took the classic backwards step and temporarily moved back to my dad's house. My parents had split up when I was twelve and whereas my mother, who worked for the City Council, had moved in with a new man a few years after the separation, my dad, a retired teacher, had found companionship in Sheldrick, a German shepherd. Although he was welcoming of my humble return, I felt like a third wheel between him and the hound and he made it quite clear that it was a temporary solution. I reverted to my teenage years, listened to Pearl Jam a lot, wallowed in depression and considered my next move.

*

A month into my despair and in a worrying, nightly habit of eating entire packs of Jammie Dodgers and washing them down with cans of Skol, I received an email from an amiable but vulgar Glaswegian pal. He had spent the last two years living in Shanghai and boastfully told me what a wonderful time he was having. As a result, I decided that moving abroad was the answer to my woes. I spent an afternoon on the internet in the local library where my plans fluctuated wildly. At two o'clock I had almost signed up for a TEFL program in Honduras and two hours later I'd convinced myself that, despite being a very average player, being a football coach in Ghana was the way forward.

Half an hour before the library shut (I'd been strictly informed of this by a Neanderthal looking worker furiously pointing at an imaginary watch on his wrist), I found myself flicking through pictures of Hong Kong's Victoria Harbour and decided that it looked excellent. Feeling a sudden surge of adrenaline, I excitedly researched more. Although fairly sure that the type of people who write long passages and say, "life-changing!" and "I found myself!" on travel forums are people that I wouldn't like, I was swayed by the abundance of positivity towards Hong Kong. Everyone seemed to love it. The forums also informed me that it was relatively easy to find a job and that most people spoke some level of English.

The move qualified as being spontaneous, a word I don't often associate with myself. Within a week of hearing from my Scottish friend, I'd quit my job (one of the few perks of being a temp is the five-day notice period) and booked a flight by dipping heavily back into the NatWest overdraft that I'd recently cleared. I had eight hundred and nineteen pounds left which I thought would be enough to see me through until I found work. I figured that getting a job and a place to live would sort itself out, which was ambitious given my recent struggles with work and accommodation in my own country.

The decision stirred a mixed response from my friends, some of whom thought, "fair enough, good luck," and others who saw it as running away from the reality of cold weather and working life, which is exactly what it was. At my leaving do, a tattooed colleague condemned my move abroad, calling me a "deserter." I gently reminded him that I wasn't absconding from the army, to which he responded, "Well, whatever you are, you're running away from real life." Due to his tendency for occasional violence, I didn't challenge him again. However, I actually find this "real life" conundrum annoying. Why does "real life" have to be shit? If real life is waking up freezing cold at six forty-five, trudging through the rain past saucer-eyed students returning from nights out, getting on a bus with people who smell of nicotine and depression, worrying about swiping my card a minute late, at a job which I despise, to try to save up for a mortgage on an undesirable house at a rough end of Leeds, then count me out. For now, anyway.

CHAPTER TWO

I arrived at Hong Kong late afternoon on a Friday feeling grubby and jaded after securing fewer than three hours sleep in thirty hours during two flights where after twenty-nine tries, I had finally but not without controversy, beaten the in-flight entertainment at Chess on level seven difficulty. The victory was tainted as I'd undone a move which would have led to him (does in-flight entertainment have a gender?) winning. After long haul flights, my facial hair and finger nails seem to grow worryingly faster than usual and my breath is tragic, meaning that my aim for a fresh start was dented by entering my new city of residence feeling like a grubby homo sapiens.

I walked through the plush, shiny airport that had air conditioning on uncomfortably high, picked up my spectacularly effeminate, fuchsia suitcase and took the first taxi I was offered by a grinning, buck-toothed man who had a mole on his cheek with two long grey hairs sprouting out of it. No matter how tired you are, the taxi ride from the airport is always a time of child-like excitement and optimism. I stared wide-eyed through the window as we buzzed past a colossal shipping yard, over an emphatic bridge and then into a land of bright lights, skyscrapers, beeping horns and Chinese people – lots of Chinese people. I don't know what I'd been expecting but this came as a shock.

After nearly an hour, the taxi pulled up abruptly on bustling Nathan Road where fortunately my taxi driver turned out to be not only hairy, but also honest. In my fatigued state and having not really paid attention to a five minute spell on a currency exchange website, I tried to pay him a thousand dollars for a hundred dollar fare. A cool eighty quid would have been a pricey start to my adventure so I appreciated the old man giving it back to me. There was definitely a moment where he considered exploiting my stupidity but thankfully his morals overruled.

Out of the taxi with a good first impression of the locals and a lessened opinion of myself, I noticed that I was actually far from the only foreign face and there were people from a host of ethnicities milling around in the constantly diverging crowds. This included a smiling Indian man wearing a mid-nineties Real Madrid shirt who politely / aggressively insisted on helping me with my bags. Having already nearly ballsed up with the taxi and not wanting to get done over within my first hour in Hong Kong, I assured him that I was capable of carrying a single suitcase on my own. His next move was to speak in increasingly hushed tones and ask if I wanted, "a watch, a suit, weed or cocaine." I respectfully declined.

It was getting dark by the time I arrived and I could see the neon lights of Hong Kong Island glistening across the water. Exhaustion overcame my desire to explore and I checked in to the accommodation that I had booked two days previously – Apple Hostel, in the Chung King Mansion, Hong Kong's grimiest corner.

I hate hostels. Sharing a room with a bunch of sweaty strangers is bearable for a couple of days but I was likely to be here for a while. I got my key from a grumpy teenage receptionist, dumped my suitcase in the corner and clambered onto a stained mattress on the bottom tier of a rickety bunk bed in an eight-man dormitory that had clothes and bags strewn across the floor and smelt of energy drinks. I soon drifted into a deep sleep but was awakened by the sound of a European man, who was probably too old to be a "backpacker" (I think thirty-two is the cut-off for backpackers. After that you start thinking: Stop pissing around and get a job, you should have found yourself by now) shuffling around in the bed above. When I naively looked up to see what he was doing, he slammed down the cover of his laptop, put his head down and pretended to be sleeping. A poor cover.

I struggled to sleep after that, feeling anxious, my scattered train of thought constantly returning to the lyrics of an irritating Avril Lavigne song that I must have heard at some point during the day. I gave up on the notion of a good night's sleep and got up at half six, took a shower and with an instant coffee from the Seven Eleven as my fuel, headed out to explore Hong Kong. It was a sunny, humid morning and despite the early hour, there were plenty of people starting their daily grind – businessmen, street vendors, pyjama-clad ladies carrying baskets of fruit, elderly folk pushing rickety trolleys, carrying giant piles of cardboard and portly, tattooed workmen strolling around topless and smoking.

Outside of the detritus of Apple hostel, my first impressions of the city were good. With the wanking Dutchman ordeal a distant memory, I took the Star Ferry to Wan Chai, and was blown away by my first look at Victoria Harbour. Seeing the hundreds of colossal skyscrapers stretching across the island was mesmerizing. With the bright glare of the sun reflecting off the shiny skyscrapers and into the shimmering water, my heart started to pound with excitement and to use a well-worn phrase, I felt the hairs on my neck stand up. It gave me a smug satisfaction to know that this gotham city-esque metropolis was going to be my new home.

I aimlessly wandered around Wan Chai and found myself in a crowded Pacific Coffee shop on Lockhart Road where I ate a dry sausage roll and watched the day unfold. Wan Chai is a bustling, lively hub with bright lights, high rise buildings and a mixture of pleasant and decidedly unpleasant smells. Lining the streets are innumerable signs of varying shapes and sizes jutting out of the sides of the buildings advertising ageing strip-joints and twenty-four-hour clubs, each competing with one another to get your attention. I don't like the phrase "people watching" – it suggests that you think you are above everyone else and is always used in annoying travel guides, but if you're going to do it, Wan Chai is probably one of the better places to choose. I sat and watched a bizarre contrast between last night's aftermath and the new day starting, with smatterings of drunken Westerners stumbling out of doors and onto the street, squinting in the morning light and amalgamating with sharp-suited locals, ignoring their existence, talking on smart-phones as they headed to work.

It was going to take a while to get the hang of Hong Kong.

After finishing my sausage roll, I decided to go shopping. Given my lack of money, work or place to live, this was probably not a pressing issue. However, I wanted to consolidate my fresh start and saw changing my appearance as being of paramount importance. On arriving in Hong Kong, I rated myself, perhaps over-critically, as a five out of ten. My modest self-esteem levels have certainly been influenced by my mother's inexplicable decision to name me after Greek mythology. During an alarming, at times painful, growth spurt in my teens I'd rocketed to six foot two but I have never managed to fill out my tall frame, becoming used to ill-favoured terms such as "lanky" and "gangly." I don't go, and never have gone to the gym for the simple reason that I really don't enjoy it. It's not fun. Perhaps if I had been single over the past few years, I might have done so, but I'd had a girlfriend, so becoming more aesthetically pleasing to females wasn't a priority. Also, there has never been a point where being stronger and more muscular would particularly benefit me – my lifestyle has never required any heavy lifting. When you turn twenty-four it seems that everyone loves the gym. In recent times, whenever I see my friends, it is probable that they will be in possession of a protein shake.

My face is neither pleasant nor unpleasant – just an elongated man's face with pale blue eyes and with a few wrinkles forming around them, which I actually quite like because they might trick women into thinking that I'm more intelligent than I am. Due to my build and too-long face, being compared to the well-known English footballer Peter Crouch is like water off a duck's back. On one occasion in 2007, however, a girl on drugs told me that I look a bit like the American pop-star Justin Timberlake, which I still dwell on with pleasure.

My hair is a dark blond (preferable to mousy brown) and seems to be constantly stuck at the awkward stage – not sure whether to be put up at the front, or into a side parting. As the first part of my Hong Kong reinvention, I'd got a twenty pound haircut the day before I left. Spurred on by Beckham's latest do, I'd opted to go for a short back and sides and spiked up at the front but the barber had cut it too short which drew unwanted attention to my small, but sticky-out ears. For the past year, I'd been going for a rugged stubble look which I never really pulled off. The stubble was, at least, multi-purpose, acting as a useful alternative to fingernails when scratching itches on my upper body. I opted to approach Hong Kong clean shaven, with the aim of appearing smarter, classier and more mature.

Despite several attempts over the years to become a fashionable man, I've never managed to quite get it right. Being tall and thin doesn't help matters. Like most men in their twenties, I do have a "going out" outfit of a well-fitting shirt, smart jacket, a nice pair of chinos (inspired by Dawson Leary) and some trendy pointy shoes but I've worn it so much that I no longer get the, "I look good tonight" spring in my step. In general, most expensive shirts I buy never quite fit right. They always seem to be too big and baggy so I look like a teenager who has borrowed his dad's shirt to try to get into a nightclub. Any T-shirts I buy from the H&Ms and Top Shops of this world almost invariably tend to shrink within one wash, ride up my back and become way too short in the sleeves, revealing too much of my spindly biceps. I always find myself indecisive in the jeans department – a brief flirtation with skinny jeans was brought to an abrupt halt when a friend whom I don't really like called me Peter Crouch in Pete Doherty's clothing the one and only time I wore them.

Anyway, such faux pas were to be forgotten. I walked the twenty minutes to Causeway Bay, where the rent for shop space is the most expensive in the world, and during a ruthless two hour blitz, fought through the obscenely busy crowds, made sizeable dents in my credit card and bought: six T-shirts – two expensive numbers and some cheap backups, four new pairs of jeans – one pair skinny (my friends weren't here to judge), one pair of real CK boxers, and six pairs of fakes, a pair of trendy checkered shorts and – despite not having a job – three "work" shirts. Putting on new boxers and a fresh, new-smelling T-shirt bred confidence. I left my spree feeling exhausted but happy, buoyed by excitement at my fresh start.

*

After the shopping spree, things started to move quickly. The following day I found somewhere to live. I went with the first estate agent I met – a greasy but agreeable local called Kenneth who was a Lynx Africa-wearing middle-aged man with decent sales English but a poor grasp of the language in any other sense. He answered the majority of my questions with, "can" or "cannot" which took a while to adjust to.

"Do I have to pay two months deposit for this one?"

"Can."

"Does the flat come with furniture Kenneth?"

"Cannot."

"Will the hole in the wall be fixed before I move in?"

"Cannot."

On a Friday afternoon he showed me two pokey flats in North Point – one of which was currently missing a toilet – a decent sized effort in Causeway Bay that was nice but nearly twice my budget, then finally, a tiny but well-situated place on Jaffe Road in Wan Chai.

I opted for Wan Chai as, despite its obvious dodgy-ness, it's one of the most convenient places for a foreigner to live. You have everything you want on your doorstep; most people in the district can speak some level of English and there is the option of vices should you fancy letting your hair down: as I'd witnessed the previous morning, plenty of pubs, all-night bars, strip clubs, massage parlors and prostitutes. Just to clarify, this is merely coincidental and not the reason I chose to move to Wan Chai. I have never slept with a prostitute and I don't think I ever will. If you do it once then you are forever condemned to the category of men that have paid for sex. Once or on a thousand times, you are in the same category and I've made the conscious decision not to join. That said, I don't feel really strongly about it and slam my fist on pub tables, veins pumping out of my head as I aggressively voice my opinions about sexual equality and the objectification of women. It would be annoying if I did. I don't dislike all men that do sleep with prostitutes – in many situations it's probably a reasonable option which works well for both parties so who am I to judge? After all, prostitution is the oldest profession in the world. (That is one of those chronically overused bits of trivia. You see people's eyes light up when the opportunity to say it crops up. It's in a similar vein to, "Do you know that you eat over one hundred spiders in your lifetime?")

As the price of rent is astronomical in Hong Kong, Kenneth had lined the pockets of his too-tight black corduroys by helping me to move into a tiny bed-sit of a flat on the 21st floor of an old tower-block. Instead of "tiny bed-sit" the Hong Kongers call them "serviced apartments" which sounds misleadingly more pleasant. Kenneth cheerily informed me that a "top class" cleaner would sort out my flat twice a week. The day I moved in I noticed that there were flies buzzing around in my bathroom so I was unsure if Kenneth's description of her abilities was accurate. My plan was to stay in the flat for a few weeks, possibly months until I got myself sorted, at which point I would start to rent a *proper* flat somewhere else.

Apart from the first day when the cleaner had covered the place with cheap bleach and disinfectant, I was hit by a musty, damp smell when I entered my flat, which I decided I would counter by purchasing – for the first time since the teenage Bob Marley phase – some scented joss sticks. Questionable. The grand tour didn't take long. A living-room, which was also a bedroom, complete with a slightly less than double double-bed with a hard, but surprisingly comfortable mattress, no kitchen – a temperamental microwave, sink and small fridge probably don't even equate to a kitchenette but it just about did a job – and the classic, Asian style "wet room" which was for the toilet and shower. If feeling lazy, it was possible to use the toilet and shower, while using the sink to brush your teeth, all at the same time. I'd be lying if I said I didn't successfully prove this hypothesis within my first hour in the flat.

As with anywhere on Hong Kong Island, it was noisy. Surrounded by busy roads, there was a constant buzz of traffic and idiots impatiently beeping their horns outside. Something else that Kenneth neglected to tell me was that the man in the flat directly above had an infuriating DIY habit, clattering about and drilling, seemingly directly into my skull, for most waking hours.

I considered making the flat more homely and personal, flirting with the idea of buying a trendy painting, a plant, or some bean-bags. (Do people actually sit on beanbags?) After deliberating for a while but knowing deep down that I wasn't going to bother, I decided against any sort of home improvement and decided to live with my shabby white box. I wasn't going to be here for long so there seemed little point. Basically I am lazy and unimaginative. I had got my PlayStation 3 with FIFA though. So that overruled everything.

*

There is a good mix of local Hong Kong folk and foreigners or "forinjers" – locals can't pronounce it properly – in Wan Chai. Amongst these forinjers, or gweilos (slightly more offensive than mispronunciation, meaning "ghost person") are a highly disproportionate number of middle-aged English men who are escaping ex-wives and ugly financial situations back home and enjoying cheap beer and the attention of attractive Filipinos.

It is a perfect example of the overused description of Hong Kong being where the East meets the West. You can have a McDonalds then head to a pub called the Queen Victoria to watch a Premiership football match, but on the way you'll see Chinese street-food stalls selling god knows what, elderly women wearing pyjamas burning incense and monks strolling along the street. (There are countless phony monks who ask you for charitable donations. Excited and naïve, when I first encountered a monk I gave him fifty dollars as my good deed for the day. An hour later, I saw him and a group of other "monks" sitting in a park drinking beer, smoking and watching a horse race on an I-phone.)

Something that was going to take a while to adjust to was the sheer number of people in the area. In fact, this wasn't exclusive to Wan Chai but pretty much all of Hong Kong. There are just far too many people; there are loads of people everywhere, all the time. It's frustrating. Especially if you are rushing to get somewhere and there are hundreds of people in front of you walking at the pace of a dying rat. Hong Kong is thought of as a fast-paced city but this is not reflected by the walking speed of the locals, who saunter around showing no urgency whatsoever. Many of the slow walkers have additional irritating behaviour, such as having their eyes glued to an I-phone ("Are I-phones making the world worse? Discuss…"), having zero awareness of their surroundings, and perhaps most infuriatingly, stopping suddenly, with no warning or deceleration, causing a reasonably-paced walker such as myself to plough straight into them. Crashing into people was never an issue in Leeds but it happens daily in Hong Kong. It's hell.

CHAPTER THREE

Two weeks after getting my new pad and for all the glitz and glamour of settling into such a renowned world city, I was unfortunately hampered by a shopping-spree-induced lack of finances and the increasingly pressing issue of finding a job. While I was pleased that I'd found somewhere to live, I hadn't had any luck with employment. All I wanted was a job that paid for my rent and living costs that I didn't hate – surely not too narrow a specification?

My expectations of work and working life have become more realistic over the last few years and I was aware that I would probably not find a job that I loved or even particularly liked. I couldn't have less of an idea as to what I want to do for a long term career. I have no discernible skills and the few things I'm passionate about (the usual – football, music, films etc.) are, due to limited talent, unlikely to lead to a glorious celebrity career. How do people decide what they want to do? Or do you just wake up one day, with a pregnant wife whom you're not sure you love and whatever job you are in at that point has become your career?

While at university, I'd contemplated applying to do a PGCE but decided against it as – consistent with the cliché – the only reason I was considering teaching was because I couldn't think of anything else. Over the last couple of years, with people approaching their daunting late twenties and struggling to find a better-than-terrible career, there had been a huge influx of old schoolmates and university acquaintances who'd become teachers. This is fine and good for them – worthwhile work, good holidays etc. However, most of them seemed to spend so much time moaning on Facebook that I was unsure how they found the time to teach.

I tried hard to find inspiration but found only mouse mats and free stationery at careers fares where I sought advice from the campus advisors but to no avail. There is an irony that people who work as careers advisors don't want to be doing it and don't know what they want to do with their own lives. They probably become teachers.

Through desperation, at the final fair I went to, I had a long chat with a muscular, charming Royal Marine and decided, for about four minutes, that I had found my chosen path. I would have been a truly dreadful marine. I had a similar epiphany when I found out that you could earn good money working on an oil-rig. I was reading the pamphlet through blinkers, only focusing on the potential forty grand starting wages, overlooking the extremely tough physical labour, long hours and spending months at a time at sea with only men.

My oil-rig phase outlasted my plans to join the marines by about ten minutes before I saw sense and found myself trawling back to the HSBC tent to see what opportunities there were for a man who would be lucky to secure a 2.2 in Sociology. Even the bright-eyed, badge-wearing bank employees didn't give me the assurances I was after and I found myself about to graduate with fewer ideas about my career path than I'd ever had.

Despite the nature of the job, I classify the call centre job as my first "proper" job by the definition that I had to wear a tie and had to be at work for forty hours a week.

It was woeful.

My role was officially "Customer Services Officer" but this is misleading and overplays my skill-set. My one and only job was to ask people three security questions. If they got two of them correct they could be passed on to somebody else, somebody more important, who could actually discuss their bank account – somebody qualified to tell them their balance or even cancel a standing order.

"Where did you open the account?"

"What's your mother's maiden name?"

"When was the last time you withdrew money?"

All day.

My plight wasn't helped by the fact that my pungently perfumed team leader Carol seemed to despise me for reasons unknown. Carol had recently landed a promotion from her dubiously-titled previous role as "floor walker" and was revelling in the new-found power, flaunting her success with a dramatic change of hairstyle, a range of expensive new blouses and a visible enjoyment at making my life hell by criticising me for failing to hit the startlingly unrealistic targets that she set. Hitting targets in an inbound call centre is, in essence, completely stupid. How can you control how many people call you?

The only relief was my lunchtimes spent with Naveen, an odd middle-aged colleague. Although I made it subtly clear that I wasn't really interested, his only topic of conversation was cars – especially his car which had recently had alloy wheels fitted. Despite blatant attempts to make the place cheerier with lurid colour schemes, TV screens playing BBC News 24 all day (which we weren't allowed to watch during calls, making their existence fairly pointless), posters of attractive, smiling customers and – most depressingly – the personalization of desks by veteran colleagues with flowers, family photos and soft toys, there remained a strong, underlying sense of misery and failed dreams.

Prior to this I did the usual stuff that teenagers and students do. Here's a brief job history in chronological order with a more realistic summary than on my CV, which I've realized after two futile years should definitely not be in "Comic Sans" font.

- *Paper round.* (It took me until I was twenty two to realize that this didn't deserve a third of the space on my CV.) The rite of passage for all twelve to fourteen-year-old boys and it was actually considered quite cool amongst peers to be a paper boy. What wasn't cool was doing a Sunday round where all the papers had their bastard supplements to carry, so weighed an ungodly amount. So heavy in fact that a bike was rendered useless as you couldn't carry it over your shoulder and had to walk. Doing this in January, in the North of England, was hard labour. I eventually got asked to leave / was sacked when, after number of complaints, and a tip off from a snide, informant girl who worked the Monday round, they found out that I'd dumped a bunch of papers in a nearby bin. Following some basic calculations, I worked out that my wages were one pound and ten pence an hour.

- *Jack Fulton's Frozen Food.* This represented a solid salary increase as my starting package was two pounds and a penny an hour. It was a Saturday job which entailed a man chucking boxes of frozen food at me from a truck that I had to catch and take to a storeroom that was an irritatingly, illogically, long distance away. I was never truly respected by the delivery man as my regional accent isn't particularly strong so he assumed I was posh. This was probably why he chucked the heavy boxes with extreme force, while scowling. A vivid memory is that during one shift he chopped his finger off in the truck door. Pretty horrendous.

- *Subway.* I enjoyed this job. It was OK. The perks were, that if I gave free sandwiches to pals, they would reimburse me with beer at the pub later. A highlight was closing the shop early and crafting a giant bagel using four pieces of bread moulded together then putting every ingredient inside it. It didn't taste much, but what a sight. A lowlight was that every Sunday I worked with a violent thug a couple of years older, who had mugged my friends and me a few years before. The topic was never mentioned by me or him, but we both knew.

So, not blessed with a wealth of experience, I was hoping for a slice of fortune in my Hong Kong job search. Since arriving, I'd spent hours trawling through job websites (the ones where you kid yourself that you have a chance of getting employment because you have done "quick apply" for over a hundred jobs) first on Apple hostel's and then my new apartment's infuriatingly slow internet.

The positions that I thought I might have a chance of getting were either in recruitment or teaching. There was an abundance of jobs in both fields. There are always lots of jobs in recruitment which I find confusing. If there are so many recruitment consultants, why is it so difficult to get a job? Who are they recruiting, more recruitment consultants? I don't actually know what a recruitment consultant does, which was probably reflected in my sub-standard answers on application forms. I spent a whole day (over two hours), filling out arduous forms – or more specifically completing one, then copying and pasting the answers and tailoring them to the differently worded questions – but got no luck.

I was disappointed that there was no space for a man who was so many different positive adjectives: confident, experienced, loyal, committed, hard-working, passionate. Who wouldn't want such a man working for them? Or, does every applicant for every job ever possess similar skills? Having got either no response, or the generic, "After considering your application...." Knock-backs from four recruitment places, I decided to focus solely on becoming a teacher, which I'd been told by an arrogant cousin, who had spent a year in Hong Kong before university, was "a piece of piss."

I fired my CV off (a CV is always "fired off" as opposed to "sent" – you're more confident it will succeed) to what seemed like each and every school, kindergarten and language centre in Hong Kong. I had two unsuccessful interviews. At the first one,

Rainbow Tots, I turned up in a new shirt and shoes but then felt suitably daft when the interviewer rolled up wearing shorts and flip-flops and the questioning took place on a small plastic chair in the middle of a room with solar system mobiles floating uncomfortably close to my head while chubby, snot-covered, Chinese kids crawled around my feet.

The second interview was with a sharply dressed, middle-aged recruitment agent, who intrinsically told me every detail about Hong Kong's Education system. It seemed a bit more like it until he told me that the current available position was, again, in a kindergarten, then told me to do an impromptu ten minute class with him pretending to be a baby. He pretended to cry at one point. Seeing the failed interviews as damaging learning experiences, I fortunately found success on my third interview at an apparently renowned, yet terribly named, adults language centre called Super English.

After struggling with a hastily hand-drawn map, I eventually found Super English located on the nineteenth floor of a rundown industrial building in Kwun Tong. Despite the shabbiness of the building, the school itself was a shiny modern effort, smelling new but let down by a vile wallpaper colour-scheme of bright white, slime green and orangey brown. On entering, I was met by an unmanned, semi-circular reception desk. Adjacent were a number of tables and white plastic chairs scattered about in no particular order on a shiny wooden floor. There was a coffee machine which had an "out of order" sign hanging from the front. The paper sign was browning and the text was faded suggesting that the school had been out of caffeine supplies for some time.

Beyond reception and the miscellaneous seating area, the torso of the school was subdivided into six square, clear-glass segments, which I presumed to be classrooms. Inexplicably there were a number of toy musical instruments sporadically hung from the ceiling around the school. I recognized one of the toys as a real ukulele. It seemed something of a waste to use it for ornamental purposes. That said, people who play the ukulele tend to be pretentious, grinning idiots so at least it was being kept away from them.

Just past the glass-walled classrooms was a small computer area where two Chinese women of indeterminate age were reciting broken English into the microphones of their headsets. At this point, they were the only other people in the building. One of the women looked at me, so I smiled. In response, she looked scared and quickly jerked her head back to her computer screen.

Not knowing what to do, I stood uneasily by the reception area, got out my phone and checked through my inbox which currently had two messages – both from my network provider – welcoming, and rather over-excitedly "congratulating" me on signing up with them.

After two minutes, my mindless phone activity was interrupted by the entrance of a small but muscular Chinese man with longish hair combed into a nineties boy-band-style centre parting. He introduced himself, with a slight Australian accent, as Kit, and despite the hours he presumably spent in a gym, offered me a feeble, limp-wristed handshake.

He apologized for keeping me waiting then beckoned me into one of the square rooms. He seemed more nervous than I did. Once it was established that I could indeed speak English, the interview was fairly simple. After a few standard questions which I answered confidently with internet-advised buzzwords, the questioning soon took an informal tone and after ten minutes, I was offered the position.

My delight at securing a job was swiftly replaced with dismay when Kit told me how it would take at least four weeks to process my visa. I should probably have known this but didn't and hadn't prepared for it financially. I congratulated myself with a Tsingtao beer when I arrived home but the joy was tainted by worrying what on earth I was going to do for the next four weeks with no money.

Inevitably, I had to make a humbling phone-call home to my mother, who didn't seem too surprised or annoyed at my latest shortcomings, and agreed to help me out until the first paycheck. I think she quite enjoyed the opportunity still to be looking after her son, who was comfortably too old still to be tapping her for cash. You should probably stop sponging off your parents at twenty-one, not twenty-six. She ended the phone-call with a light-hearted, yet also self-congratulating, "What would you do without me?"

CHAPTER FOUR

The visa waiting time gave me an opportunity to explore Hong Kong some more. I took trips to Hong Kong's guidebook tourist sites – the Peak, Mong Kok Ladies' Market and Stanley – with varying success. I didn't really know what to do when I arrived at the Peak. The view was undeniably marvelous but I didn't have a camera or anyone to talk to. I missed the stupid things you say to people when you see a famous sight, "Wow. Can you see that?" (It's unlikely you'd be facing the other way.) After twenty minutes of shuffling through crowds and taking a photo of a smiling Chinese couple who seemed pleasant before telling me the photo was "no good" and I needed to take it again – twice, I turned and rather sadly ambled back down to the taxi-rank.

In the taxi, which smelt worryingly of cheap whisky, I decided, in a flash of determination, that I needed to do something to get out and meet people. Aside from job interviews, the only conversations I'd had were during the exchange of money for food items at cafés and Seven Elevens. It was starting to become startlingly apparent that I didn't know anybody. I was starting from scratch. I was going to have to be pro-active and actually look for friends. How does a twenty-six-year-old man look for friends?

In the past when I've been traveling or on holiday, I've been perfectly content without making friends. I find that the, "How long have you been traveling?" "Where are you going next?" "Have you learnt the lingo?" sort of conversation quickly becomes boring, tiresome and slightly depressing – conversations for the sake of being sociable when much of the time the people asking the questions don't really care about your answers and only want an excuse to talk in depth about their own worldly adventures and show off their irksome, Rosetta-Stone Spanish on you. Another particular gripe with travel friends is when people, usually girls, insist on showing you their travel journal. Photos, I can just about deal with, but when a girl shows me a crumpled bus ticket that she got four years ago in Peru, I couldn't be less interested.

My previous stints abroad had been spent with friends or my then girlfriend, so aggressive sociability wasn't necessary. My attitude had to change, otherwise I was soon going to get sick of my own, fairly average company. I was going to have to eat some humble-pie, go out and actually make an effort to get to know people. I was going to be "that man" – the man who is in a foreign country alone and clearly desperate for company – the man who looks for any hint of an olive branch to invite himself into other people's lives.

After returning home, I showered, put on a new T-shirt, khaki shorts and flip-flops and went out to a nearby internet café which was usually frequented by foreigners. I had no reason to be checking the internet. It was my façade. As I was scrolling through the BBC Football gossip column, a tall, wiry man of similar age to me came and sat down at the computer next to me. I started to sweat. I felt nervous. I bit the bullet.

"Alright mate," was the best I could manage.

"Alright," the man answered not looking away from his computer screen which was struggling to open his Facebook account.

Silence.

We didn't talk for the next two minutes.

"For fuck's sake," the man finally said. "These computers are shit."

An opening.

"I'm nearly done. Do you want to use mine?" I asked the man.

"That'd be great. Cheers," he said. Then, "I'm Adam," and offered an outstretched hand.

From that point, it wasn't too bad. Once the initial ice had been cracked, I remembered that talking to a man was actually relatively easy. We talked for ten minutes. Adam was twenty-five and from York. He was in a similar boat to me; he had just moved to Hong Kong and was starting a teaching job soon. He was in a slightly more secure boat though, as his school was paying for him to live in a luxury (by Hong Kong standards; pokey by Leeds standards) apartment in Central. We arranged to go out for a drink that evening and I was pleased.

At nine o'clock, we met at the Seven Eleven and strolled to Carnegies bar on Lockhart Road. During the five minute walk, it seemed as though Adam and I were destined to get on famously. He seemed like a decent, normal man and small talk ran smoothly. However, upon getting to the empty bar which smelt of urinal soaps, things took a turn. Adam ordered a coke. He was teetotal. This sounds pathetic but it put me on edge. I'm not one of those dreadful people who brag about how much they drink with a militant precision ("I had seven pints, four tequilas and two Sambucas last night!") but I am a man and I enjoy drinking beer.

Should I ask him why or would that bring to the surface a horror story of a drunkard, abusive relative? Maybe he just didn't like drinking? This is sad but my opinion of a man changes when he says he is teetotal. Similarly to when you meet someone who tells you five minutes into meeting them, unasked and with great pride that they are in a long-term relationship. While I certainly don't think less of the teetotalers and long-term relationship boasters as people, I do question how exciting the night ahead is going to be.

Despite the lack of drinking, there were many reasons why Adam and I should have got on. We were from the same part of the world, of similar age, starting a new life in Hong Kong – we were at the beginning of a new adventure.

But it just didn't work.

Sometimes with a man, you can't put your finger on it but it just doesn't click. There were too many silences. I found myself not knowing where to look and filling silences by nodding and examining my beer bottle. It was a normal Corona bottle – there was nothing worth examining. When the silent spells finished, we tried to resume conversation at the same time, talking over each other clumsily. Things I said sarcastically, he took seriously. At times, I couldn't work out if he was joking or not. He supported Man United.

After half an hour, I found myself having *nothing* to say and Adam seemed to be the same. It was tragic.

In a bid to resurrect our new-found friendship from its spectacularly dying embers, Adam took out his I-phone and said, "Have you seen this video?" and showed me the YouTube clip of the talking dog. I'd seen it before, and while it is undeniably amusing, I found myself laughing exaggeratedly and pretending it was the first time I'd seen it. I was already being dishonest. It just wasn't happening. I didn't dislike him, he didn't dislike me but it just wasn't happening. We weren't going to be friends.

*

In a similar vein to trying to pull a girl on a night out, I eventually made my first Hong Kong friend when I wasn't actively looking for one. Two days later and still feeling disheartened by the Adam failure, I met a twenty-eight-year-old Danish man called Sander. Our paths crossed on a ferry-ride to Lamma Island, where he, in typically over-confident Scandinavian style, came and sat in an empty seat next to me.

"Hey man, what's up?"

Unless you are introduced through someone else, or lager or football is involved, it's not normal English behaviour to start chatting to someone whom you have never met before, so naturally I was caught off-guard by this tall, tanned, bleached, blond-haired man suddenly interrupting my alone time.

"Alright," I stuttered, feeling uneasy.

"I'm Sander. What's your name, man?" He spoke in near perfect English with a probably-learned-English-through-watching-every-episode-of-*Friends* American twang. He exuded confidence and clearly thought very highly of himself. This was likely inspired by his striking appearance. He was unarguably handsome; a chiseled handsomeness that would have hit the heights of film-star good looks if not tainted by a slightly protruding chin and oversized jaw. He had frosty blue eyes and unblemished skin that had clearly undergone extensive pampering to be so smooth and bronzed. When did it become acceptable for men to moisturize?

The ferry-ride was forty minutes and I figured there was no escape, so decided to put my scepticism aside and be sociable. We discussed the usual things: where we were from, what we did and why we were in Hong Kong. He told me he worked, unsurprisingly, as a financial advisor in Central and he lived on Hennessy Road in Wan Chai, close to my apartment. Like me, he had only moved to Hong Kong recently, so it suited us to befriend each other. The conversation ran freely for the duration of the ferry-ride, and by the time we arrived at the island, we had got to know each other quite well. After we walked down the pier, Sander pointed at an attractive, young Chinese woman and said.

"That's what I'm doing this afternoon!" then winked at me.

Willing to overlook the wink, I agreed to give him my phone-number. Again, this is a situation that Englishmen feel unnecessarily awkward about. Due to potential homosexual undertones, it's always a bit nervy when you ask a man you've only just met for his number. For Scandinavians, it's apparently no problem at all.

"Hey man, let's swap numbers and go for a beer sometime!"

"Sure."

I watched him strut over, kiss the Chinese girl on the forehead and walk off in the other direction.

Two days later, on a Thursday, I got a call from Sander.

"Hey man, let's go out tonight. I need to meet some girls."

Before I went to meet him, I felt nervous. My preparation was similar to going on a date; think about what clothes to wear, try to apply the appropriate amount of aftershave – not quite as much as if it were a date with a girl, decide whether or not to gel the hair. Does Sander deserve gel? Will he be wearing gel? My mind was racing. Despite being safe in the knowledge that Sander was a confident loud-mouth, I still had to have a quick think about what things we could talk about; Hong Kong and football were the safe options. I wanted to steer clear of politics and religion. Mostly due to my limited knowledge of both but also due to the fact that both subjects are not, in my eyes, fun conversation on a night out and often cause fallout. I remember a bad time in my life in sixth-form when every one of my close friends whom I went to the local pub with became really into politics and talked about it all the time. As an alarmingly ignorant teen, I neither knew nor really cared about the conflict in Israel or whatever was the hot topic at the time, so I suffered months of frustrating pub trips, being cast to one side and barely talking, only contributing occasionally when trying to steer the conversation away from war, and closer to which girls were attractive, or whether Leeds were going to get promoted. This was a tough transition to make and one that I rarely succeeded in doing.

I got a taxi and met Sander in Oysters in Lan Kwai Fong, which is the main drinking area in Hong Kong. It has two main streets in an L-shape on steep, cobbled roads, packed with pubs, overflowing bars that call themselves clubs and fast-food places. It started out as a place for the Brits to debauch with drink and prostitutes in the early nineteen hundreds and underwent a major renovation in the 1980s where it became synonymous with the disco scene. Nowadays, it feels like you are in Malia or Magaluf, albeit with an older average age and less belligerence. While those treacherous Club Med places (both of which I've been to and thoroughly enjoyed) are aimed at English louts who hope to sleep with as many people as they can over a two week blitz, Lan Kwai

Fong caters for all ages and people from all different walks of life. It's commonplace for fifty-year-olds to be out dancing in the streets on a Saturday night.

Oysters is a small, dingy bar on a sloping side street, just away from the main action, which smells slightly of vomit and has an outdoor seating area. It was nine o'clock when I arrived and saw Sander standing, leaning / leering on the bar chatting animatedly with a French-looking woman (I'm quite good at identifying French people – they usually wear Converse trainers) with enormous breasts. Fortunately, he spared me from having to break up his conversation by shouting, "Troy. Hey man, what's up?" and swiftly ordering two Tsing Taos. "Speak to you later," he said to the lady and patted her firmly on her arse.

"How you doing man?" he asked through noticeably beery breath. I assumed that he'd been here for a while. He seemed to be the sort of man who'd have no problem going out alone. We sat on a pair of too-small plastic stools outside the front of the bar and talked while sipping our drinks. It was pleasant. Sander asked me why I'd moved to Hong Kong, to which I gave a wishy-washy answer about "a fresh start," but neglected to tell him about my cheating girlfriend. His answer (to his own question) was – said with only a slight smile – "Simple. Women and money. In that order!"

I learnt that he'd been transferred from his banking job in Copenhagen and was going to be running his own team over here. Quite what his team would be doing remained unclear. He kept ordering drinks and refusing to let me pay so I assumed he was probably earning a decent whack. To my relief, he was in the eighty-two percent of European men who are football fans, and was happy to exchange easy anecdotes about ex-girlfriends and stupid behaviour of friends back home. One good thing about being abroad is that you can exaggerate your stories greatly and there is no-one there to say, "That's not what happened."

Strictly speaking I'm not a liar, but I'm a firm believer that it is acceptable to adjust your stories slightly if it makes them better. Sander and I traded tales and I'd say that we were having a good time. We'd had three drinks each and it was getting towards midnight when suddenly I realized that Sander had been in the toilet for ages. I scoured the bar and couldn't see him anywhere. Feeling uncomfortable in my own company, I got a text message, "Sorry man, that chick wasn't gonna wait all night! Have a good one!"

He'd gone. Brilliant! After thinking our night was in its preliminary stages, I found myself gingerly nursing the rest of my drink, queuing up in the rain for ten minutes then getting into a taxi and going home. Was that a successful evening or not? I asked myself.

One issue with my new companion was that I didn't think I actually liked him. He had the potential to be good company but he was arrogant, didn't really listen and he was sleazy – unbelievably sleazy. I'm realistic though and I was aware that I needed him. He was currently my only potential friend, so I was far from spoiled for choice. Comparable to your first day at secondary school – you don't realize it at the time but the person that you sit next to in your form room is the person you are going to be sitting next to for the entire year. You might not like them but you learn to make the most of it.

*

Over the following three weeks, Sander, who was averaging eleven hours a day, and I, who was working zero hours a day and consequently starting to go mildly insane, met up several times to go for food and beers. I'd developed an unhealthy habit of wanting a beer every night and Sander was seemingly happy to oblige. When you are doing next to nothing during the day, beer helps to differentiate between day and night. We usually met at Spicy Fingers pub, which if you had a good arm, was a stone's throw from my apartment. It is a decent enough pub, offering a "Crazy Hour" between six and seven when drinks are half-priced. Crazy hour isn't that crazy. It was usually Sander and me and a smattering of other men who had just finished work and were nursing a beer, not talking much.

After becoming used to, and sort of enjoying it, just being the two of us, I became concerned and envious one night when Sander texted me to say he couldn't make it as he was going for a drink with a new work colleague called Kris.

Kris, a six year veteran of Hong Kon, had hit it off with Sander and subsequently introduced him to his group of friends. After the abrupt emergence of Kris and his pals, I felt ostracized and demoted to Sander's number two drinking pal. This didn't do a whole lot to improve my already flailing social confidence. He invited me to join them, but not wanting to be a charity case, and not particularly liking the sound of Kris, I initially declined. I'm not ordinarily one to judge people before I've met them, but this man Kris really didn't sound like someone I'd like. The spelling of his name caused roughly thirty per cent of my scepticism; I struggle with the spelling of Chris. It should always, in my opinion, be spelt with a "Ch."

After a third night in a row of solitude, I eventually accepted Sander's offer to join Kris and "the boys" for a night out. We were, unsurprisingly, meeting in Armani Bar, which is a pretentious bar in Central which does things such as "Models Night," when women are only allowed in if they are – or resemble – a model.

As they had gone out straight after work as bankers do, I had to turn up alone. Rather shamefully, I found myself changing into my smartest suit. My cynical intuition told me that I wasn't going to like these men but still I clearly felt as though I had to impress them. Already feeling uneasy, I got in a taxi and headed to the bar.

I found Sander and three other men sitting outside on the balcony, laughing rowdily, with two bottles of champagne on ice sitting on the table. Sander beckoned me over and I shook hands with Kris who looked almost exactly as I had imagined him; a towering man in his late twenties to early thirties with rugby-player muscles, a shaved head and very deliberately groomed designer stubble.

"Alright, mate. We have another weekend warrior on board, boys!" Kris spoke in a deep, public school, southern accent.

My emotions were mixed. While I was pleased with myself about how accurate my imagined image of Kris was, I was also concerned by this phrase, "Weekend warrior." The phrase clearly stirred a response as Sander poured me a glass of champagne and feeling spectacularly uncomfortable and stupid, I joined in the toast.

"To the weekend warriors!"

The other two men introduced themselves as Rob and Mark. Mark was a slim man with sun-bleached blond hair and an arrogant look comprised of pointy features and a smirking smile. He'd removed his suit jacket but was still wearing a loosened tie, with the top two buttons of his shirt undone.

Rob was a short man, who thought this needed to be compensated by wearing what was definitely a very expensive suit, diamond ear studs and a gold ring on his thumb. I dislike thumb-rings. Rob looked really young – he had the face of a friend's annoying younger brother. You see these people frequently in Hong Kong; young men working for big banks. Man / child hybrids with chubby faces, bright eyes and grinning mouths, openly delighted that they are earning decent money at a young age and pretending that they earn even more than they do. Even though they wear suits that have been expensively tailored, they look too big for them. They wear too much aftershave and too much hair gel. Their overconfidence is irritating. They talk about their work a lot and always refer to their company, proudly as "We." ("*We* made a twenty million dollar profit last year" or "*We* are a client-based company. Some of *our* clients are...")

I had a token, introductory small talk with the men who were clearly unimpressed by my pending job as a teacher. Even when I told a funny story, complete with accent, about a Korean man at Pacific coffee who had fallen over and spilt coffee on my lap, they didn't seem too interested. Inevitably enough, all of the men worked in finance. Kris had the same job as Sander but I gathered was his superior due to his experience. Mark was an Investment Banker and Rob, a Portfolio Manager. I don't know the difference between the job titles but didn't want to further alienate myself from the group by daring to ask.

Kris was evidently the ring-leader, pouring the drinks and dominating the conversation with tales of rugby nights out and a stag do to Thailand that he'd been on recently.

"You have to go to Bangkok boys. It's fucking amazing. Ten quid for a blow job! Gotta watch out for the chicks with dicks though!"

This unbelievably average comment stirred raucous, over the top laughter from the others, especially Sander. Despite the free flow of champagne, I wasn't enjoying myself at all. I tried to join in with the "banter" – I hate that word – by telling a couple of exaggerated stories from my own trip to Thailand but the men didn't really seem to care and I found myself trailing off gloomily. We stayed in Armani Bar for two long hours before Kris told us to drink up as we were heading to Lan Kwai Fong.

"Yeah, enough of this cockfest, let's get to business!" said Rob, who would surely require ID to get into the bars and proceed with this sinister-sounding "business".

"Tonight's gonna be peng!" replied a giddy Mark.

"Peng?" Is that even a word? This was the breaker. I don't want to try to be friends with someone who says "peng." When the others stopped to have a cigarette before getting taxis to Lan Kwai Fong, I made a transparent excuse about irritable sinuses and set off walking home. I sensed my early departure would have little impact on their evening but still felt a pang of hurt when imagining the likely possibility that Sander was joining in a badmouthed review of my less than "warrior"-like performance.

I later found out that Mark spelled his name "Marc." So I had been out with three men called Sander, Kris and Marc. Although Sander just about gets away with it due to being Danish, there was no such excuse for the others. I was glad I went home.

CHAPTER FIVE

Despite the unsuccessful night out with the spectacularly stereotypical bankers, all in all I had enjoyed my unemployment phase. Four weeks of lazing around, sightseeing and undeserved drinking had been mostly good. However, it is not a sustainable nor particularly well regarded lifestyle and I was relieved when my visa finally came through. I was starting to get cabin fever and questioning my value to Hong Kong society.

In order to validate my visa, I took a return ferry trip to Macau. I very nearly refrained from gambling and came back on the first return boat but succumbed to temptation and lost five hundred dollars playing a combination of roulette and an Egyptian-themed slot machine that I didn't understand. Despite my lighter wallet, I was in high spirits when I returned and my passport was stamped. I was legal to work in Hong Kong. Good.

I started on a Monday in mid-September. I was given three hours training by a flustered, coffee-smelling Kit and then told I would be taking my first class in the afternoon. It was all very rushed; I'd had four weeks training to be a security man at the Call Centre.

To summarize – it's easy to switch off when someone describes their job so I'll try to keep it brief – I was going to be teaching small classes of one to five adults. This meant going through whichever book / level they were on, doing some exercises and generally just talking a lot in English – something I am, hopefully, competent in. Each class was an hour and there were twenty-five in a week with Wednesday a half-day and, tragically, Saturday being a normal working day.

My first class was with a portly policeman in his thirties called Dixon. He was thrilled to be meeting a new teacher and was an affable, friendly man with decent English. The first half hour was spent answering personal questions that Dixon fired at me. "Do you have a girlfriend?" caused him to chuckle. After I answered "no" and got a sharp sinking feeling, he started to laugh hysterically and tell me, proudly, how beautiful Chinese women are. Afterwards, I checked an essay he'd written in scrawled handwriting, which was almost unreadable. I gathered it was something to do with seagulls and oil spills, and marked it an A, which it certainly wasn't, then talked some more and it was done. It was fine – enjoyable even.

Barring a few thorny English grammar questions that I didn't know the answer to and one nerve-wracking class with a Russian man with piercing eyes that suggested he'd probably killed someone, I got through the next three days relatively unscathed and was in self-congratulatory mood that I'd landed a decent gig.

This satisfaction came to an abrupt halt when on Thursday I was informed that I was going to do a *social class*. This was an entirely different proposition to what I'd signed up for. Kit, who had neglected to tell me about this duty in the interview, casually told me that there could be anything up to forty students and that the classes are all about "having fun". Organized fun is not something I necessarily like the idea of – especially when the fun is organized by me. I am not a fun organizing kind of man. Hell.

The main problem was the fact that, out of the group, the level of English-speaking ranged from people who couldn't understand "hello" to seasoned students who, honestly, probably had a better understanding of the language than I do. How do you cope with that?

Before my first social class, I'd been horribly ill-advised by a middle-aged teacher called Les – who was, for some reason unknown, allowed to wear running trainers to work – that you didn't need to prepare any material.

"Just show up," he nonchalantly informed me. "They just want to practice talking to you so they'll ask you some questions and it will flow naturally from there."

Utter bullshit. On arriving into the large room, I found sixteen adults sitting down staring at me, expecting me to do something.

"Hi, I'm Troy. Nice to meet you all," I greeted with forced enthusiasm, before realizing I had nowhere to sit and had no idea where was a suitable place to stand. "How's everyone doing?"

Cue the unbearable sound of a few mumbles and then silence. Oh shit, I thought, heart beginning to pound, a trickle of sweat working its way down my forehead. Usually in stressful situations my mind races, however in this one, it went totally blank. This lasted for what seemed like about six years but was probably twenty seconds. I need to buy some time, I thought desperately.

"Right, let's get to know everybody. Can we go round the class and everyone tell me their name and their job?" Excellent move; I quickly estimated that this would give me about ninety seconds or so to plan an entertaining activity for sixteen grown-ups of differing ages and English levels.

It started.

"I'm Karl, I'm an office worker."

"I'm Didi, I'm a housewife."

"I'm Candy, I'm a shipping clerk."

I nodded approvingly trying to look interested despite the turmoil my head was in. This was going far too quickly.

"I'm Marco, I'm a personal trainer."

One student said, "cannot", so details of name and employment remained a mystery.

"I'm Coco, I'm a graphic designer."

Got it, I thought with a wave of excitement. Let's play the name game. Everyone likes the name game. Always a big hit at Christmas parties – a good game, a solid game. It's going to save me. Fresh with confidence after my inspirational idea, I hit a roll and even asked a few follow up questions to the remaining introducers.

"OK, good to meet you all. We're going to have a bit of fun today." (I'm never going to say that again. Predicting fun is an absolute no go – far too much pressure.)

"We're going to play the celebrity name game. Everyone write the name of a celebrity on a piece of pa…"

"What means celebrity?" questioned Frankie.

"A celebrity is a famous person, Frankie. Like Lady Gaga for example," I replied, thinking that teaching was a good career choice after all. I expected a cheap chuckle here. I don't know why – it wasn't a joke – but I did. And it didn't come. Confidence slightly knocked, what followed was an even greater blow.

"Is this where people ask us questions and have to guess who we are? I've played this before," said Connie, a middle-aged lawyer, in near perfect English.

Fuck you Connie.

"Me too," from Paulo whose trousers were far too short.

"So have I," from Lam.

Ah, bollocks! A half-hearted, stiff smiling, "Well you guys should be good at it then," was all I could muster.

The bunch that had played it before weren't interested and didn't want to join in. One lady said she was going to the toilet but put her coat on and took her bag with her and two others remorselessly took out their mobile phones. They had probably played with Les, who gave me his pearls of wisdom prior to the class. What a bastard. Three other students had no idea what was going on despite me explaining the rules three more times.

"Watch the first game and then you can join in next time," I told them to deaf ears.

"What?"

How do you explain to someone who doesn't understand anything you're saying that they can't play? I was left with nine contenders who seemed to understand, scribbling down the names on slips of paper.

I realized nine was still quite a big group and I hadn't actually worked out a system. I decided in order to kill time – as opposed to killing myself, which was starting to seem a better option – that I would play it one at a time. Eight students question the remaining one: the celebrity. The first questioner to guess the celeb wins a point. It must work. It has to work.

So it began. Coco was the celebrity.

Marco stepped up to ask her a question.

"What's your name?"

For fuck's sake.

"No Marco, not quite the idea," I said, my patience in danger.

After spending a while explaining the rules concisely for a fourth time, we went again. This time, first question duty was passed on to Marian. I fancied her to deliver. She seemed OK. Marian was going to be the saviour.

"How old are you?" she asked.

"Twenty-eight" replied Coco.

This was good so far. Next question.

"What's your job?"

"I'm an office clerk," replied Coco.

Unless there are some famous office clerks in Hong Kong, It was safe to assume that Coco still didn't understand the game.

After the two false starts, we eventually got going, and it was OK-ish. To a few chuckles, Marian, who was quickly shaping up to be my favourite student / person in the world ever, managed to guess that Cherry was Michael Jackson. Next, to further giggling, it turned out that Dennis, the joker, was Jacky Chan. Hilarious. It was flowing, it was working. Next up, a little quicker than the previous rounds, Marian scored another point when guessing that Ringo was also Jacky Chan.

Round four. Candy was the celebrity.

"What's your job?"

"I'm an actor,"

"How old are you?"

"About fifty-five,"

"Where are you from?"

"Hong Kong,"

Marco stepped in. "Are you Jacky Chan?"

"Yes!"

Excellent. Three Jacky Chans in a row. Round five. Marco is in the hot seat.

"What's your job?"

"I'm an actor,"

I feared the worst.

"Are you Chinese?"

"I'm from Hong Kong,"

I might know this one.

"Are you a man or a woman?"

"I'm a man,"

Marian's eyes light up.

"Are you Jacky Chan?!"

I was getting angry now. Why didn't Marco change his name? Come on Marco. Something had to be done.

"Is anyone *not* Jacky Chan?" I asked smiling, but gritting my teeth to the point that I was about to bite through my chin.

Two of the remaining three students shook their heads.

Then Coco answered. "I'm not. I'm Coco."

That was it. I'd had it. Why had I decided that moving to Hong Kong to teach English was a good idea? It had been a huge mistake. I hated everything. At least this charade must have killed off most of the class? I thought. I glanced at my watch. It was one sixteen. Forty-four minutes left.

Fuck teaching.

CHAPTER SIX

After the steep, near vertical, learning curve of my first social class, things got better quickly. I asked the advice of other, more responsible teachers, and managed to up my game. I learned my first pieces of Cantonese, "hm sic" – to not know how and "aiya" which is useful as it can be used to portray surprise, irritation, shock or pain. Hong Kong folk say it *all* the time. It's a good expression and we should have an English equivalent. Steadily the normal classes became auto-pilot; pick up a book, work through it and talk a lot in English. If not necessarily difficult, the job was exhausting as I had to be chirpy and talk for eight hours. Men aren't programmed to talk that much.

A problematic area was dealing with "Why?" questions. "Why do we use the third conditional?" Third what? Although sometimes, "You just do," would suffice, occasionally, the students would demand a detailed explanation and cause my heart to pound and my temples to sweat irrefutably. Given that I was an English teacher, the questioning was probably fair enough. Rather than spending my own time reading up on grammar, which is fairly horrible, I found that developing skillful dodging techniques was less time-consuming and managed to conjure up a few. Here are some:

1) "We'll cover that in the next class, Lam." (We won't. I hope he forgets.)

2) "I'm afraid we don't have time to discuss that now, Ken." (If there are forty minutes left this one is not so good.)

3) "As your homework, find out the answer to the question you just asked and tell me next time."

4) My personal favourite: "Ah good question, Winky! Now does anyone know the answer?" (If none of them knows, revert to 1.)

5) If none of these work, just talk really fast about things that sound like they are relevant but actually aren't. Keep talking until

34

the student gives up and says, lying, to spare themselves and me, "Ah OK, I get it."

NOTE: These tactics don't work with French people.

*

Despite the small gripes, which were down to my limitations rather than the job itself, after one month I felt comfortable and settled in to the new job. For the first time in my ailing career, I was finding work to be adequately worthwhile and rewarding. Lots of English teachers abroad are extremely annoying, believing that their work is comparable to that of Amnesty International, and dodging questions about what they were doing before they became a teacher; but it is a nice job. During successful social classes, seeing forty people smiling and enjoying themselves is gratifying. It felt as though I was having a positive impact on people and, unlike my previous job, what I was doing actually mattered a bit – if I pulled a sickie, people would notice.

The majority of students were local or from China. (I was beginning to notice a subtle animosity from "Hong Kong people" towards their "mainland" compatriots. I gathered it was something to do with milk powder and rent prices but didn't want to risk fistfights in my class and gently shifted dangerous conversations to friendlier topics, such as barbeques or I-phones.) Helpful to living in Hong Kong, I'd drawn the conclusion that I liked the local people. Smiling Chinese people make me smile. Despite some shocking English names (For example: Dracula, an office worker, Octopus a piano teacher and Adolph, a dentist), rush hour on public transport, chicken feet being a popular snack and a few other startling cultural differences, my experiences were generally favourable and I found the majority of Chinese students to be polite and friendly.

Aside from the Chinese, there was an eclectic mix of people from other nationalities who, for one reason or another, were learning English in Hong Kong. The job was a good way to meet a wide range of people from all different backgrounds (a phrase taken straight from my dormant CV). There were two Brazilian friends whose husbands were pilots. They fit the stereotype and were just beautiful; it was fairly painful just to spend time with them. It's unusual for me to spend an hour talking to attractive women who actually listen intently to what I have to say. With sterling professionalism, I managed to keep any impromptu erections well hidden.

There were five or six French folk who were all pleasant enough but asked lots of awkward questions and made me feel uneasy. As touched upon previously, they were wise to my shirking techniques and less placid than the Chinese, so demanded better teaching, which was not altogether unreasonable.

There was also a group of about ten Koreans and Japanese who always hung around together and kept inviting me to go out for drinks and, oddly, massages with them after work, no matter how many times I politely declined. Perhaps most excitingly, one student, a thirty-year-old man called Kratos, was from Kyrgyzstan. I'd always wanted to meet someone from Kyrgyzstan. Unfortunately he was a bit of a dick.

Although it was meant to be an adult school, low earnings over the last couple of years meant that the rule had been loosened so that high school kids could also come along, or more specifically, be forced to go by their parents. In Hong Kong, children are put under an obscene amount of pressure. Some of the kids had extra-curricular activities every night of the week and it was clearly not their choice. It seems rare to meet a Hong Kong teenager who isn't multi-lingual and grade eight on at least one instrument. It's even rarer to meet an eighteen-year-old lad who has a girlfriend, which is a shame.

About twenty percent of the students were teenagers, most of whom were knackered from school and didn't want to be there. Something I noticed about the teenagers was that almost all of them set their watches to be ten or fifteen minutes fast. Despite this, they were almost always late which was both confusing and irritating.

Out of the teenagers, Leroy, was comfortably my favourite. Leroy was an overweight fifteen-year-old who had a non-specified "mild learning difficulty" and spoke very limited English. He was constantly in a fantastic mood, breaking out into fits of laughter at inappropriate times and frequently standing up in the middle of a class and talking to himself in Chinese and / or his own language.

Not long after I started, we had a school talent show. The usual stuff came up. Opening proceedings, a group of girls sang a Taylor Swift number before there was a high quality solo version of, 'My Heart Will Go On,' by a middle-aged Japanese lady. A couple of lads then did a comedy / magic show that was poor and it was unsure as to whether they were deliberately messing up or not. I don't think they were. After this, a businessman from Shanghai surprised the masses by reciting some heartfelt poetry.

The show had been a relative success and the thirty or so members of the audience were eagerly anticipating the final act, which Leroy had ambiguously called, "Martial Arts." The murmuring died down and suddenly all the lights went out. Leroy burst on to the stage wearing a Karate outfit, complete with black belt. The black belt was made from paper, so I assumed he hadn't actually attained it.

The lights came back on, and loud Korean dance music started to boom out as Leroy whipped out a pair of nunchucks and proceeded to whirl them frenetically around his head. As far as I was aware, there was no correlation with the music.

The whirling went on for the duration of the dance track, by which time Leroy was red-faced, sweating and exhausted; while the audience was relieved to have escaped the performance unhurt. After the music stopped, he threw the nunchucks on the floor then screamed for a good few seconds before ripping off his shirt and standing topless as the spotlight shone on him. The crowd was stunned into silence but after a few seconds came a scattered applause that never really got going. He didn't win.

One of the largest groups that came to the school was housewives and retired women. Most of them were fairly lovely women who were just looking to pass a bit of time and meet new people while their husbands brought in the dough, and probably entertained mistresses across mainland China. The housewives would always ask me, "Have you eaten lunch yet?" regardless of whether it was ten a.m. or six p.m.

There was an interesting lady in her sixties called Angela. Her English was almost perfect so I think she just enjoyed the company. One time, over a dubious soya-bean drink, she told me the story of how in the nineteen-sixties, her husband escaped the then horrific Communist China and swam to Hong Kong. If he had been caught, he would have been shot instantly. After making it across successfully, he arrived on Hong Kong shores with no money, clothes, or ID. Fifteen years later he was running his own highly successful building company.

Aside from the housewives and students, I met professionals from all different trades. For example, in one day, I might see a doctor, a pilot, a chef and a security-guard. I was starting to build a strong rapport with Dixon, the policeman, who came in on his lunch break every Monday and Friday. The third time I met him, he handed in his homework from the previous class. The assignment was to write about a story that has happened in the news recently. His story was entitled, "SUAREZ FINED FOR BITING IVANOVIC."

I read Dixon's story and was amused to discover that he had copied an article from the local English speaking newspaper. I'd read the article earlier that morning and I was fairly sure that he hadn't changed a single word. I started laughing and Dixon joined in. Knowing he'd been rumbled, he began to apologize, admitting that he found the set work painfully boring and just wanted to practice speaking English.

From that point on, we settled into a pleasant routine of talking, almost entirely, about football. Despite being an Arsenal-following Chelsea fan, he had a good knowledge of the game and gave me solid tips on who to pick as captain for my Fantasy Football team. Our friendship was consolidated when we went to a nearby sushi café one evening after a lesson. Dixon struggled to contain his sheer delight when I misjudged the wasabi causing my nose to feel like it caught fire and my eyes to stream uncontrollably.

In general my colleagues were alright. Kit, my muscular Australian-Chinese manager was a nice enough man. I wasn't sure what he did apart from staff rotas but he was at work when I arrived and still there when I left every day. He also came in on his day off to "check how things are going," which I questioned. He usually wore a vest for this so I think the opportunity to show his ample biceps to female colleagues was the main motive for the unpaid overtime.

There were four other teachers at my centre, two working full-time and two part-timers. I hadn't seen Les since my first week and his name was never mentioned. Working identical hours to me was a thirty-something, massively camp Australian bloke called Aiden, who was friendly, although we rarely got beyond work chat, "Busy day today?" or "What classes have you got?" I assumed he was gay but couldn't be totally certain. Does it get to a point with someone where you're allowed to ask, "Are you gay?" or is that not acceptable?

Something odd about Aiden was that if you asked him a question, and his answer was "yes," he sternly replied, "Oh god, yeah!"

For example, "Did you have a good weekend Aiden?"

"Oh God, yeah!"

"Do you want a coffee Aiden?"

"Oh, God. Yeah!"

I wasn't sure what this was about. Sometimes it was inappropriate. I did notice, if his response was negative, he simply said, "no."

Aiden was not a cool man. His social life almost definitely consisted of spending most waking hours on his laptop. He brought his laptop to work which was totally unnecessary. I assumed him to be the kind of man who angrily commented on YouTube videos, overusing exclamation marks, saying, "Whoever clicked "dislike" does not know what they are talking about!!!!"

Aiden lived in Tin Hau which was quite close to me and therefore we took the same MTR train route home. Fortunately we had an unspoken arrangement whereby one of us would stay at work for an extra three or four minutes, allowing the other to get to the train station and get away. Small talk with a colleague after work for half an hour is hard work / irrefutable torture. There was once a dreadful situation where I didn't leave it long enough for Aiden to get out of the traps. As I was walking, I saw him at the traffic lights a few metres ahead. He also saw me, but we pretended it hadn't happened. I veered left over the road to take a slightly longer route to the train station so I'd avoid him.

My plan backfired.

He'd had the same idea and decided to go to a cash point to give me time to overtake. As I'd taken the slower route, we ended up at the platform at exactly the same time both knowing that we'd tried to avoid each other. Not ideal and a confirmation that Aiden and I were to be forever stuck in the "colleague" zone.

The other full-time teacher was Vicky, an overweight, grey-blouse-long-skirt-wearing middle-aged woman from somewhere down South in England and arguably the most miserable woman I've ever met. All I established was that she had lived in Hong Kong for twenty years and had worked at Super English for nearly as long, which was possibly why she had such a chip on her shoulder? At first I assumed she was just quiet but she was actually just astonishingly rude. She didn't even acknowledge me when I entered a room. Not even a nod.

The first day I started, she asked me where I was from and where I lived in Hong Kong, but after that, she never asked me another question. She moped around the place scowling, occasionally criticizing people for treachery such as turning the air-conditioning up, or not refilling the coffee. After a few weeks, it got to the point where I had to avoid the staff room at lunch as I couldn't bear sitting near her. It was worse than work and even worse than Naveen at the call centre – the hardest hour of the day.

A twenty-two-year-old American girl called Nicola worked part-time some evenings. She was a petite blonde girl with dubious pink highlights and an eyebrow piercing, who was fairly attractive although I think I got it into my head that she was prettier than she actually was because I saw her so much. I think it made my life more interesting if I did find her attractive so I decided to fancy her a bit. Work is always more bearable if there is a potential squeeze there. It makes it worthwhile putting on a fresh shirt each morning and doing your hair.

She was a chirpy woman but could be quite trying – one of those women who ask irritating questions that you have no way of knowing the answer to. For instance, she asked me if I thought she would be able to take all of her baggage through airport security when she went back home for Christmas. I'm sorry Nicola but I just have no idea. I don't know.

There was also a local guy called Jason who seemed to work as and when he felt like it. He was fine but had an annoying habit of saying passively offensive remarks to me all the time. For example, "Wow. You look tired today. Didn't you sleep last night?" Or "Why haven't you ironed your shirt?" He also made sure to tell me about any spot, scratch or blemish that I ever had on my face. He didn't seem to appreciate that people are fully aware of these confidence knocking irritants and don't need reminding. I wasn't sure if he was deliberately being a dick, or trying to joke with me. If it was the latter, I didn't get it.

CHAPTER SEVEN

Something positive that also happened during my first few weeks of working life was that I secured two more friends to add to my steadily rising tally. The first was a man called Dom from Dudley. I first encountered him on a Saturday night around twenty minutes after Sander had done his usual trick and left me sitting alone at the bar in Oysters considering whether to go home or not.

Befriending an Englishman was something that I needed. It's always welcome to meet someone from your own country. You share things in common. You have mutual points of reference. You can cite TV shows such as "Knightmare" or "Noel's House Party" and no follow-up explanations are needed. You can both appreciate that a man in the bar looks like Ross Kemp with hair.

Dom approached me at one a.m.

"Alright mate, what you doing out here?" he asked in thick, West Midland dialect.

After Sander's American English twang, a regional English accent was refreshing to hear. Although the Birmingham accent doesn't sound overly intelligent, I like it; it's friendly. (I don't really have a regional accent myself, just a deep, neutral voice that drones monotonously. I've flirted with having a thicker accent. At university, cringingly and on the back of the Arctic Monkeys' success, I decided that a Yorkshire accent would make me seem cooler so I'd exaggerated it a lot. I was a dick at university.)

Dom and I ordered a couple of lagers and got chatting. He told me how he had moved straight out to Hong Kong after graduating from, by his own admission, "a dreadful university with an utterly pointless degree." He'd managed to land a job working as a native English teacher in a local school and had enjoyed it sufficiently in his first year that he'd signed an additional two year contract which he was midway through.

He told me that he'd been out with some of his Chinese work colleagues but they had all "eaten loads, taken too many photos on their I-phones, then left". As he was sufficiently oiled, he'd decided to stay out on his own for more drinks and, unashamedly, in hope of catching a lady's eye. Lamentably for him, he'd met me instead. His story wasn't dissimilar to mine and we found that we shared a lot in common. In general life story anyway; in appearance, not so much. Dom was a huge, muscular man. Back home, he'd played basketball at county level and claimed that he'd nearly got into the England schoolboys team. A lot of men you meet in pubs claim to have played sport at a high level at some point in their past. Why is this? (I have unfortunately been one of those men and I still get a sinking feeling remembering a night when I told a bunch of people that in my teens I'd played for Leeds United youth team and was close to becoming a professional. I remember I got to the point where I believed my own bullshit and started to enjoy the fake past I was creating for myself. Of course I added the whole, "I fucked it when women, drugs and booze came along," which is how all fictitious pub stories of past glories end.)

I believe my first impressions of people to be pretty solid and I had no reason to doubt Dom. Besides, he was six foot six and ridiculously well built – to the point that the first night I met him, not one but two women asked if they could touch his biceps. In twenty-six years on this planet, I don't think I've been asked that once. In fact I know I haven't. I would have remembered and probably made a note of it.

In contrast to the sheer size of him, he had one of those friendly, likeable faces with dimpled cheeks and an expressive smile that, when in full force, caused his small brown eyes to almost completely shut. He wore a small, sparkling stud in his left earlobe and had a trendy, heavily-gelled side-parting hair-do. Over recent years, I've altered my opinion regarding musclemen. I used to have a preconception that musclemen liked fighting and shagging and not much else but I've since met several men who have disproved my assumption. This is, in part, due to the fact that almost every man in their mid to late twenties seems to be an avid gym-goer, so the ratio of musclemen I now meet is much higher than in previous years. I still hadn't signed up to a gym in Hong Kong and Dom recommended that I should "definitely" join his gym, because I "needed to." He then felt guilty about his choice of words and back-tracked. "I just mean the facilities there are top-class so everyone needs to join." It was an unconvincing retraction but I appreciated the effort, and belated kindheartedness.

We stayed out for a few hours and had a jovial, beer-fuelled conversation, when his biceps weren't being groped, about traveling experiences, retro cartoon shows and the archetypal banker-wanker who was common in Hong Kong. Owing to my recent meeting with Kris and his idiot friends, I had quite a lot to say about this. Inspired by Sander's confidence, I had no problem asking Dom for his number and we arranged to meet for a game of squash the following Wednesday. In a state of inebriated arrogance, I'd overplayed my squash-playing skills, making myself out to be a competent player when the reality was I hadn't picked up a racket in six years.

I got the solo taxi home that night feeling pleased. I am no ladies' man and never have been but for a twenty-six-year-old man, out alone, I honestly think it is easier to pull a girl in a bar than befriend a man. I had succeeded that night. I was going home alone but I'd secured a potential new pal which was a great coup

*

After introducing Dom to Sander, the three of us smoothly formed a beer drinking companionship. Sander was wise to the fact that his banker friends and I were not going to become best buddies so he divided his social life between the two different groups and his ever-growing harem of women.

I was extremely grateful for the addition of Dom. One on one with Sander was too much. As a duo, I'd have to let his questionable behaviour slide but now, whenever Sander made a lewd comment or a bad joke, Dom and I would share a glance. Sometimes a glance is all that is needed. Although Sander was a friend, Dom and I wholeheartedly agreed that he was a clown and our mutual opinion of him helped to solidify our own friendship. We were on a good run and for the first time in years I found myself genuinely excited about going out at the weekend.

Foreigners living in Hong Kong are generally less guarded and much more open to talk with strangers. If a stranger approaches you in a bar in Leeds, it is usually a precursor to violence. This affability meant that on nights out, the three of us would get talking to an eclectic mix of people from different nationalities, professions and ages. You could be talking to a twenty-five-year-old builder from Auckland one minute and then a forty-year-old Argentinian musician the next. A lot of people were probably lying but nevertheless, I enjoyed the variety.

One small issue was that both Sander and Dom were considerably better looking than me. I couldn't work out if this

43

was a good thing or not. Did being with them increase my own average or did it simply highlight my inadequacies? Although happy to talk with females, I was rusty and lacking in confidence. (I say "rusty" insinuating that there was a time in the past when I was a ladies' man. There wasn't.) Despite his looks and the confidence that bicep-groping must breed, Dom surprisingly lacked confidence romantically too, becoming shy and quiet around girls.

Sander was, undeniably, frighteningly good with women. Aside from a glaringly obvious jealousy, I don't have anything against ladies' men per se. It does depend on the type of man though. I'm partial to hedonistic men whose womanizing is just one branch of a high-octane, vice-ridden lifestyle. With these men, I think: fair enough – you're good at what you do and I can't compete. I do, however, struggle with the other type of ladies' man – the boring ladies' man – the man who is dull, unimaginative, poor company and generally just shit during any social setting where a potential squeeze is not present. I've met several men like this and they make you question your existence. When I see a man that has never made me laugh, ever, charming an attractive girl into hysterics, I wonder what I am doing so wrong in this inverted world.

With any type of ladies' man, I wonder if it sometimes gets boring. Do ladies' men not get tired of saying the same chat up lines and following the same well versed routine over and over again? Is it similar to when you have a good joke or a good story and you tell it to everyone you know? By the time you're saying it to the fifth person in a week, it's still pleasant to receive the good response but it's also a bit depressing and you end up bemoaning your lack of variety. Does a similar thing happen with ladies' men? Probably not. Definitely not.

Whereas Sander would seemingly never go home alone, Dom and I tended to end out nights in Big Pizza or Ebenezer's Kebab house at four a.m. with our only female interest coming from tired prostitutes who smelt of chili sauce.

*

More exotic than a man from Dudley, the second new friend that I acquired, and third overall, was a Filipina lady. As Wednesday was my half day, I usually tried to make the most of it by getting out to one of the islands, or hiring a bike then wishing I hadn't when the chain came off, which happened every time. One Wednesday in late October, however, I was low on energy and decided to have a lazy afternoon drinking tea, playing FIFA and watching YouTube videos, which invariably leads to watching porn. I was excited at the prospect of my slob afternoon and barreled into the house in a good mood, eager to turn on my PlayStation and put the kettle on.

I was surprised to see that my flat wasn't empty. I found Carmella, my Filipino cleaner sitting on my sofa, with her plump, bare feet up, sound asleep. I decided not to wake her up and smiled to myself as I went and changed into baggy shorts and a classic Fiorentina shirt – perfect attire for lounging. I must have made enough noise as, when I returned, I saw a startled looking Carmella had woken up and was vigorously rubbing her eyes.

"Good afternoon," I said, laughing.

"Mr Troy, I'm so sorry. I must have fallen asleep!" she replied, in her jaunty Spanish-like Filipino accent. She was mortified. I considered pretending to be annoyed as a cheap gag but decided against it.

"No problem. Do you want a cup of tea?" I asked her.

"I've never done this before. I'm so embarrassed!" she replied.

"Seriously, it doesn't matter. Out of interest, how long have you been here?"

"Not long, maybe ten minutes?" she said, then started to grin. "OK, maybe nearer to three hours."

Previously, I'd always said hello to Carmella and been polite but I'd never really had a proper conversation with her. Filipina women have excellent faces; they look cheeky and mischievous with big eyes and constantly grinning mouths. Carmella fit this description perfectly and even had a broad smile on her face when she was asleep. She had shoulder length, ink-black hair and always wore a large flowery headband. Her work uniform was consistently a white vest top, three quarter length leggings and some ragged, blue flip-flops.

We had a cup of tea and talked animatedly for the next hour or so. Like most Filipinas I'd met, she was very talkative and funny, with good English. She told me how she had been living in Hong Kong for nearly seven years. She had graduated from a university in Manila with a first class degree in Economics but had struggled to find a good job. She was working as a waitress to make ends meet when she fell in love with one of the chefs and they got married within three months.

Her husband decided that they weren't earning enough to raise a family so advised her to go to Hong Kong to make some money before they had children. The initial plan was that she would do two years working as a maid in Hong Kong and send home all of her wages, while he would save as much as he could from the restaurant. It hadn't worked out that way unfortunately. Carmella went back to the Philippines after one year to attend the funeral of her grandfather. When she arrived she found that her husband had done a runner – taken all of her wages and disappeared. Too distraught to face the situation, she saw moving back to Hong Kong as a better option.

She had made good friends and the wealthy Chinese family she was working for in Sha Tin had been good to her. She looked after the daughter and did all of the cooking and cleaning. Despite the heavy workload, she'd enjoyed it and was made to feel like part of the family. She'd been given a decent wage and had her own small room in the house which was better than many of her friends, who had to sleep on sofas or fold out beds in the living-rooms. She lived and worked for them for nearly three years but left when the daughter became a teenager and was deemed old enough to look after herself. She'd departed with a heavy heart and told me how she missed the daughter especially.

After leaving, Carmella had had a succession of jobs working with other families but the living conditions were always worse, she was paid less and she was not treated anywhere near as well. Subsequently, she started to work cleaning serviced apartments and had been doing so for the last three years, working long hours six days a week.

After listening to Carmella's interesting and touching story, I told her about my own barely comparable motives for moving to Hong Kong. As she had opened up to me, I felt comfortable telling her all about Imogen and my dissatisfaction back home. I felt like a bit of a dick, moaning about my inane, middle class "difficulties," in comparison to her own tale, but she seemed interested and offered a sympathetic ear. She said Imogen sounded like a "fat cow," and despite being inaccurate, I enjoyed her speculative decision that Imogen must be overweight.

"So how long will you stay in Hong Kong?" she asked after a short lull in conversation.

"The plan is to stay for one year and then go back to England."

"Just one year? That's what I said. I bet you stay for longer," she said with a knowing smile.

"I won't. How much do you want to bet?"

We shook hands on twenty dollars.

"So be honest, have you had a few naps at mine then?" I asked her, as she was standing up to leave.

"No. This is the first time," she said then started to grin again. "OK, maybe not the first time. After doing your flat, I'm done until the evening so I sometimes relax for a bit after."

I laughed and told her that she was welcome to relax at mine whenever she wanted.

She duly obliged. The following Wednesday I came home and found her sitting with two cups of tea ready and we slotted into a pleasant routine of drinking tea and coffee and chatting for an hour or so every week. One Wednesday, after we had eaten a paella dish that she had cooked, she invited me to come out with her on a Sunday.

"I've told my friends about you," she said. "They want to meet you. Will you come?"

I assumed that they went for a picnic in Victoria Park which on Sundays is overflowing with Filipino and Indonesian maids enjoying their day off and partaking in suspect dance routines, but Carmella had something else in mind.

"Sunday is our party day!" she told me, beaming. "It's like your Saturday night. We meet up early though. Do you think you can handle it?"

*

Unsure exactly what I was getting myself in for I agreed to join her and her pals the following weekend. Carmella met me outside J. Forrest in Wan Chai at midday. She was wearing a tight black dress and high heels and her face was heavily made-up, wearing thick red lip-stick and heavy blue eye-shadow which drew attention to her large, sparkling brown eyes. She had gone to work on her hair too – it was immaculately straightened and smelt of coconut. It was a far cry from her work outfit.

I had never been to J. Forrest before and naively assumed that it would be a pub where we would have lunch and a few beers. We entered the building through an innocuous-looking side door. Most good bars, pubs and restaurants in Hong Kong have low-key entrances and are on higher floors, so if nobody introduces you to them, you'd never think to go there. We headed up some steps, and I heard loud, bad club music beating. A delighted Carmella grabbed my arm, then we entered the pub which was heaving full of people, dancing and drinking as a machine fired wispy, white smoke into the crowded dance floor. Bearing in mind it was early afternoon on a Sunday, this wasn't what I'd anticipated.

Carmella led us over to the centre of the dance floor where she introduced me to her friends. Over the course of the next ten minutes, she must have introduced me to at least fifteen Filipino ladies, of varying ages, all dressed to the nines, grinning and dancing. It was bizarre.

Although I couldn't hear properly and any conversation was a struggle over the noise, I could tell that her friends were incredibly friendly, especially when they forced me to dance. This was alien to me at this time of day and without having touched a drop of lager. I collared a bar man who was doing the rounds and ordered four San Miguels for myself, Carmella and two of her friends whom I'd been clumsily dancing with.

I looked round and took in my surroundings a bit more. On closer inspection, I noticed that there was certainly a type of person in here. Almost every single one of the women was a Filipina, most of them wearing tight-fitting black dresses, and every single one of the men was white, over forty and not particularly good at dancing. I pondered the situation. Were the women prostitutes?

"So, this is what we do on our day off!" Carmella shouted, then insisted that I pirouette her around while she sang along to a repetitive Taio Cruz number. Carmella was clearly well thought of in the bar, and over the next hour, she chatted animatedly to most of the women and three men bought her a beer.

"These guys are so friendly," she told me, then winked. I was unsure what the wink meant.

We stayed in J. Forest until about two o'clock by which point I was semi-drunk and hungry. Carmella and her friend Angel asked if I wanted to join them for a snack. We left and went down to street level where I bought myself and each of the girls a slice of soggy pepperoni pizza from a fast-food stall.

"Are you enjoying yourself Mr Troy?" Angel asked me.

"I really am. What a good way to spend your Sundays."

After the barely edible nourishment, we headed over to Lockhart Road and a bar called the New Makati. It was exactly the same as J. Forrest, only there was a foam machine in this one. The last time I'd seen such a machine was in a club in Malia where I had badly cut my hand on broken glass when doing a "Klinsmann" dive into the foam. In the New Makati, Carmella bought me a Strobe – an alcoholic energy drink which actually feels like it is rotting your teeth the moment you pour it in your mouth. We continued to dance when a middle-aged English man unsubtly danced into my vicinity and introduced himself.

"Can't do this back home, can you?" he said, clearly itching for a conversation.

Frank was a fifty-three-year-old estate agent from Watford. He'd lived in Hong Kong for four years now and said moving here "saved his life." Bit over the top, Frank, I thought. He seemed a nice, albeit half-cut, man though and I was happy to talk. His bright red nose and the strong smell of whisky suggested that Hong Kong was actually in the process of ending his life early but I toasted his life-saving anyway.

"Perhaps you can educate me here, Frank. What's the deal with these pubs on a Sunday? Are the girls prostitutes?" I asked.

"Not exactly. It's just the maids' day off. Some of them will sleep with fellers to try to earn a bit of extra money, some of them won't. They are great girls though, aren't they, the Filipinas?"

Happy with Frank's shrewd assessment – he seemed a man familiar with prostitution and women in Hong Kong – I shook his hand, we tentatively said we'd see each other again and I went back to find Carmella. Carmella was visibly drunk and she and Angel were sexy dancing with an Arabic man who had not one, but three, Strobe drinks in his hands and was taking sips from each one – wild.

I had thoroughly enjoyed my Sunday out but had already started putting drinks on my credit card so thought it best to leave before irreversibly damaging my finances. I thanked Carmella and jerkily tried to shake the foam off my trainers before heading out of the club. I got outside and was met by bright sunlight. A real shock to the system, after being in places resembling night-clubs all day.

Similarly to when leaving an afternoon showing at the cinema, it took a while to readjust. It was three forty-five, and outside there were respectable citizens doing the sort of thing that you should do on Sunday – going to the shops, having a coffee, taking their children out for lunch. I stumbled home, and decided that it had been my best Sunday since Leeds had beaten Man United in the FA Cup.

CHAPTER EIGHT

I was enjoying the expat (why is expat such an annoying word?) lifestyle and pleased with myself for moving to Hong Kong. Although Hong Kong is not the sort of place you can ever feel fully settled in, my life had started to fall into a well-structured routine and despite it being one of the reasons why I'd left England, I'd fallen very much into a "live for the weekend" mentality. The crucial difference was that I was now enjoying my weekends.

Although I worked on Saturdays, I generally went out on Friday nights for a meal or a few drinks, then Saturday would be a night out with Sander, Dom and any acquaintances that any of us might bring along. Sunday day time would usually be spent bedridden with a hangover, or strolling aimlessly around Wan Chai with Dom, occasionally losing heavily to him at squash. He was so much better than me it was embarrassing. Once, he quite obviously eased up and deliberately missed a few shots, which is one of life's biggest insults.

I occasionally joined Carmella, her friends and the middle-aged men for questionable Sunday activities; then, without fail, every Sunday evening was arduous: Skype calls to people at home, repeating details of my unspectacular week to family members who complained of poor connectivity and a blurred video. The end of the phone-call signified the end of the weekend. And then it started again.

In November, I managed to disrupt the routine after an ill-fated trip to Macau. Sander, Dom and I took the hour-long ferry-ride over on a Sunday morning and had a decent day strolling through the old town, sightseeing and eating some nice but overrated Portuguese food at Fernando's restaurant. It is seen as a trendy place to go and more than one (two) excitable expats had claimed, "It's the best restaurant I've ever been to!" It is basically a replica of Nando's, which itself is overrated. (People get disproportionately excited about the PerriPerri sauce at Nando's just as they do about the dough balls at Pizza Express. They're balls of dough – they are fine. They are not "amazing" as many giddy girls have you believe.)

Of course, with us being men, a pleasant sightseeing and dinner trip wasn't enough, especially given that we were in one of the gambling capitals of the world. So instead of going back on the eight o'clock ferry as we had planned, we decided to go to the Venetian, initially for a beer and a look round, just for an hour. Predictably, it didn't work out that way. We got seduced by the bright lights and dollar signs and decided to go five hundred dollars each on a roulette game. The money vanished within five minutes. Three spins of the wheel and we had lost the lot. Instead of putting us off, this only whetted the appetite and I found myself aggressively marching towards an ATM with plans of making the money back and doubling it. It didn't happen. I lost a further three thousand dollars.

The wheel cruelly mocked me on my final spin. I'd put one hundred dollars on zero. If zero had come in, I would have won back what I started with and be up one hundred dollars. The ball flew out, spun around, then dropped down into the right section. I began to feel my heart racing. It was all going to be fine. Zero was going to save me!

It didn't.

The ball bounced off the outer rim of zero and settled smugly into its arrogant neighbour, thirty-two. I still hadn't learnt my lesson and had time to lose a further thousand dollars playing Sic Bo dice, another mindless, no-skill-involved game of chance. By the time we left the Venetian, I had seven hundred dollars (about sixty quid) left in my account. And it was three weeks until pay-day.

I familiarized myself with fried rice much more than I would have liked over the subsequent weeks. It was a testing time. Four days before I got paid, I had the indignity of taking my pot of worthless change to HSBC and emptying it out on the counter. After the unfortunate customer services woman spent ten minutes counting it all, and to the anger of everyone else in the queue, I got fifty-three dollars back. It just about took me over the line. I vowed afterwards that I would never gamble again. But we've all heard that before.

*

Despite the bleak November, my day to day, week to week existence was pretty standard. I didn't mind – in fact I quite liked

– having a set routine. It meant that time was going by incredibly quickly. When I heard the first Christmas songs being played in Starbucks, just how quickly the year had gone actually startled me. I'd been in Hong Kong for nearly four months. It felt like I'd just got there.

Sander had gone back to Denmark for a month, but happily I didn't have to suffer from a bout of severe homesickness, which would likely have accompanied a solo Christmas in Asia. After Macau, Dom was also broke and after initially planning on going home, couldn't afford it, so he and I organized a Christmas Dinner at the Pawn – a classy but unsociably expensive English bistro in Wan Chai. Including ourselves we managed to get a crowd of seven people together. I invited Carmella who brought Angel, and Dom came with a couple of giant, but amiable, men from basketball: Cody, a cool American and Ben, a dozy man from Sheffield, who brought a Thai girlfriend, attractive but guilty of having a terrible paw-print tattoo above her breast which suggested a promiscuous past. In the event it was a memorable Christmas. We did a secret Santa, with usual hilarity at the joke sex presents, and after Carmella's flirting with a barman secured us a free jug of mulled wine, drank heavily enough to sing Christmas carols in the streets.

After the success of Christmas, the same crowd gathered again on New Year's Eve and had a solid night out at a rooftop bar in Central. I disagree with the increasingly common, "New Year's Eve is overrated" stance and enjoyed seeing the fireworks and celebrating midnight by throwing my T-shirt off the roof with Dom – an act that saw us banned from returning to the bar.

Sander returned in mid-January looking slightly plumper after the festive season. He had tried to counter this weight gain by intensively tanning and looked about three shades darker than when he left. Unless there had been a bizarre heat wave in Scandinavia, I assumed he had spent more time on the sun-bed than off it over his holidays. With his pearly white teeth, this new fatter, browner Sander actually looked fairly ridiculous, but he was far too vain to be criticized to his face. He went quiet for an hour when Carmella joked with him that he looked like a Filipino.

With February came the excitement of Chinese New Year and a few extra days off. Carmella, Sander and I went to Ocean Park on one of the bank holidays, which was a drastically bad decision owing to half of China opting to go at the same time, celebrating New Year's jollities by spitting, smoking and shoving.

The second day of the Chinese New Year was more successful. Dom and I decided to walk part of the Hong Kong trail, culminating in a dinner for two at the Jumbo restaurant – a restaurant on a boat. What's not to like about a restaurant on a boat? The contrasting fortunes of the two days – one dreadful, one excellent – were a good reflection of my wider feelings towards Hong Kong. On some days I would be so sick of the crowds, the pollution and the humidity that I would wish I was back in England, but on others I would love the place and feel lucky to be living in such an incredible city.

In other events of note in February, I had a brief, unsuccessful fling with an Irish girl whom I met at Al's Diner in Lan Kwai Fong. After managing bunglingly to secure a dance-floor kiss on the Saturday night, we arranged to meet up at Pacific Coffee the following Wednesday. I'm unsure about daytime dates but went with an open mind.

It was dreadful.

For starters, she was only nineteen which was a big age gap and something she had neglected to tell me on the Saturday. She also looked nothing like my Saturday night memory of her, and while I had put on a shirt, she'd arrived wearing grey joggers and fake Ugg boots – a look I've deplored since university. Worse still, she was wearing some large, thick-rimmed glasses with plain glass in the lenses. Awful.

We realized almost instantly that there was zero in common. My brain failed me in that I could think of nothing interesting to say. When her best effort was to tell me that she still had feelings for Connor, her ex-boyfriend, I decided that there was probably nothing much I could say even if I had been on top form. She also told me that she was leaving Hong Kong to move to Shanghai in two weeks, at which point I wanted to ask her what the logic of meeting up for the date was. After nursing a caramel latte for twenty strenuous minutes, I took the initiative and told her I was doing some private tutoring that afternoon. She was totally aware I was lying but noticeably relieved that the pain was over.

The failed date made me consider my stalling romantic life. Since splitting up with Imogen, there had been very little. Barring a one-night stand in November with an overweight Canadian girl whom I'd met when she was dancing on the bar in Carnegies, there had been nothing. At the work Christmas party, I'd considered trying it on with Nicola but after deliberating for too long, wondering whether it would be a good idea, I missed the chance; and later in the evening saw her kissing a local man who, to his credit, actually pulled off the white suit he was wearing.

It wasn't so much the lack of "action" that I was concerned about – this would have bothered the nineteen-year-old version of me – I was more worried that in six months living in such a vibrant, exciting city, I hadn't come anywhere near close to getting a girlfriend. I'd not been seduced by the "Asian persuasion" as idiots say or got "Yellow Fever" as even bigger idiots say. It's not that the local girls aren't attractive, but call me old-fashioned – I see being able to have a conversation with a girlfriend as fairly significant. I'd seen enough fat, rucksack-wearing Americans having queasy, baby-talk conversations with their beautiful Asian girlfriends to decide that I didn't fancy going down that route.

On the flip side, my confidence with girls, whose first language is the same as mine, was also failing and I was suffering from a different communication barrier. In the time that I'd been together with Imogen, the rules of the game seemed to have moved on and left me behind. I still felt like a teenager but girls had now turned into actual, grown-up women. Grown-up women are intimidating. How do you initiate a decent conversation with a grown-up woman? What do you say?

Despite English not being his first language, Sander didn't suffer from either of my insecure pitfalls and was perfectly accomplished in having thumb wars with twenty-year-old locals or discussing the stock-market with thirty-year-old New Yorkers. How did he do it? Being around him was a depressing confirmation that there clearly wasn't a shortage of available women in Hong Kong and it was definitely me who was doing something wrong.

CHAPTER NINE

At the start of March, it had started to get much warmer. On a Thursday afternoon I had to go to Manning's, one of Hong Kong's main chemists, which is everywhere, to stock up on hay-fever tablets for the season. Hay fever is something that has tried its best to ruin my summers since I was ten. I'd hoped that moving abroad would abolish the problem but apparently whatever pollen affects me the worst is everywhere in Hong Kong. You'd think somewhere along the evolution of humankind we would have managed to shed being allergic to grass and plants by now.

I extremely un-fondly remember the day I first became aware of my pollen allergies. It was the summer holidays between year seven and year eight at school. My friend Rodney (I have never met anyone else called Rodney. It's a great name. The world would be a better place with more Rodneys) and I had gone to the park to kick a ball around and ride down perilously steep hills on our bikes, when three girls from a school nearby came over and started talking to us.

Despite our collective inexperience with girls, they seemed to like us and suggested a game of spin the bottle, a game that a couple of my friends claimed to have played and which was rumoured to be excellent. The five of us made our way to the small bit of a wood behind the skate park and sat cross-legged in a circle. Rodney reckoned he'd kissed four girls in a week when on a family camping holiday in France earlier in the summer so he was quite cool about the situation. I, however, had only ever kissed one girl at the school fair in year six and it was debatable whether it actually counted, so I was suitably terrified and excited about the imminent future.

A Kappa-tracksuit-wearing girl pulled out a bottle of Mountain Dew, spun it and it landed on Stacey, a pretty girl whom I'd decided that I would probably like to marry. Now it was between me and Rodney– huge pressure. Rodney spun. The bottle picked up pace and whirled round for what seemed like twenty minutes, then slowly ground to a halt and landed on me.

I was delighted. I moved over towards her and was getting overwhelmingly excited until, just as I was looking at her, ready to tilt the head, the whole moment was destroyed by an uncontrollable sneezing fit.

"Achoo!" Not once, six times in a row, culminating in a thick, green slug of snot landing on my trouser leg. I'd never sneezed six times consecutively in my life before. Why now? I panicked afterwards and instead of sticking around, did what every twelve-year-old would do, and picked up my Argos-bought Kalamundo mountain-bike and sped off as quickly as I could. By the time I got home, my eyes were so puffed up and blood-shot that my face was almost unrecognizable. The following week when term started again, my pal Rodney told our whole class about what had happened and finished the tale by telling me that he had kissed all three of the girls after I left. What a bastard. Is that when men start being bastards, at age twelve?

*

Fortunately, Hong Kong is pretty lax in that things you'd need a prescription for back home are bought in chemists' at relative ease. As I got to the counter to pick up my tablets, I noticed, as a man does, that two attractive young women had just entered the shop. They were the classic combination of one blond and one brunette, both wearing alluring summer frocks and with full hair and make-up in force. My limbs tensed up and I felt my heartbeat increase.

Despite my running nose, I found myself forgetting about my reason for being in the shop, and everything else in the world for that matter, as my itchy eyes fixated on the two girls. I fumbled around and managed to pay for my hay-fever tablets. On leaving the shop, I realized that I would miss the two girls, in two senses of the word. I would literally miss them as we would fail to encounter each other, and I would miss them in that I would feel sad about their absence in my life. The latter, similarly to when you have noticed an attractive girl in a bar, then you tell yourself that you will go and talk to her after two more drinks. However, by the time you have almost plucked up the courage to approach, she leaves. It always results in approximately five minutes of heartbreak.

I didn't want a trip to buy hay-fever medication leaving me heartbroken so I started to think: Is there anything else I need from the chemist? After deliberation, I decided, rather than leaving, I would head over to the protein supplement area and possibly make a rash purchase of a muscle-building substance that I would never use. As I headed over to the aisle, already doubting my moral compass, I made eye-contact with the brunette of the pair or, more specifically, she noticed that I was staring at her.

She had lost interest in the tinted moisturizer in her hand and surprisingly held my gaze. Is she actually interested in me? This isn't normal? Then I looked back and examined her even more closely. No. It can't be?

I recognized her mahogany hair and the glowing chocolate brown eyes that were framed by long, mascaraed lashes. I recognized the dimple in her cheek when she smiled through her full pink lips. When my brain had finally processed the exquisite view, it hit me. I knew this woman. It was Sophie.

*

I hadn't seen her for about three years but it was definitely her. I went to school with her. She was in my form. We were even in the "friends" category throughout year ten and eleven. I also used to absolutely, unrequitedly, love this girl.

There is one in every year of every school. The girl who is the most attractive, the coolest, the nicest; the one that every pre-man falls in love with. I was unable to avoid the trap and fell for her something rotten. During the formative days of spin-the-bottle and short-lived relationships, where you held hands during break time and split up at lunch time, she'd largely slipped under the radar. However, over the summer holiday between year nine and year ten, she possibly subconsciously, probably deliberately, decided that she was going to be "the one".

She was in the first batch of girls to develop breasts but hers seemed to have grown incredibly quickly. Either that or she opted for an extremely effective push-up bra. She'd also had her hair done and started wearing grown-up women's make-up. Unlike many girls who struggled with the early days of make-up, caking their faces with dark orange foundation, Sophie, with the advice of a knowledgeable older sister, managed to apply hers perfectly every day. She also started wearing the most incredible perfume I've ever known. I still remember the sweet vanilla smell to this day. It must have been a popular brand because I frequently come across it. If I catch the scent when in a shopping centre or a night club, it always takes me back to being a love-struck, spotty fifteen-year-old. It's just lovely. (The perfume, that is. Not being love-struck and spotty – that was a traumatic combination.)

Her summer transformation also seemed to change her attitude and whereas she was fairly introverted before, she now had a newfound confidence. Maybe it was just that everybody now wanted to talk to her? By the October half-term, she had stratospherically risen to become the most popular girl in year ten and glided around the playground seemingly hovering above the tarmac with a goddess-like aura, while the rest of us minions stared at her, goggle-eyed, vying for her attention.

Every boy fancied her, and every girl wanted to be best friends with her. Despite her new-found school celebrity status, she wasn't a dickhead. She was kindhearted, funny and friendly, which was unfair. It was difficult to find a flaw and therefore impossible to stop myself from pining for her. Fortunately, she was in my form so I got the opportunity to work my limited teenage charms on a daily basis. Continuous bad behaviour from Ismael and Madjid, the class clowns / bullies, who sat at the back, beat-boxing badly and making offensive comments, led to a giant slice of luck; the class seating plan was overhauled and changed to alphabetical order and I found myself sitting next to Sophie, much to the jealousy of the other, cooler, tougher, better-football-playing lads. The main aim of morning and afternoon registration was to make her laugh, which fortuitously, was fairly easy to do. She laughed at my average jokes and joined in with my varying-quality impressions of classmates and teachers.

We exchanged numbers and would text each other frequently in the evenings. Not talking about anything particularly interesting. But I found it unbelievably exciting. I remember the nervous wait after texting her the first time: "Hi Sophie, How are you? Up to much tonight? Xx." I'd opted for two kisses which was potentially risky.

I rode an emotional roller-coaster in the hour-long spell afterwards when I was waiting for her response. Twice there were false alarms. One was from Orange telling me that my credit was running low. – Why do you always get that one when you're waiting for something important? – The next equally unexciting message was from my friend Matt, asking if he could borrow a pair of shin-pads for football training. As a result, I hated Matt and considered not bringing my spare pair out of spite. Finally, third time lucky, my phone finally buzzed and it was indeed

Sophie: "Hi. Im gr8! Just watching *Eastenders*. Who do u think shot Phil Mitchell?! xxx."

Wow. I'd never been so excited to hear Phil Mitchell's name. The message was cordial. And it had three kisses – a quick recap informed me this was one more than I'd sent her. She must be interested? I sent back a message regarding my theory as to Mitchell's shooter and we continued to text each other for the rest of the evening. (As a result of this success, I changed my mind and did take the shin-pads in for Matt.)

The good thing about text messages is that you have time to think about it so you don't say anything stupid. Whereas, in conversation, my brain's filter doesn't always work properly, text messages cancel out this problem. I've always believed myself to be a solid texter. I was in dreamland, thinking, irrationally, that if this friendship continues, surely the natural progression is that she will definitely become my girlfriend at some point soon?

The dreamland era didn't last long. During one of our text conversations, Sophie informed me that she had met a new boyfriend at a party. "He's really nice Troy – U will luv him! x"

I was devastated. And why did she assume I'd love this bastard? Did she really think that was an appropriate thing to say? She must have known that I was hopelessly in love with her.

Despite this tragic revelation, we continued to sit next to each other in form class. Whereas, previously, this was undoubtedly the highlight of my day, I now dreaded it. Almost every conversation, she told me about this new boyfriend, Ryan.

Of course, Ryan was three years older than her. I could have predicted that before she told me. He was at sixth form in a school a few miles away. He also, obviously, drove a car. Why wouldn't he drive a car? Sophie decided I'd want to know about Ryan's sporting success, his good grades and his plans for university. I couldn't have wanted to know less. I hated him.

Inevitably, I met him when, one afternoon after school, as I was standing with Sophie waiting for the bus, he pulled up in his Ford Fiesta. He got out and swaggered over to us – a six foot four monster of a man wearing a G-Star T-shirt and baggy jeans.

"Hello, love!" he said in a thick deep Leeds accent then proceeded to kiss Sophie passionately for about a minute, oblivious to my existence. Eventually, he introduced himself without making eye contact. "Alright, mate. I'm Ryan," and offered a handshake. I hated that I had to shake his hand. This was torture. Is this what life had in store, having to shake hands with people like Ryan? I watched as he lit a cigarette for the pair of them and they strolled over to his car, his arm lazily slung round her neck. She doesn't even smoke? I thought to myself.

My turmoil continued for weeks, with Sophie constantly talking about Ryan and me leaving every form class feeling suitably gutted. In hindsight, I should probably have just stopped sitting next to her and asked to sit with Matt, who was unhappy with his own seat next to Ismael, who thought that punching someone in the arm was the height of humour. I couldn't bring myself to do it though because I still had an irrational glimmer of hope that she had feelings for me too.

We would still text each other most evenings, discussing the day's events, or her telling me what gifts Ryan had bought her. I was perplexed as to why an eighteen-year-old boy had so much money for gifts. I still got excited when my phone buzzed with a reply from her but she would often take up to three hours to reply, which made for a long time of waiting and yearning.

Shortly after Christmas, things between her and Ryan took a turn for the worse and one day after school she broke down in tears outside ASDA. "He's such a dickhead, Troy. Rachel saw him kissing some tart in the pub last weekend. I can't believe he's done it!"

I was, of course, delighted about this development, yet for some reason unknown, I defended Ryan.

"I'm sure he didn't do anything. He loves you Sophie. You can tell that just by seeing you guys together."

"Oh Troy, do you think so? Really? Because Rachel has never liked him, so she could be lying. What do you think?" she managed to respond while her sniffing subsided.

I gritted my teeth and responded, "Yeah, he wouldn't do that. Rachel's probably just jealous that you have a boyfriend. She's a total bull-shitter anyway."

I barely knew Rachel so this fleeting accusation was probably unfair.

Over the following weeks, the trouble with Ryan continued. If it wasn't rumours about his fidelity, it was stories of shouting, slammed doors and late night drunken arguments. Almost every day Sophie would tell me about how much of a dickhead this guy was, and I kept finding myself defending him. I had such strong feelings for her so I always wanted to cheer her up and couldn't bear to see her upset.

One day, she asked me straight up, "Should I split up with him?"

Despite every single part of me thinking, "Yes! Leave the wanker and go out with me," I feebly responded, "No, you should talk to him. Sort it out."

At the beginning of February, they broke up. She came in to school with blotchy eyes and rosy cheeks one day, said they'd split up, and that was that. Given the timing, in my schoolboy stupidity, I thought, with Valentine's Day approaching, I would finally tell her how I felt. I picked a fancy card for close to five quid which was a real fork-out for the fifteen-year-old man, and meant that I had to live off bread rolls with no filling at lunch for three days. I spent an age deliberating over what to write in the card before finally going for, "Sophie, I think you're great. Do you want to go to the cinema with me next week? Love from Troy x."

Valentine's Day morning, I was terrified. This was the biggest thing I'd ever done. The most scared and excited I'd been since going on The Ultimate at Light Water Valley. My heart was pounding and my head felt like it was ready to explode by the time I arrived in the form room. During the previous day's planning, I hadn't thought how I would actually get the card from my pocket into her hand. I couldn't do it in the form class, as if other people saw, I'd get ribbed. My impromptu plan was to sneak it into her bag during morning registration. I skillfully pretended to tie my shoe laces as a decoy, then successfully smuggled it in. As we didn't share any classes together, and didn't hang around in the same group at break times, I had to wait until afternoon registration before I would get her response. It was a torturous wait.

By the time I was heading upstairs to class I was even more nervous than the morning. It's done now, I thought. No turning back. I borrowed some of Matt's Lynx Africa and sprayed loads of it all over my jumper in preparation for what was going to be either the best or worst moment of my life.

I arrived at class to see Sophie with two other girls around her. One of them was holding a heart-shaped balloon and the other was tucking into a giant Toblerone mountain. As I made my way over, my eyes caught sight of at least ten opened envelopes on the table. The three girls were in buoyant mood, giggling and chattering about all the attention that they had got. Upon further inspection, I saw the girls had put their cards into separate piles. The largest pile was, of course, Sophie's.

I felt like I had been punched in the gut. Everyone had sent Sophie a fucking card. She finally noticed me and called me over, "Hey Troy. Thanks for the card. That was so sweet. You are such a good mate."

Even in my age and lack of experience with anything, I knew that it was all over. No reference to the cinema invite and a huge reference to being good "mates" which I knew immediately was all it was ever going to be. I didn't sit with her that class and the next time I saw her was outside ASDA after school, holding hands with a rugby-playing scally from year eleven. Devastated – my first taste of heartbreak.

It took me a while to get over it all but by the summer I had managed to get a sort of girlfriend called Laura. We met at a Barn Dance and had a fleeting, sexless two-month relationship. Barring a mutual dislike of Simon Cowell, we didn't share a whole lot in common but everyone was getting girlfriends and boyfriends so we were a convenience to each another, stopping us from being outsiders.

The fling helped and after a few months, I managed to stop thinking about Sophie every waking moment. We stopped sitting together in class and gradually drifted apart. We chatted at parties and saw each other in the parks, pubs and clubs of the local underage drinking phase in subsequent years, but we were never close again – more acquaintances, than friends.

And that's the story of Sophie. Until now anyway; by some unbelievable twist of fate, she was in Hong Kong, standing right in front of me.

CHAPTER TEN

❝Oh my God!'' she said disbelievingly after taking a moment longer to recognize me than I had her, "Is that you Troy?"

She threw her arms round me and we embraced, the scent of strawberry shampoo gladly – heroically – fighting through my blocked nostrils, while her pal stood on looking a bit anxious. After the excitement died down, I gathered myself and managed to ask normal questions as to what she was doing in Hong Kong. She told me that she'd arrived four weeks ago and was here on a two year placement with Ernst Young, before I told her my own tale, glossing over my reasons for leaving Leeds as fancying a change of scenery.

"Right, let's have a proper catch-up tomorrow night," she decided, after ten minutes of frivolous chattering had become too much for her noticeably impatient pal. "Here's my number. Call me and we'll go for drinks. I can't believe this!" She flashed a smile then headed out the door. I was stunned.

I looked down to realize that I'd been holding a pack of extreme weight gain Kreotine for the duration of our chat.

I got home feeling giddy and struggling to regain a regular breathing pattern. This was the feeling of teenage lust coming back to me after a long absence. I was just about to calm down with a shower when my phone vibrated:

"Can't believe we saw each other! Anna's gone home now, so wanna have a coffee in 10mins? X."

Without hesitation, I replied.

"Sure. Come to mine. My apartment is on the road behind the chemist. X."

Seventeen seconds later.

"Send me your address and I'll be straight over."

I had ten minutes, possibly fifteen to prepare. I didn't want to go all-out attack as this wasn't a date. It was merely meeting up with an old friend, albeit an attractive female one, for a coffee. I couldn't change as she'd just seen me and it would be obvious that

I was making too much of an effort. I had, however, developed a large sweat patch on my back which was the breaker. I took off my top and without having consciously thought about it, found myself doing some bicep curls with my dumbbells for the first time in three weeks and the fourth time I'd used them since their purchase. It was fairly pathetic behaviour but immediately after doing weights, my swollen arms would create the illusion that there was at least some kind of muscle there – a good trick.

I did one hundred bicep curls and fifteen press-ups, took a thirty second in and out shower, then changed into my newest casual wear, grey joggers and a loose fitting plain white T-shirt. I wanted to look like I'd been lounging. Not like I'd been aggressively doing weights. A quick brush of the teeth and two generous sprays of CK One and I was ready. (Since adolescence, I have always put a spray of aftershave behind my ear after a friend's self-proclaimed womanizing older brother once advised us that girls "loved it." I wasn't sure of the validity of his claims: but some twelve years later, I still find myself adhering to his worldly-wise rule.)

Weights, shower and change had taken me approximately seven minutes. This gave me a tiny window of time to create a better image of my flat. I fake swept the floor, sweeping everything under a well-positioned brown mat, then sprayed the place with fruity air freshener. I regretted this decision as it probably made the place smell like I'd just been to the toilet and wanted to conceal the evidence.

Finally, I had to consider music. My laptop, which was ageing, took at least five minutes to start up but was fortunately already on and I thought a bit of background music wouldn't go amiss. It would make for a better mood, cover up any potential breaks in conversation and, if I did it right, it was an opportunity to appear cool. There was a time when I would have just put shuffle on my I-tunes and not thought much of it but I had fallen foul of that once or twice. Once notably, I had a house party at mine and shuffle shot me in the foot. To start with it played two Boyzone tracks in a row; I only had three Boyzone tracks out of thousands so this was wretched luck. After I'd taken an aggressive ribbing (including a severe dead leg from Ismael whom I deliberately hadn't invited but had shown up anyway) and had just about managed to laugh it off, things got worse; an hour later a song that I had recorded with a year eight high school band came on. It was a terrible song, sung by me in a pre-pubescent attempt at an American accent and I had no idea it was still on my computer. I'd learnt from my mistakes though and wasn't going to get caught out this time. Fuck you shuffle.

I flirted initially with the idea of putting on a band that was popular when we were in school but thought that would come across as trying too hard, cheesy and possibly even a bit creepy. Next, I considered putting on some drum and bass music, but stopped because I don't like – and despite several attempts – never have liked it. I finally settled on Frank Ocean's Channel Orange which I liked and hopefully (and misleadingly) would make me appear knowledgeable about modern music.

I set the volume to an ambient background level, then placed the laptop slightly skewed in the corner of the flat so as to appear as though no effort had been put into the music selection. The doorbell rang. She had been exactly ten minutes; deep breath.

"Hey. You found it OK? Come in, I'll just put the kettle on," I said.

"Hi. Yeah. Well I thought it would be nice to have a cuppa after such a coincidence."

I gave Sophie a tour of the flat with a well-practiced (not particularly funny) ironic estate-agent, silly voice. She seemed to enjoy it and sat down while I fought through shaking hands and managed to make two cups of coffee.

"So, tell me again. When did you get here then?" I asked her.

"Three weeks ago. It was a spontaneous decision. They said there was an opportunity out here and I said I was interested. The next week I was booking tickets, a bit of a whirlwind. It still seems surreal that I'm living in Hong Kong. Even more surreal is that I'm in your flat!"

We chatted animatedly while drinking our coffee. It was easy to talk to her and I was pleased with my long-term memory for remembering what kind of things made her laugh. She was talkative, but not just about herself and seemed interested in my own story.

After some deliberation we finally agreed that the last time we had seen each other was three years ago at the Original Oak pub on Christmas Eve.

"Don't you remember?" Sophie asked me, cheerfully. I was glad that her Yorkshire accent hadn't deserted her in London.

"A group of us had a game on Deal or No Deal on the It-box. We did really well but you messed up right at the end. We could've got twenty quid but you went for the wrong box and we got 60p!"

I have a largely frowned-upon habit of drinking too heavily on Christmas Eve so I couldn't recall the game. Besides, I have wasted many hours, and lots of 50ps on the It-boxes over the years, so despite her angelic presence, it wasn't too surprising that this particular game had not stuck in the memory. In fact, the only particular game I remember was a game called Football Crazy when I managed to get "Lundekvam" as a Southampton legend and won eight pounds.

Nonetheless, I was flattered that Sophie remembered our last meeting so clearly. The reminiscence made me get that welcome warm feeling that is difficult to describe without sounding like a drip. The feeling is most commonly associated with meeting up with an old friend from school and by the third pint you talk about old times, exaggerate how good they actually were, and feel happy with nostalgia.

Unfortunately, during my last year in Leeds, such nostalgic nights were often ruined by futile attempts to chase the past highs. Someone usually suggested, "Let's go to Basement" (a club we frequented as teenage idiots), and we'd get there feeling happy and excited, then walk in and realize that we were the oldest group of men there, and that time had, in fact, moved on.

I utilized my train of thought by telling Sophie a story about how a mutual school friend of ours had been turned down by an eighteen-year-old girl recently because – in her words – "he was too bald". This led us to chat for a while about old school friends which was enjoyable, and at points we were both laughing hysterically. Sophie had an endearing trait, which I remembered from school, of making a weird snorting noise when she laughed a lot. The snort would make her blush, but then, with embarrassment, she would start laughing – and snorting – even more.

As the Frank Ocean album was approaching the midway point, I asked Sophie if she wanted another cup of coffee and gladly she accepted. After I returned from my cupboard of a kitchen with two freshly-brewed mugs, we talked more about what had brought her to Hong Kong; she cited disillusion with London life. I knew she had gone to Durham University and wasn't surprised when she told me that she'd got a first class degree which had qualified her for a top graduate scheme in London.

"What they don't tell you is that in these schemes you start well below even the bottom tier of the ladder. The first three months of the job were unbearable. I'd worked so hard and was so happy to get the job but it was awful. I don't want to sound big-headed but at Durham, I had loads of friends and a brilliant social life. When I moved to London, it was the exact opposite – I was nobody. It was really difficult to take."

"I'll bet," I offered, annoyed with myself for not having a clever comment to make about the pitfalls of the mid-twenties London dream.

"Apart from the demoralizing work, I loved the London life for the first year, and met some people whom I thought were great."

My heart irrationally sank at this point as I was aware that at least one of these "great" people was probably a boyfriend.

"But after a while, I realized it was bullshit. It was so competitive. Even going on a night out was competitive – where to go, which bars to be seen in, etc., which DJs were playing. – DJs are idiots. I needed to leave."

I nodded, interested by the story. I had considered moving to London. In fact, I had applied for several jobs there, but never got past the first interview. Three of my good friends from Leeds had taken the plunge, and were enjoying varying levels of success.

A bunch of friends and acquaintances from university had also gone and though most of them had Facebook statuses boasting about how great their lives were, coupled with photos in swanky wine bars or at gigs of little-known, soon-to-be-huge bands, I wasn't sure how many of them were actually enjoying it. There were never any photos of small flats without heating or bank statements.

"It's not what you know but who you know," she said dejectedly.

This overused saying irks me. I have been on this planet for nearly twenty-seven years and have got to know quite a few people in that time. I have never once in that time met someone who said, "You seem like a good guy. I can get you a great, well-paid job." This, "who" person doesn't seem to exist. Maybe I'm just not very good at networking? Networking can piss off.

Sophie told me she'd lived in Hackney for two years and spent a few months in Shoreditch before the Hong Kong offer came about.

"I just couldn't turn it down. It's an adventure. I've spent my whole life in England so why not have some time away?" I agreed with her wholeheartedly and went on to talk about how great Hong Kong was, overplaying the activeness of my social life by namedropping bars that I'd never been to.

After nearly an hour of engaging conversation, Sophie eventually told me that she had to get home as she had a Skype date with her sister. I overlooked the annoying phrase and was thinking about how much I'd enjoyed catching up over the last hour, when I realized that the Frank Ocean album was in the final seconds of the last track.

Now trying to hurry the exit up, I opened the door and said,

"Looking forward to tomorrow night!" and gave her a hug, while also moving subtly forwards to get her out of the flat. I managed to shut the door just as, "It's Raining Men", by Geri Halliwell was starting. I'd got away with it.

The afternoon had been, to use a soppy word, lovely – just lovely. So lovely in fact, that my feelings had seemingly jumped in a time-machine and gone back eight years to when I was hopelessly in love with her. I still was. Could I say, still was? More a case of a lengthy hiatus; but now I was again. Definitely.

CHAPTER ELEVEN

About an hour after Sophie had left, I was coming to terms with the fact that I had just met the first girl I loved, by complete chance, in a Hong Kong chemist's. It was a pretty good story so I called Sander to tell him about my afternoon.

"That's cool man. She hot?" he replied in a calm, unconcerned manor after I spilt out my story with childlike giddiness.

"Isn't it amazing though?" I continued.

"Yeah it is. Last week I fucked a Swiss girl that I met in Thailand last summer," Sander said and I could just picture his mouth breaking into a smile. Sander is one of those people, of whom there are far too many, who brings every story back to himself. Most of the time when I am talking I get the impression that he is just listening out for a chance to tell his own, better story on the same subject. It was annoying but I was not letting this Scandinavian prat ruin my jubilant mood.

"I'm meeting her tomorrow night. Which bar do you think I should suggest?" I asked.

"Hmm. What time are we meeting them?" he responded.

"We?"

"Yeah. You said she has a friend so obviously you'll want someone to take care of her, right?"

"No I don't think her friend's coming. Will probably just be me and her." In a case of improbably unfortunate timing, my phone beeped. It was a text from Sophie:

"Hi. Still can't believe it. Thanks for a great afternoon. I'm bringing Anna tomorrow so do u want to bring a friend? You name the bar and time xx."

Dom was currently on a basketball tour in Guangdong so it would have to be Sander. Bollocks.

"Come to mine at seven tomorrow night then," I told him.

I had only recently had a haircut, but keen to look the part for the evening, I went to Kwan's Barbers after work the next day. Whereas getting a haircut in England was an overpriced chore – where I had to endure conversing with a pink-T-shirt-wearing idiot telling me, in graphic detail, about his conquests in Ibiza (he was always going to Ibiza – how much was he getting paid?) – in Hong Kong it was an underpriced privilege. For less than five pounds, the enigmatic, middle-aged Kwan gave me the works. The language barrier meant zero conversation was required or expected and I could, if I wanted, close my eyes while he gave me an immaculate cut, followed up by another rinse, head massage x2 and a cleaning of the ears – superb.

While I was still feeling refreshed and semi-confident after my trim, Sander arrived at mine at five to six, over an hour earlier than I'd said to him, wearing an expensive turquoise T-shirt. I knew it was expensive because he had told me twice that it cost ninety quid. He had gone for some questionable hi-top trainers which I complimented him on despite not being a fan.

"So, where are we meeting the girls?" he asked, lighting a cigarette even though he knew I didn't like him smoking in my flat.

"Delaney's first, then we'll see what they fancy?"

I'd opted for an Irish-themed pub which was a five minute walk from my place in Wan Chai. Lots of people moan about Irish Pubs or "Plastic Paddies" as the haters call them (these are the same sort of people who are delighted to tell you that Diet Coke is "actually worse for you than real Coke!"), but I have no problem with them. I figured it would be a good place to start the night as it was not too noisy; we could talk and catch up properly. Sometime after turning twenty-one, I stopped liking bars that are too loud to talk in and now question if I ever did actually like them.

I put on two-thirds of my best outfit – chinos and white shirt – but mixed things up by wearing some Adidas trainers to try to appear a bit casual. I looked at myself in the mirror and thought I looked reasonable. I'd had a beer though so this could have been a case of beer goggles. We had arranged to meet the girls at eight, which gave Sander time to beat me twice on FIFA while we supped two more Coronas to build up some Dutch courage.

"So, did you two fuck?" Sander asked after infuriatingly dinking in a penalty with Thomas Sorensen.

"It's a long story but no," I replied before giving him a brief rundown of events, to which he laughed, then patted my shoulder in a friendly, yet incredibly patronizing way.

"I think you have unfinished business!" he smirked.

We got to the pub early, just in time to secure a decent seat before the place busied for the eight until nine happy hour. Sander went up to the bar, and as usual got a couple of drinks and refused to take my money.

He sat back down and we waited. Sander was not nervous at all. He was fine. This was just a Friday night to him. To me, it was a lot more. I was terrified. Sophie and I had got on exceptionally well before, but one thing I was concerned about was that maybe I was being too self-deprecating. Taking the piss out of yourself is one of the easier ways to make a girl laugh, but on the flip side, it is more likely to make them see you as a mate rather than a potential boyfriend. Everybody knows this but as someone who's fallen foul of it exactly three times, I was desperate to avoid it this time. How many girl "mates" do men actually have anyway? If you are mates with a girl, the likelihood is that one side (usually the man) is after more – "He'd do anything for me, we're so close!" – Ah, shut up, you know he wants to sleep with you!

At half-past eight, the two girls arrived both looking even more glamorous than they did at the chemist's. Sophie had clearly spent a while getting ready. She had done something with her hair – it was bigger and wavier – and she was wearing more make-up. She'd gone for a green and red floral dress which was almost definitely from H&M and was wearing uncomfortable looking high heels. She looked stunning.

I regretted the Adidas trainers.

Anna, her pal, had also made a sizeable effort to impress. I didn't really take her in before but I now appreciated that she was a good-looking girl. She also was wearing a floral dress – probably the other part of a two-for-one offer, I considered – and she had straightened her long, blond hair.

"Show time," Sander whispered as we went to greet them.

We said hello and I gave Sophie a hug, which sadly gave me a slight erection. Bad start, I thought and started to blush, hoping that she hadn't noticed. I gave Anna a clumsy kiss on the cheek. She moved her head too quickly and I kissed her far too near her mouth. (Once you reach your mid-twenties, it is expected that you should give women a hug and peck on the cheek as a greeting. I wish it wasn't. There is too much opportunity for error.)

Sander gave Sophie a longer hug than I did and, without any problem, kissed Anna on both cheeks. We headed over to the table and ordered some drinks. I sat next to Sophie in the corner seats and Sander and Anna sat opposite. We had polite four-way conversation for a while. Sophie told us about how difficult it was finding a flat when she first got here and how it's better money but longer working hours at Ernst Young in Hong Kong. Anna told us how she had only lived in Hong Kong for two months but thought she could spend the rest of her life here. I doubted whether she had thought this through thoroughly but didn't comment.

Sander was on good behaviour. I didn't like to admit but his conversation skills with women were phenomenal. He was undeniably talented. He asked the right questions, smiled and laughed accordingly. He painted a good picture of himself as a kind, confident and charming man. I could see through the bullshit but even the brightest of girls usually didn't. His confidence helped to put us all at ease and he gained an exaggerated laugh with an anecdote about one of his workmates falling asleep in the toilet at Delaney's and waking up at six a.m. in a locked pub.

Half an hour and a couple more drinks passed when Sophie asked me if I wanted to join her for a cigarette. I would have liked to spend a few minutes alone with her, but I don't smoke. Sander accepted the invitation and the two headed outside. Sitting with Anna, a girl I didn't know, I felt a bit nervous but she immediately started talking – a lot. She had an accent I recognized as Northwest England; Bolton, Preston, or one of those towns.

"Oh my God! I can't believe you met Sophie here. I think it's amazing!" she started.

"Yeah, I know, it's…. ."

"I love Sophie. She's great. I met her when we were having a cigarette after work two weeks ago and we've become like sisters!"

I'm not sure you can develop quite that strong a relationship with someone over two weeks but I nodded and smiled. I was starting to think that Anna might be a bit impulsive. And annoying.

"Oh my God. We got so drunk on Wednesday. I had two glasses of wine, four shots of vodka and two bottles of beer. It was an epic night!" Anna continued, confirming my thoughts. "Epic" is a chronically overused word. If you are talking about the Lord of the Rings trilogy, that's fine; it's appropriate. If describing drinking heavily in a bar, it's not.

72

After what seemed like ages, Sander and Sophie returned giggling.

"Right, we're going to Azure. The girls have never been before," Sander told us.

"Awesome. I've heard it's sick!" said Anna. We got up and headed out to the taxi-rank.

Azure is a relatively posh bar, on the twenty-ninth Floor of a hotel in Lan Kwai Fong. Like most of the bars in Central, it is criminally overpriced, but I still like it. Lively enough to dance, but also with the option of sitting in a quieter area or playing pool. I was hoping we would get a mixed doubles game of pool later as it was the one thing I knew that I was better than Sander at. For that very reason, he would probably claim that pool is shit and refuse to play.

Sander sat in the front of the taxi, which gave me a chance to talk with Sophie in the back. Anna had fortunately quieted down a bit so Sophie and I reminisced about our school days some more and had a laugh discussing what our old classmates were up to nowadays. She informed me that Sarah Scott now had two kids and worked in a chippie and I told her that last time I saw Imran Younis, he was kissing another man. Helped by the drinks and conversation with Sophie, I was feeling fuzzy by the time we get to Lan Kwai Fong, and started to wonder if it was acceptable to try to kiss her later on in the night. I decided that I probably would.

We got into the bar and Sander ordered a bottle of Grey Goose Vodka and Sprite for our table which we drank greedily and quickly. I continued to chat about old times with Sophie, while Anna and Sander were playing some kind of drinking game involving dice. I don't know where the dice came from. Did Sander take them out with him? A pulling prop?

Our conversation turned to more serious matters when Sophie resumed talking about her parents' break-up. She almost started crying at one point but held firm. I consoled her and found that my arm was round her waist.

She looked through her vodka-blurred eyes into mine and said, "I'm so happy to see you again Troy. I know we were only kids but I've always missed you."

"You too Sophie," I replied, "like you wouldn't believe."

I wasn't sure if I was imagining it but her face seemed to be moving towards mine. My heart started to pound and I felt a rush of blood to the head. Did she want to kiss me?

Suddenly, I felt a cold, wet finger shoved deep into my left ear.

Snapped out of what was possibly an invented moment, my excitement made way for disgust as I turned round to see Sander laughing hysterically with Anna.

"What the fuck are you doing?" I asked him, before realizing that Sophie was also laughing and pretended that I was amused too, my scowl swiftly turning to an unconvincing, flat smile.

"Hey, chill out man! Come on, it's Friday night – time to dance!" Sander said, then led the way to the dance floor. We followed him and Anna asked me, deliberately loud enough for Sander to hear, "Is he single?"

Timberlake's new song, which I happen to like, was playing and we jostled to the middle of the now-crowded dance floor. I'm a poor dancer at best, but over the years have managed to develop a kind of slow, repetitive movement that qualifies as dancing but isn't really. It doesn't get much attention, but I would prefer that than to try to dance seriously and get scowled / laughed at. (For something that is such a large part of socializing, very few people are actually good at dancing. It is a strange form of socializing. People stood around, moving their bodies but not actually going anywhere. Of course, it also acts as a major mating ritual; is that the main purpose? If aliens were to come to earth and see a dance floor at one a.m., I think they'd be suitably confused.)

Unlike me, Sophie was a good dancer – classy and sexy. Of course she was. In what was now a bit of a drunken stupor, I forwardly dived straight in and put my hands on her hips; the romantic tactics of a seventeen-year-old in a Ben Sherman shirt. She accepted this and we danced together, laughing and singing the words to the music. I knew all the words to the chorus but not the verse, so when it came, I tactically took a long swig of my drink and kept the glass there so I didn't have to suffer the indignity of getting the words wrong.

Unfortunately, the next track was Gangham Style which I didn't find particularly funny the first time I heard it. Now, on the eight thousandth time I'd heard it in the last six months, it was becoming a little tiresome. Sophie further went up in my estimations by saying in my ear.

"I'm so sick of this shit song," before, "I'm going out for a cigarette."

She mouthed the universal smokers-on-a-dance-floor action to Sander and he immediately stopped dancing with Anna and nodded his head.

"You take care of this one," he said pointing to Anna who was now doing the horse-riding dance. Jesus. I humoured her but, to her annoyance, didn't do the dance and we danced near – but not with – each other throughout a Calvin Harris number. Following that, a nonsensical Rihanna track came on where I shook hands with a drunk, rosy-cheeked Chinese man who claimed to know me but I was certain that we hadn't met before.

After a while, I noticed that Sophie and Sander hadn't returned so I headed out to the balcony smoking area to meet them. I even decided that I would have a cigarette. I was drunk, it was a good night. I'll smoke, I thought to myself, and became excited at the prospect of it. I stumbled towards the door and in my good mood, did the irritating drunk man thing of wanting to shake the bouncer's hand. Bouncers must get so annoyed by this. Or do they enjoy the celebrity status? Either way, it took me a while to convince him.

"Shake my hand mate," I slurred as the tall, muscular Filipino looked back at me.

Eventually he reluctantly grasped my sweaty palm then opened the door to the smoking area. Buoyant, I walked outside and dodged in between people on the now crowded balcony.

Then I saw it; unmistakably.

Sander had one hand on the back of Sophie's neck, and the other on her waist and she had both arms draped round his neck. They were kissing passionately.

I was stunned, and devastated. My response was to turn around and head back into the bar. As I walked back in, feeling abruptly sobered, Anna staggered towards me, drunk and loud, "Do you want some coke?" she asked.

Without thinking about it, I replied, "Yes," and we made our way to the toilets upstairs. Anna was holding my hand and dragging me along which was annoying but she had offered to give me drugs so I didn't say anything. Cocaine seemed a reasonable short term solution for my shattered heart.

*

Since arriving in Hong Kong, I hadn't touched drugs, apart from one afternoon on a junk (a traditional Chinese ocean-going boat often used for recreational uses by expats), when I'd shared a joint with a rugby-playing South African man. As it had been over a year since the last time I'd smoked weed, it went straight to my head, and coupled with a bout of sea sickness, had ruined my day.

Like many people, I'd succumbed to peer-pressured experimentation as a teen, and under the guidance of a reckless friend whose cousin was a local dealer, we spent sixth form working our way through the food chain, from cannabis up to cocaine. The most fun in my own experiences was undoubtedly ecstasy but it came with the slight snag that the next two days of my life were always an unbearable combination of nausea, anxiety and self-loathing. Having an excellent time for six hours to have a dreadful time for forty-eight hours is not a fair trade off.

I seldom bothered with drugs throughout university. There was the odd silly night out fuelled by MDMA or MKAT which became huge for a few months while it was still legal and sold as plant food. These nights usually resulted in having grossly over-sentimental conversations with friends, then being so embarrassed the next day that I didn't want to see them ever again.

At the start of my working life, cocaine had started to become the popular drug of choice among my friends and I'd tried it once or twice. It turned me into an over-confident narcissist but it was undeniably enjoyable. The issue was the price though. Spending forty quid – a full day's call centre graft – on a small packet of powder which was probably more flour than cocaine was not practical. Coupled with the amount you drink when on cocaine, it was easy to spend a week's wages within a few hours that you wouldn't remember the next day.

*

So that's my brief drug history. It was about to resume now. Anna handed me a small packet and said that I should go into the toilet first and she would wait. I clasped the packet in my moist hands and giddily made my way to the toilet. I headed into the cubicle and I was happy to see a ledge on the side which was perfect for organizing the lines. You're supposed to feel like a rock star when you snort cocaine so kneeling in a strangers' piss and snorting it off a toilet seat damages the image a tad. I noticed that Anna had given me a massive bag, full of loads of powder. My inexperience meant I couldn't guess how much of it there was or how much it was worth. It was definitely a lot. Why did she have so much?

I clumsily poured out a generous amount on to the ledge, put the packet back into my pocket, and proceeded in chopping it into two lines using my provisional driving license. I then realized that

I was out of cash so had to use an old Seven Eleven receipt to make my snorter.

I rolled it into a well-crafted cylinder then leaned over the ledge and snorted the larger of the two lines in one go. My nose stung sharply and my right eye started to water. I could tell that this was good quality cocaine. I took a powerful sniff then prepared myself to take the second line. Just as I was doing this, there was a loud knock on the door. At first I thought it was Anna, getting impatient.

"One minute," I managed but to my shock I heard a man's voice.

"Open the fucking door!"

Shit.

"I'm on the toilet mate. Give me a min…"

As I was speaking, the Filipino bouncer whom I'd shook hands with a few minutes previously had climbed up the door and was looking over the cubicle. I had been caught red-handed.

CHAPTER TWELVE

"Come out of there now. You're fucked!" He looked livid. I was terrified. What a terrible five minutes.

I opted for an accepting, deeply apologetic stance. I opened the door and tried to say sorry but before I could speak, the bouncer had got me in a strong head-lock – a vice-like grip. With his arm round my neck, I could barely breathe but managed to splutter. "Look, I'm sorry. You caught me. I'll go. I won't come back here again."

"Too late for that," he said.

I started to panic. What was going to happen? Best case scenario was that he gave me a slap and told me to fuck off. What was the worst? He pulled out his walkie-talkie with the non-head-locking arm and talked hurriedly in Tagalog. He then released me from the headlock but kept a firm hand on my shoulder.

"Follow me," he said, then led me out of the toilets, past a large queue at the girls' toilets. I didn't see Anna. Then he pushed me along past the crowded bar area where 'Take Care' by Drake was playing. Not many people paid attention to what was going on but those who did probably knew exactly what had happened – a man being led out of a toilet and pushed along by a bouncer is fairly self-explanatory.

He escorted me out of the bar and to the lift. This was not a time to be standing waiting for a lift, I thought. After a ten second wait, it arrived and he shoved me in hard enough for me to stumble and my back to smash into the adjacent wall, causing a sharp pang of pain. He pressed ground floor. Then he turned round, looked at me, didn't say anything and absolutely cracked me in the face. It was one hell of a punch and it nearly knocked me out. I gathered myself and stayed on my feet. Lifts are awkward at the best of times. A lift when the only other person in it has just punched you in the face is beyond awkward. It was ridiculous. I stood, silent, holding my face.

We finally got down to the ground floor and he grabbed my shoulder again and pushed me outside. With it being the height of rainy season, it was now lashing it down so I was soaking wet within two seconds of being outside. I tried to wipe the water out of my eyes and to my horror, noticed that there was a police car waiting outside the hotel.

The bouncer spoke quickly and aggressively to two young-looking policemen as they both scowled exaggeratedly, one nodding his head while the other shook his. The policemen were both wearing black berets and clad in short-sleeved pale blue T-shirts, which were gradually becoming navy as the heavy rain drops stained them. They were both small but one was sturdy with lean muscle and the other was incredibly scrawny with pipe-cleaner arms thinner than my own. Their waistlines were dominated by weighty, police-related equipment; a walkie-talkie, a truncheon, a gun and some handcuffs which the sturdy officer had some difficulty in un-attaching.

"Please put your hands behind your back," he asked politely.

I duly obliged and felt my body shudder as the cuffs were clamped on, painfully cutting into my wrists. Being handcuffed is an extremely low ebb. The action momentarily jolted my frazzled brain into reality and I realized with a sudden clarity the trouble that I was in.

I've only had one previous brush with the law when I was caught taking a piss behind a KFC one Saturday night. On that occasion my punishment was an eighty pound fine. I fancied that I was in more trouble this time.

Cocaine, like alcohol, affects me (and everyone else I'd suppose) depending on my mood and the environment I'm in. Safe to say, right now was not a good time to be feeling wired from the line I'd just had. My mind was racing and I was terrified. The spindly policeman showed surprising strength in pushing me into the car, saying the classic "watch your head" as I manœuvred my tall frame into the back seat. For a moment, my brain went off on an unhelpful, police-related tangent as I tried to remember what the alcoholic officer in The Bill was called.

The stronger-looking officer sat in the back with me, annoyingly opting to sit in the middle seat, so our legs uncomfortably touched. The thin officer shook hands with the Filipino bouncer, who looked satisfied with his night's work, then got into the front seat and started up the car. He didn't look old enough to drive. They didn't say anything to me.

I stared out of the rain-soaked window as the police car zipped past the Bank of China building and cursed my bad luck. Despite the predicament I was in, my mind kept drifting back to the sight of Sander kissing Sophie which was a further punch in my vodka-polluted stomach.

It was only a five minute drive from Lan Kwai Fong to the nearest police station on Arsenal Street in Wan Chai. The car pulled up in front of the station and the driver came and opened the door for me. The two policemen chatted animatedly in Chinese.

They stood on either side of me and walked me into the station where they talked to a couple of other policemen and a female officer who was sitting at the front desk looking bored. They took off my hand-cuffs then told me to remove my belt and my shoes. I put them into a gray plastic tray, similar to airport security.

"Anything in your pockets?" asked stickman.

"Yes. Here you go," I said and handed over my wallet and my ten year old Nokia 3310, which I'd bought on the cheap in Mong Kok Ladies' Market.

"Is that everything?" asked another cop.

I nodded, but then my heart sank as I remembered I still had the cocaine in my pocket.

Fuck.

Why did I not flush that down the toilet? What bad decision-making! I've never fared well under pressure – never one to step up in a penalty shootout. What should I do? I decided that I would be in more trouble if and when they found it so, resigned, I pulled out the crumpled bag and placed it in the tray with the rest of my belongings. This didn't stir as much of a response as I might have expected from the policemen whose facial expressions didn't change. "Thank you," one of them said then signaled for me to put my hands behind my back to prepare for the cuffs again.

I was then led, stocking-clad, to the cell. The floor was cold and sticky. My trousers were also falling down, and due to being handcuffed, I couldn't pull them up. I tried to shuffle my hips for support but it was a struggle and by the time I'd got to my accommodation for the night, my trousers had dropped well below my waist and were in serious danger of dropping to my ankles. Fortunately, they just about managed to stay up and I arrived at the cell with a small slither of dignity intact. The policeman fumbled with some keys, opened the door, then gently prodded my back, as I stumbled into the small cell.

"Wait here," I was instructed.

Unsurprisingly, the cell was grim. It was about half the size of the small bedroom in my flat, and complete with a horrible, pungent odour, which I recognized as a mix of sweat and urine. There was a small metal bench, which was presumably meant to be a bed, with a grubby, ripped pillow and in the opposite corner, there was a metal, seatless toilet. There were no windows so it was sub-tropical temperature and unbelievably clammy; a piss-smelling sauna. I sat down and sank into the classic stance of a broken man. Knees apart, elbows on them, and face in hands. I was drunk, and fairly wired so the whole situation hadn't totally sunk in yet. I sat like this for what was probably an hour and tried to gather myself. I didn't have a clue what the time was.

What was I going to do? I had no idea about drug laws in Hong Kong. Due to the old British rule, I imagined they were similar to back home. I certainly hoped so as I'd watched several episodes of Banged up Abroad and the justice system in some Asian countries wasn't appealing. Thai jails don't look very welcoming at all. Sander had recently told me that if you're caught in Singapore or Malaysia with drugs, you could face the death penalty. My trail of thought turned to intense paranoia. I could have just ruined my entire life. How much cocaine did I have on me? Enough to be charged with dealing, supplying?

I vomited in the toilet, tasting the Grey Goose vodka again as it came back up. Life was so much better when it was going the other way. What a disastrous downfall I'd suffered in the last hour; a strong worst-hour-of-my-life contender. I washed my face using the trickle of water from the tap and resumed my head in hands position, this time on the toilet. Improbably, I drifted into a sleep and I was startled awake when the door opened and a hard-faced, spectacled policeman entered my cell. I tried to stand up but because my elbows and all of my weight had been on my legs, I had contracted severe cramp. My legs were numb, and crumpled under my weight as I slumped straight back down onto the toilet seat.

The policeman gave me a glass of metallic, lukewarm water which I desperately needed. I felt reassured by this mild act of kindness and when the feeling had come back to my legs, I stood up and followed him out of the cell and into the corridor. The numbness had been replaced by an extreme case of pins and needles which was coursing through my calves but I managed to stagger along just behind the policeman.

We walked past the entrance area and through some double doors until I saw a sign saying: Interrogation Rooms. The policeman withdrew a large set of jangling keys and opened Room B. I entered the lifeless gray room which had nothing in it, bar an old, splintered rectangular table and two chairs opposite one another.

"Sit here," he told me and I obliged, relieved to take the weight off my lactic-acid-filled legs. Two minutes later, the door opened again, and another police officer entered, dressed in a different uniform suggesting a higher rank. I was looking down at my feet, mentally preparing what I was going to say in what could be a defining moment of my life.

What happened next stunned me.

CHAPTER THIRTEEN

The high-ranking police officer sat down in the chair opposite and I raised my head and looked at his face. It was Dixon – the football-loving student from Super English.

Whenever I'd seen him before, he had been a grinning, cheerful man. Usually clad in baggy, combat shorts and a dated Chelsea shirt, he appeared chubby, friendly and harmless – like a favourite, funny uncle. In this new setting he exuded a tougher, hardened manner. He seemed five inches taller and looked stronger, more powerful. His face was redder and the skin on his neck looked thick and leathery. His eyebrows seemed to have shifted into a more sinister angle and I spotted previously unnoticed wisps of graying hair creeping out the sides of his black beret.

Having seen him at least once a week since I started my job, I knew quite a lot about Dixon. Although the predominant topic of most of our classes was sport, I'd also learnt a brief synopsis of his life-story. The third time we met, he had told me in detail about the difficulties he faced when, just three months after meeting her, his girlfriend had fallen pregnant with his daughter. She was in her final year of university at the time, while Dixon had just graduated from his police training school and was working long, unsociable hours. In Hong Kong, it is still largely vilified to have children before marriage, so to avoid the chastisement of their families, they had rushed into a low-key budget wedding before revealing the pregnancy. By virtue of the wedding, his wife's wealthy father had bought them a new apartment in Tseung Kwan O to raise the baby. Four years after his first daughter was born, his wife gave birth to twin boys leaving Dixon with a tough job supporting his large family. Despite being "more intelligent" than him, Dixon's wife had never had a job, becoming a devoted full-time mother and housewife.

It was remarkable that this man whom I knew almost to the point of being friends was now staring me in the eye, and responsible for making decisions that could potentially ruin my life. I'd assumed he was a normal police constable. I had no idea that he was in such a lofty position, as he had never wanted to talk about his work. I looked at the badges sewn on to his white shirt, and noticed he had a red crown attached to his shoulder pads, which quite probably signified a high ranking. I had to contain myself from saying his name. He uttered some instructions to the two other police officers in Chinese and they swiftly left, shutting the door behind them. I presumed he was saying something along the lines of, "I'll take it from here lads."

"Hello. I'm Dixon Cheung, the Chief Superintendent of the Hong Kong Police Force. What have you did?" he asked, his eyes widening and a deep-set frown forming on his face.

For a second I totally forgot what was going on and considered correcting his English; he always struggled with tenses. My teaching clearly hadn't been particularly effective if he was still getting it wrong.

"I've made a big mistake, Dixon," I told him, having to make a special effort not to slur my words and deliberately using his name now in the hope of building an allegiance. "I've never done anything like this before. A man in the bar asked if I wanted to take some drugs. I was drunk, I said yes. He gave me them, and I got caught taking it in the toilets."

"Do you know how much drugs you had on you?" Dixon asked.

"I have no idea. They aren't mine. I swear," I told him, suddenly starting to feel extremely nauseous.

"You have nearly three grams of cocaine. We are awaiting test results to see how pure it is. This is a serious offence," Dixon told me sternly. "Don't call me by my name. I know who you are Troy. I'm surprised by what's happened tonight. You will return to the cell now while I think about what happens next."

With that, we stood up and he escorted me outside where the police constables were eagerly waiting to drag me back to the cell. I saw a clock in the hallway. It was nearly five a.m. I had work in just over five hours. I got back into the cold cell and sat down, legs shivering. I simply couldn't fathom what was happening. This was the second time that I'd had bleary eyes and a stinging nose in Dixon's company. However, on the previous occasion, it was due to my erroneous wasabi portion. This time the circumstances were much less cordial. Perhaps knowing Dixon was going to help me? Maybe he would go easier on me, give me a reprieve?

The booze was wearing off now, and I was starting to feel extremely dehydrated. The beginnings of a hangover were crashing in. I waited for twenty minutes when the door opened again and Dixon entered alone.

"Come with me, Troy," he said and I followed him out and back to the interrogation rooms. Feeling slightly reassured that he was calling me by name, we resumed our positions in the seats, and he looked at me.

"You're a good guy. I know that. But what you did is not good. I hate foreigners taking drugs in my city. I hate it." He raised his voice at this, looking angry. Even through his broken English and strong Chinese accent (probably the least frightening accent in the world) he sounded intimidating.

"You have enough cocaine to be dealer. I believe you that it's not all yours but you can go to prison for this."

"What? I can't go to prison!" I replied, too loudly and feeling a lump forming in my throat and a bead of sweat trickling down my back.

"You are lucky that I know you. I am going to speak with my colleagues and try to help you. There might be something we can do."

"I'll do anything if I don't have to go to prison."

"Go home now. You need to sleep. But come back here tomorrow at seven p.m. We will talk then. I doubt you would, but don't think about leaving Hong Kong because you are on our systems now."

With that, I was led back to the entrance of the police station where I picked up my things. I didn't say anything, and left. It was nearly six a.m. I started the short walk home, too tired to think. I would think tomorrow. The roads and pavements were still damp from the previous night's downpour and it was starting to get light. If I got home soon, I could get three hours sleep before work tomorrow morning. Jesus. As I arrived at my building I heard the first of the morning buses screeching and hissing its way past.

*

I had that abominable experience where it felt like I hadn't been to sleep at all when the alarm sounded. I'd inexplicably opted for the most annoying alarm tone I could find; simply a woman saying, "It's nine o'clock. Time to wake up," over and over again; infuriating and the outstanding reason for my waking up in a bad mood on weekdays. I rolled out of bed and was abruptly hit by memories of what happened last night. I got a feeling beyond sinking feelings. Devastated, scared and confused – an ugly combination.

I couldn't call in sick for work as I'd already had three isolated sick days. One of which I'd slept in and in an act of cowardice, hadn't dared to ring and tell them, so I was on a last warning now. I probably couldn't afford another sick day for the next six months. Given my adventure last night, and subsequent lack of sleep, the commute to work was horrific. I had run out of money on my Octopus card so needed to buy a manual ticket. There was only one coin-operated machine working and to continue my wretched, recent luck, a mainland Chinese tour group of ten elderly people were standing in front of me. Instead of just buying tickets for everyone in one go, they had decided to purchase each ticket individually. My day was bad enough as it was and I didn't fancy showing up for work late because of this lot. Finally I got my ticket and after sprinting down the escalator, managed to get on the train which would, barring any other delays, get me to work on time.

The train journey itself was shit. I tried to think about other things than my pending overseas imprisonment. My thought processes are anxious and erratic when I have a hangover, so the best I came up with was, "How deep underground are we? If I flew directly upwards, passing through the train ceiling and the ground above, where would I come out?" Not particularly useful.

After pushing off the crowded train and unsteadily pace-walking through the hordes of people that are always everywhere in this stupid city, I finally got to the school two minutes before my first class of the day. The events of last night had feasibly changed my life drastically but I didn't have the energy to think about it now. All I could think about was the fact that my head was pounding, I was sweating, my stomach was churning and imminently I was going to be holding a social class discussing the differences between formal and informal English, which I hadn't prepared a thing for. Hell. I wish that sometimes in life you could just be honest and it would be OK. Why couldn't I have just called Kit and said, "Look, I got arrested for possession of cocaine last night. I'm absolutely fucked. I also feel like shit and the girl I might love has probably slept with the sleaziest man I know. All in all, I don't think I should have to come in to work today."

The day was rough. There was a time in my teens when even the heaviest of nights on the booze would only result in two hours of grogginess. Nowadays, a heavy night leaves me with two days of nausea, sickness and self-loathing. Why is that? I stumbled in, jaded, and didn't even have time for a coffee before the social class. To my relief, only seven students had shown up so I didn't have to put on a great show. I told them all that I'd got a heavy cold, which didn't explain the pungent whiff of stale alcohol, in a bid to excuse myself for the upcoming poor class. I got through it reasonably unscathed. Marian and a couple of other heroes were in a talkative mood so the class turned into a group discussion talking about the price of rent and housing concerns in Hong Kong, rather than when and where to use formal language. I had five more classes to go but my head really was pounding now. I splashed water on my face, had a lukewarm, stomach-stinging coffee and ploughed on.

There was a hairy moment in one class where a business man asked me why I had told him that "at all" was one word. He had sent an email to his American boss who had corrected his spelling and bemoaned his lack of professionalism. I clearly remembered giving him this misinformation the previous week, but went for the easiest option – and denied it.

One thing about teaching is that even on the worst days, time goes reasonably quickly. I took a nap on the toilet for twenty minutes during my lunch break which gave me sufficient energy to complete the day. In a rare stroke of luck, the student in my last class failed to show up so I could leave early. I was due a bit of good luck. I was hoping that the cancelled class wasn't things balancing out. I needed a bit more. At least, I had time to go home and freshen up before heading to the police station to hear Dixon's proposition.

It's clever how your brain works at times. It can be very quick to vanquish bad memories. My day at work had been dreadful, but by the time I'd arrived at the MTR station, I had forgotten about it and my mind had moved on. On the way home, I thought about what was in store. How could I help? What could I possibly offer the Hong Kong Police Department? I would do anything they asked though. So long as I didn't have to call home and tell my mum I'd been arrested for drugs abroad and might be facing a lengthy prison sentence, I would do *anything*.

At home, I managed to hold down a cheese toasty and drank my fourth coffee of the day, then took a cold shower and dressed for the police station. I decided to put my work clothes back on, in an attempt to look more respectable than I did last night, which wouldn't be too challenging. I drew the line at a tie. I set off early for the walk down Gloucester Road to the police station and arrived at ten to seven. After a deep breath, I walked in. A short-haired female officer seemed to recognize me and directed me to take a seat in the waiting area.

The police station looked different to how I remembered it. At five a.m., the bright lights reflecting on the shiny white wallpaper had seemed brash and sinister, intensifying my negative mindset. Also it had been extremely quiet. The only other people I'd seen who weren't involved in my arrest were a couple of receptionists and a cleaner. This had caused an eerie atmosphere. I remembered the over-amplified noises of footsteps marching past my cell, heavy-duty police shoes squeaking and echoing on the shiny linoleum corridor.

Now, at dusk, and with a less fuddled brain, the station exuded a much more normal day-to-day feel. As I sat waiting, I watched as police officers finishing their shift walked past, jovial and chattering away loudly and the night-shift staff came in putting on a façade of cheerfulness when probably hating their colleagues who were off to the pub or home. Phones were ringing and walkie-talkies crackling as the night's work began to take shape.

I was surprised that I wasn't attracting any attention. I wondered how many people Dixon had told about my situation. A drunk and, by the looks of it, homeless, elderly Chinese man was causing much more of a stir as he barreled into the station shouting what, even to the locals, appeared to be gibberish. I watched as it took five policemen to escort him into the back rooms and most likely into his room for the night, while he sobered up; which could feasibly never happen.

After the drama of the drunkard, I noticed a fairly frightening anti-ketamine poster, featuring a skull with fire in its eye-sockets, on the wall. I was staring at it, trying to decipher the relevance of the skull and what the Chinese text might mean when a door banged open and Dixon marched over stiffly and greeted me.

"Hell, Troy. You look better but still very tired," he said. I was constantly getting told that I looked tired by Chinese people and had tried hard to stop taking it insultingly. Besides, I *was* tired. I was shattered. I stood up and followed Dixon out of the bustle and down the corridor to the interrogation rooms. Before he opened the door he turned to me and said, "I'm going to introduce you to my colleague who will explain things clearer than I can. My English is poor."

I was apprehensive about who I was going to encounter behind the doors but relieved to hear that I would be talking with a better English speaker. In spite of all of my casual lessons with Dixon, his grasp of the language hadn't improved much, if at all, and I feared that I wouldn't actually understand large parts of the upcoming critical conversation.

The door opened and I saw the splintered wooden table in the same place as the night before. Sitting opposite me was an attractive policewoman in her late thirties with shoulder-length, curly hair which had been dyed light brown. She had a wide mouth that dominated her face and looked as though it would be better suited smiling than scowling, which she was doing now. Dixon took his seat to the right of the female officer and he invited me to sit in the interrogation chair.

I sat down rigidly, making the effort to straighten my back as I would have done in a job interview.

"This is Detective Violet Liu who works with the drug squad."

I nodded unsurely and after waiting for an offer of a handshake that never came, felt nervous and looked at the floor.

"Good evening," said Liu in perfect English with an American or maybe a Canadian accent.

I think I fancied her.

"Superintendent Cheung has told us about events from last night. Are you aware that you have committed a serious offence?"

"Yes," I replied.

"This is a very unusual situation we find ourselves in. Normally you would be advised to get a good lawyer and most likely you would end up in prison for a period of time."

I find the expression "period of time" annoying but didn't see it as a suitable time to voice this particular gripe.

"However, given that Detective Cheung knows and likes you, we feel that there is an opportunity that could suit both parties."

"What?" I asked.

"There has been a dramatic increase in cocaine-related arrests in Hong Kong over the last six months. We believe that a group of foreigners are involved in a large-scale trafficking operation. We have a team of officers working on the case but we keep hitting dead ends. All the arrests we have got are for possession of smallish amounts. Nobody has given us any information about the main suppliers," she said. "Some of our officers have gone undercover to try to find a way in but it has been no use. We need a native English speaker to help us find a way into the circle."

"This is where you come in," Dixon added, seemingly wanting to remind me that he was there. We want you to work with the Hong Kong police. If you find out enough useful information, i. e. if you assist us in finding the top dealers, your case will not go to court and you will be free to go. What do you say?"

I was shocked. I felt lightheaded and it took a while for me to understand what had just happened. Was I really being asked to be an informant for the Hong Kong police? I was aware that I'd left England in search of an exciting new life but I'd assumed that the peak of my excitement would be ordering food at random off a Chinese menu and being served chicken feet. Not this. This was ridiculous. This was a bit too exciting.

"I'll do it."

"Good," said Dixon, as Liu sincerely nodded in approval.

The atmosphere in the room noticeably loosened and I was relieved to see Detective Liu smile at me and say, "I think you are making the right choice."

A woman's smile always makes things seem better.

"So, where do I start?" I asked.

"We believe that the cocaine you were in possession of came from the suppliers that we want. The first thing we want you to do is try to find out who your friend got the cocaine from."

"I got it from a man in the bar. I have no idea who," I said.

"Stop there," Dixon interrupted. If this is going to work, we need honesty. We know that's not true. The bouncer saw a young woman giving the drugs to you. Don't worry, she will not get into any trouble."

"OK, I'll call her tonight."

"Good."

"And then what?" I asked.

"Just try to get hold of a phone-number for the drug-dealer. Your friend must have it, or be able to get it. Then we will go from there," Detective Liu said confidently. "You will primarily report any information back to me but Dixon is leading the case so he will give you the orders."

Before I left, Dixon looked me in the eye and shook my hand. It was odd timing for a handshake but it reassured me that Dixon had my best interests at heart and I felt a little less terrified about the situation.

CHAPTER FOURTEEN

I left the station, texted Sander and got Anna's phone-number, which I remembered he'd got from her in the midst of his dice game wooing. I didn't ask him about Sophie as I didn't want to know. Sophie had texted me earlier in the day asking how my night was but I hadn't replied. Sander immediately got back to me with the number and an ambiguous, smiley wink.

I called Anna. "Hi Anna, how's it going? It's Troy."

"What the fuck happened to you last night?" she squawked.

"Sorry, I was too drunk so I left early."

"Where is my coke?" she asked angrily.

"Yes, about that, that's why I'm calling. Can you meet me at Pacific Coffee in twenty minutes?"

"OK, but I want my cocaine back," she replied frostily.

I got to Pacific Coffee early and ordered a couple of lattes and a pork Kaiser sandwich which always gives me a dodgy stomach but tastes good and I never learn. Fortunately a businessman left right on cue and the sofa became available – the best seat in the house. Anna stormed into the coffee shop with a face like thunder.

"Hello, mate. I got you a coffee," I said. I'm not a fan of when men call girls "mate" but I wanted to build up a level of unity with Anna before informing her that I no longer had the two hundred pounds worth of drugs she had entrusted me with.

"Where is it?" she asked, sitting down. She was wearing a trouser-suit which didn't really suit her but seemed appropriate attire for an angry woman. I wondered why she was dressed so formally on a Saturday.

"I lost it Anna. I'm really sorry. I was so pissed. It must have come out of my pocket."

"You did what? Do you know how much that was worth?"

"No, I don't but if you give me the dealer's number, I'll buy more and give it to you. I know I fucked up so I want to pay you back."

"I'm not giving you his number. He doesn't like me dishing it out. Just give me three thousand dollars and we'll call it even," she said, her tone becoming gradually less aggressive.

"I want to buy it for you Anna. And besides, I want to buy some more for myself. It was excellent coke from what I remember and I've got a big weekend coming up."

"Alright, fine. I'll give him a call and see if we can sort something out."

Now I'd offered to pay her back, she'd cooled down and we supped our coffees and chatted banally about our jobs for a while. She then told me that she had lost Sophie last night and ended up at a "buzzing" house party in Central until seven a.m. I bet she kissed a DJ.

"So did you get with Sophie last night or what?" Anna asked abruptly, causing me to gulp my coffee too quickly so that it went down the wrong way, causing an ungainly cough and splutter.

"No. Why would you ask that?" I asked after regaining my composure.

"She's been banging on about you all week – it's done my head in to be honest."

My self-esteem suddenly boosted, I momentarily forgot about everything shit that had happened in the last twenty-four hours. Men are quite pathetic in that sense. As soon as their ego is stroked by hearing of female interest, nothing else matters. Not even getting arrested abroad. She's been talking about me? That has to be a good thing? Perhaps I hadn't been imagining things after all.

"What has she been saying?" I asked, fishing.

"Just how you're such a nice guy and it has been amazing to bump into you," Anna continued, uninterested. "She said that you'd got fit since she'd last seen you too. I can't say I agree with her on that."

Cheers, Anna.

The butterflies that had formed in my stomach soon made way for yet another sinking feeling as I considered her reasoning for getting with Sander. If she had been talking about how nice I am, why would she then go and kiss a fucking prick of a guy? What the hell is wrong with women?

"Right. I'm gonna call Browny now," Anna said, with a rapid change of subject that interrupted my brooding and brought me straight back into the present. I could continue my romantic ponderings later on. She stood up and walked outside, holding her phone between her shoulder and her ear which seemed unnecessary as she wasn't doing anything with her hands.

I was unsurprised that the drug-dealer was known as Browny. It seemed like a suitable drug-dealer name. Approximately one minute later, she returned.

"I've placed an order for four grams. He'll give it me for three thousand. He says I can pick it up on Monday night but he lives in fucking Tuen Mun, which is miles away. I asked him if you can go and he said that it's alright. I'll give you his address and number. He says go around after eight o'clock," she told me, clearly pleased with herself for knowing a drug-dealer with a nickname.

"Nice one. Thanks Anna. I'm sorry I lost it, I'll go and sort this out."

"Alright, I appreciate that. I'm never giving you any coke again though, you dopey bastard," she replied, not joking.

I was pleased with how the exchange had gone. After initial reluctance, Anna had got me a drug-dealer's number and address and I was going to be meeting him. This should be it? All I had to do was tell the police this guy's address, then the police could follow me there and arrest him. Then it will all be over; easy enough?

I called Detective Liu and told her what I'd done. She seemed relatively pleased but less excited than I'd hoped, then asked me to hold the line for a minute. Six minutes later she returned. I had expected her to ask me to come to the station to plan the police raid on the dealer but to my surprise she said, "Just go and make the deal. Buy the drugs and talk to this guy. He is probably just a small fish but he might hold some key information."

I started to think that maybe the whole process wasn't going to be so easy.

*

Monday at work dragged badly. I was nervous in anticipation, and feeling strangely excited, about meeting Browny. I wished I could tell Dom about my adventures and that I had become an informant for the Hong Kong police. Despite the fact that I could comfortably end up in even more trouble than I was already in, it was undoubtedly a good story. Sadly, Liu had told me, quite reasonably I suppose, that if I told anyone I knew that I was an informant, the deal would be off.

Anna had given me this Browny character's address and phone-number. Work finished at six-thirty so I decided to go directly to Tuen Mun by MTR. Anna was right. It was "mileage." I'd never been there before and I was surprised to see that it was right at the end of the purple line, pretty much on the border of China.

It took just over one hour to get to Tuen Mun. Frustratingly I didn't get a seat the entire way. When I first got on, I allowed a woman to take the last remaining seat but when I got a closer look at her, I noticed that she was about thirty and neither pregnant, nor disabled. I suppose a bit of chivalry doesn't go amiss. I struggle with the giving-up-seat etiquette. Recently, after much deliberation, I'd given up my seat to an albino.

My feet sore and my thumbs aching from playing Snake on my phone for the duration of the journey, I arrived in Tuen Mun at seven-thirty and texted Browny, "Hi, it's Troy, Anna's friend. Are you in now?"

He replied swiftly, unlike a drug-dealer, "Meet me at the bridge in Tuen Mun Park and I'll take you up to my flat. I'll be there in five minutes."

The park was directly outside the MTR station. It was much better to meet there, than having to stumble around looking for his flat. This can be an issue in Hong Kong. Often the street numbers are in random orders and the housing estates all look pretty generic so it's easy to wind up in the wrong place. Twice I'd negotiated with front-door security-guards, got into buildings and knocked on the front door of completely the wrong flat. One time it was a young guy who politely gave me the correct directions in perfect English, and the other time it was an elderly woman who looked terrified at first, then extremely angry. I left as she was shouting in Cantonese, probably calling a husband to grab a baseball bat.

The park was picturesque, illuminated by lamp-posts, with a man-made pond, a few wide paths snaking around it, and trees lining the perimeter. Despite its pleasantness, it was a weird place. As I walked through the gates, I was greeted by a horrendous noise; a heavily distorted guitar with a woman screeching in Mandarin Chinese over the top of it. (I'm pleased to say that, after six ultimately unsuccessful Mandarin lessons, I had at least learnt to tell the difference between Mandarin and Cantonese fairly accurately.)

As I took in my surroundings, I saw that the middle-aged guitar-playing woman, who looked to be on drugs, was not alone. There were about fifteen live music performers scattered just a few feet away from each other, all playing different, totally uncorrelated music. There were five or six guitar players, a couple of men playing keyboards, a bongo player and three people singing – well, shouting – to karaoke backing tracks. There was also a group of five or six Filipino women crafting a fairly simple dance routine but the oldest member was really struggling and kept forgetting the moves. They were all giggling hysterically when she messed it up for the third time and she looked close to tears. There were a few people standing intermittently in the small park, watching these entertainers. A lot of the audience looked to be alcoholics, and / or homeless. This was unlike anywhere I'd seen in Hong Kong.

I headed over to an unnecessary bridge arched over a tiny pond and stood at the middle of it. As I was the only white person in the vicinity, I thought I should be easy for Browny to spot. I glanced at my watch and it was seven thirty-six. I felt a bit exposed standing on this bridge with singers and performers surrounding me. I was just considering what song I'd go for if I was expected to do a number, settling on the obvious 'Angels' by Robbie Williams, when a grubby middle-aged white man approached me surreptitiously.

"Alright, are you Troy?" he asked accusingly in a wispy, Merseyside accent.

"Yep. Browny?"

"That's me. Follow me, mate."

He was a terrible looking man. He looked reptilian. Short, unhealthily thin, with pointy features and terrible skin – jaundice yellow, decorated with spots and scratches. His bloodshot eyes were sunken, with deep-set wrinkles and dark grey bags underneath. He had matted, greasy hair stuffed under a faded red baseball cap. I got the feeling that this man probably took as many drugs as he sold.

He was wearing an old green Lacoste T-shirt which was coffee- or tobacco-stained on one sleeve, some Adidas jogging bottoms and a pair of brand new Reebok classics. I hadn't seen Reebok classics in a long time. (I remember buying a pair of white ones when I was in year seven at school and some year nine tormentors deliberately scraping their muddy shoes on them on the first day I wore them.)

What on earth was this joker doing living in a remote, very Chinese part of Hong Kong?

"How do you know Anna?" he asked me.

"She's a good friend of mine. I met her at work," I lied.

"Yeah. She's a good girl. I wouldn't mind a bit of that," he replied grinning, showing muddled yellow teeth that had clearly escaped the attention of an orthodontist.

I followed him as we entered a housing estate called Butterfly Estate which was rather unfitting for a drug-dealer. It was a number of old, dirty-looking tower-blocks with washing hanging out of almost every window. We entered the first tower-block and took the lift up to the 36th floor. In the lift he said.

"Anna says you want quite a bit of powder?"

"Yeah, that's right. We've got a party coming up next weekend so I was hoping to get four grams in?" I replied trying to act breezy, like I was experienced in the world of foreign drug deals.

"Should be alright. Don't tell any fucker where you got it from though. And I mean that," he said, and a drop of spit flew out of his mouth, looped up in the air and lofted down on to my chest. We both noticed but didn't comment. Do drug-dealers feel the same sort of awkwardness as the normal man, with situations like this? Or are they above awkwardness?

We arrived at his flat which had about fifteen different pairs of footwear strewn outside the front door. Before we entered I could hear the incessant beat of some sinister-sounding house music. The type which had no melody but occasionally makes fuzzy background noises. Exactly the sort of nonsense you would expect a drug-dealer to listen to.

We walked in and I was hit by an overwhelming stench of cannabis in the air. Peculiarly, Mario Kart 64 was being played on a huge flat-screen TV on the wall. I was surprised to see that the competitors were two young Chinese women sitting on an old sofa, which was the only furniture in the room, playing with an aggressive intensity. They were staring, glassy-eyed, at the screen and didn't even notice that we had entered the flat.

On closer inspection, they were clearly high as kites with saucer-sized pupils. That didn't seem to be affecting their performance though and I looked at the screen long enough to see that they were both fully aware of a sneaky short cut on Rainbow Road that only skilled players know about. Despite the house music blaring out, they had the sound turned up on full volume on the N64. What was it about Tuen Mun that meant contrasting music had to be played at the same time?

"Follow me, lad," Browny said and led me through the living-room to a bedroom. We walked in and I saw a Chinese man of indeterminate age passed out on a grubby mattress in the corner of the room.

"Don't mind him," Browny said and shuffled over to a chest of drawers. "Right. Here you go!" he said grabbing four milky-polythene packets.

"Wanna try it?" he asked me and I politely shook my head uttering an excuse about saving it for the party. He handed it over and I pulled the cash out of my pocket quickly – definitely too quickly hinting at my nerves and inexperience. We made the exchange before he insisted on an unnecessary handshake to officially conclude the transaction.

"OK, well you'll share a spliff before you leave, won't you?" he asked, in a tone that suggested I should probably accept his invitation. We returned to the Mario Kart arena and Browny aggressively told the girls to move. They didn't let go of their controllers and stood up, continuing to play the game faultlessly. It was a close race.

Browny pulled a comically large joint from his pocket and lit it up. This was undoubtedly the most uncomfortable I had ever felt in someone's living-room and the incoming weed would not help. Weed has always affected me quickly and negatively and I usually become a useless slump after just a few puffs. I'm sure there was a direct correlation between my peer-pressured regular weed-smoking and a complete lack of female interest during my late teens. Despite my uneasiness, I remembered why I was here and the task at hand. After gathering myself, I tried to make conversation and find out what I could about this man.

"So how long have you been in Hong Kong?" I asked him as he sucked deeply on his well-crafted joint.

"I came over in ninety-two. It's my home now. These are my people," he replied, opening his arms wide as if to suggest everyone in Hong Kong.

I cringed inside. What a crank. Despite him claiming to be local, I expected that he wouldn't speak Cantonese and asked him if he did.

"Don't need to mate. My people understand me."

This guy was dreadful. He handed me the joint, and I slyly took pathetically small drags while we continued to chat.

I stayed for about half an hour and tried to find out as much as I could about him. Despite him being a drug-dealer, I found him too ridiculous to be intimidating and didn't mind asking questions. He freely answered most of them.

I gathered that he'd left Liverpool in the early nineties when he was twenty. He had inherited some money and made some from selling drugs, and embarked upon a solo travelling trip to the Far East. After spending a year drinking and getting stoned in Thailand and Laos, he had called in on Hong Kong for a few days before going home. In his hostel in Chung King Mansion, he'd met an Indian man, bought some weed from him and got talking. The Indian asked him if he wanted to make some money by selling ecstasy.

Lan Kwai Fong was booming after a number of new bars and clubs had been built at the start of the decade; and ecstasy was making huge waves. The scene in England had exploded and therefore ecstasy was highly sought after by foreigners in Hong Kong. Both expatriates and tourists were happy to pay criminally high prices for pills; which Browny exploited, making a lot of money very quickly. I assumed he'd taken a lot of pills himself during this time as he seemed like a man running low on endorphins.

Good pills, he told me, ran out of supply at some point in the early two thousands, so he became a small time weed dealer for a number of years, supplying mostly tourists in Jordan and Tsim Tsa Tsui. After his cash-flow dwindled two years ago, he decided to move back into selling harder drugs and told me that he now specialized in cocaine and ketamine but proudly told me that he could get hold of crystal meth (or ice) if I told him in advance. He'd lived on Hong Kong Island for seven years before moving to Hung Hom for a few years and then eventually to Tuen Mun in two thousand and nine. It seemed a strange place to live but he told me he liked it out here because he didn't have to see other foreigners unless he wanted to.

We left on reasonable terms. He told me that I was in for a great weekend as the coke would "blow my mind." I shook his dirty hand for the third time in the last hour and left. The two girls had not said a word or looked in my direction throughout the duration of my visit. They were just starting a 150cc Mushroom Cup as I left.

Despite being hazy from the joint we had shared, I'd made a special effort to soak up everything he had told me, storing as much as I could in my head. Although he'd been forthcoming in giving me an overview of his life, there had, unsurprisingly, been no specific information that might help my cause; no names, no phone-numbers, no details of how the operation worked. It hadn't been totally futile though and at least I had something to report back to the police. I was pleased with my first night's work.

CHAPTER FIFTEEN

I rang Liu and described my unusual evening. She sounded interested but told me she was busy and couldn't meet me. I could hear a Chinese pop ballad playing in the background so assumed it wasn't a work-related commitment. Due to a totally needless managers' training meeting, I had a day off work on Tuesday so arranged to meet her and Dixon the following afternoon.

I woke up late and felt a misleading wave of happiness that I didn't have work. (Tuesday has long been my least favourite day of the week so it was pleasant to have it off. Whereas Monday is always a difficult return to reality, at least there can be some level of optimism at a new week, the chance to discuss your weekend with work colleagues etc. Tuesday is just a shit day. With the exception of Champions League football, nothing good ever happens on a Tuesday.) My contentment lasted all of thirty seconds before thoughts of my predicament swept, uninvited, into my freshly awakening head.

I tried to take my mind off things with a coffee and FIFA, losing three times in a row to "Simplythebeast68," the last game being a humiliating 6-1 loss. I was unable to shake my negative state and spent a good part of the morning trying to rid my head of the image of Sander snorting cocaine off Sophie's tits which was something that could feasibly have happened at the weekend.

I'd opted to take only one gram to the police, as I did actually owe Anna the drugs. Probably stupid and a dangerous idea; not ideal to be effectively dealing drugs while working with the police, but I wasn't financially equipped to give her the cash and was hoping to eradicate that problem so I could solely focus on the informant work. I picked up some eight-dollar garlic noodles from the Seven Eleven, and walked to the police station.

"Good afternoon, Troy. No work today?" Liu greeted me, looking bright and full of energy.

She beckoned me to Dixon's office where he was sitting eating fish balls out of a polystyrene box. The sound of wooden chopsticks scraping on polystyrene is a fingernails-on-blackboard one for me; horrid.

"Tell me what happened last night," Dixon asked, mouth full of food.

I regurgitated the story, telling him about the drawers full of drugs, that the guy dealt in ketamine and cocaine predominantly, and I even managed to get a smile when I told him about Mario Kart.

"Here's what I bought from him," I said placing a packet of powder on the table.

Liu examined it for a second then passed it to Dixon, who got a smear of chili source on the packet while handling it.

"Good work," Liu said. "We'll get that checked. Did he mention any names or specific details?"

"No, unfortunately not," I replied.

"OK. I didn't expect he would. We need names though. Browny sounds promising but he's not the top dog. If we arrest him early, we could ruin the chances of getting the guys above him. You've made a good start but we need more. At some point this week, I want you to go back round to his house. Spend as long as you can with him and try to find out more information," Liu continued, as Dixon nodded agreeably, wiping a stray noodle from his chin.

"I'll try. I've got a half day tomorrow so I'll see if he can meet in the afternoon. His working hours seem flexible, so should be OK."

"Good. This time really try to get more information," Dixon offered, reemphasizing Liu's comments. "Who does he get the drugs from? Who is his supplier? That's what we need. If you think it will help, place a big order with him so that he can see you're serious. If you're giving him money, he will be happier to talk to you. We can give you money if you need it. No problem."

I was relieved at this last comment, as along with everything else, cash-flow was becoming a serious issue. My job paid sixteen thousand Hong Kong dollars a month which was the equivalent of about just over a thousand pounds. This was enough to get by, but not enough to be buying large quantities of cocaine three times a week. Dixon said he would get hold of ten thousand Hong Kong dollars for me to spend in order to help. I shook hands with both police officers, which I enjoyed, and left.

On the way home, I stopped for a coffee in Starbucks and considered the discussion. It occurred to me that there were sizeable holes in the plan. What were the chances that this man whom I'd only met once, yesterday, would tell me who he got his vast amount of drugs from? It seemed ambitious. What would happen if he just didn't tell me?

The fear of the situation was waning slightly but I was now starting to experience a new, ugly emotion. I was feeling guilty. I had become involved in a process where I was trying to fuck people over in order to save myself. Fair enough they were drug-dealers and if they were all like Browny, admittedly they would be pretty horrendous human beings but was I a total scumbag for doing this? My mind flashed back to an episode of *Banged up Abroad*, where a twenty-four-year-old man from Brighton had been caught smuggling drugs from Bolivia into Argentina. He'd been given a life sentence and was probably going to be spending the rest of his life terrified and in absolute squalor. What were my other options?

*

On Thursday, I sent Browny a message asking if I could purchase more cocaine. I'd met Anna in Starbucks on the Wednesday night and given her what I owed her, so I wasn't lying to him when I said I'd run out. In a turn of luck, he replied saying that he was in Wan Chai and we arranged to meet at the Southorn Playground in an hour. The playground, in the centre of Wan Chai, is comprised of a hard tarmac football pitch and five or six basketball courts. During my first week in Hong Kong, I'd had a demoralizing experience when I'd walked through the park and asked if I could join in a game of football with some lads who were having a kick about. I'd assumed that they'd said yes and ran on to the pitch, made a good run past the static centre halves and shouted out for a pass. They had actually said "no" and were angry that I'd tried to join in.

As well as being a local sports hub, Southorn Playground also has a lawless feel to it, with local winos and drug-users sauntering around in a glassy-eyed state. Many of the footballers were tattooed and topless which Dom had speculatively informed me, meant that they were Triads. Southorn Playground and the vicinity was the only area in Hong Kong where a man had come up to me and asked for some money for "bus fare" – that old chestnut.

I met Browny by the basketball courts at seven. He was smoking despite it being a no-smoking area and looked in considerably better shape than he had done on Monday. His skin wasn't as yellow and the bags under his eyes weren't as noticeable.

"Alright, mate. Do you fancy going for some dim sum?" He asked.

This wasn't a suggestion I'd envisaged.

"Sure."

With that we walked up to Amoy Street where he claimed the "best dim sum" in Hong Kong was made. We sat down in the grubby café and ordered by pointing randomly at an entirely Chinese menu while an elderly waitress shouted aggressively at a young lad to start cooking.

"So, what are you after, mate?" Browny asked.

"Just two grams," I replied.

"No problem. I'll have to pick it up from my guy first, though. He lives round here so just come with me, yeah?"

This was promising. Without any insinuation, Browny was inviting me to see someone within his circle. Someone whom he bought his drugs from, so evidently a bigger fish? My eyes visibly widened as my heart rate increased, but now well-practiced at appearing cool when flustered due to the Brazilian students, I remained calm and replied.

"Yeah, no problem."

The boy who'd been shouted at returned with two small, wicker plates which each had twelve dumplings on. For a random order, it looked like we had picked something fairly innocuous. The dim sum was good. It was only the second time I'd tried it in Hong Kong and I was just thinking to myself that I should try it more often, when Browny stood up swiftly, and demanded we leave.

"He's fucked it up! I always get the same and he's given me some fucking shrimp shit!" Browny said, raging. "I bet the little fucker is trying to poison me! We aren't paying for this shit!" and with that he stormed out of the café.

This left me in a difficult place. I had been impressed with both the food and the waiting time and would have tipped generously. My main aim in life at this moment involved building up an affinity with Browny though, so regretfully I pretended to be upset at my delightful dim sum too and left with him. I managed to mouth "sorry" to the elderly waitress but I could just have easily – probably likelier – said, "fuck you," given that she didn't speak a word of English.

Browny lit up another cigarette then went into a barely coherent monologue about his history with the dim sum place and how they used to be like a family to him but now they had ruined the trust. From my view, it seemed as though the staff had never seen Browny in their life. He remained genuinely paranoid that the boy was actually trying to poison him. I assumed that a brain less clouded by years of substance abuse may have thought this unrealistic.

After smoking two cigarettes and making no effort not to blow the smoke in my face, Browny calmed down and the dim sum disaster was forgotten as quickly as it had erupted.

"Right, let's get to Raymond's flat then. He lives on Star Street so let's grab a cab."

We slalomed though the crowds of Wan Chai Market and on to Queen's Road where we had to wait for twenty minutes to get a cab to a street that was a five-minute walk away. Normally hailing a taxi is fairly straightforward in Hong Kong but between about six forty-five to seven-thirty the drivers are changing shifts, so it is virtually impossible. I don't understand the logic of this; surely the drivers who had just started the shift should be able to pick you up? – Apparently not.

At least twenty taxis, most of them with their lights on, drove past us with the drivers either shaking their head or scowling at us. Two drivers did a hand signal which told us "under the tunnel". They probably lived on Kowloon side and wanted to get a fare for their drive home. Waiting for a taxi is the opposite of building a rapport with someone. You both become more and more frustrated and start blaming / resenting each other. Any comment is negative or pointless filler, "What a dickhead!" or "I thought he was going to stop, and then he didn't."

Eventually a grinning, elderly taxi-driver picked us up and spoke decent English.

"Hello boys. Lan Kwai Fong?" he guessed, while pretending to do a dance, then said, "Lots of ladies tonight!" He had certainly done this routine before and the fact that we weren't going to Lan Kwai Fong didn't deter him. I appreciated the effort though and was happy to tip him when we arrived on Star Street.

We arrived at Raymond's apartment block, which was new and expensive looking and were ushered in by the security-guard. I wondered if the security-guard noticed that a drug-dealer was living in the block and if he had considered doing anything about it. Later on I saw that he was asleep on the job and decided probably not.

We got to the twenty-fourth floor and walked to his front door which was covered with red and gold Chinese decorations. Browny had given no further details about Raymond and given me no clues or tips on how I should behave. All I knew was that he was "his guy." We rang the bell which did the Big Ben chimes. I had the same chime on my door bell and almost told Browny about this but stopped myself just in time, feeling happy that I had managed to restrain myself from being so horrendously boring.

We waited a short time, then a smiling Chinese man answered the door. He looked to be around forty although I find it difficult to tell with the Chinese, they are better agers than Westerners. He was wearing a shiny Adidas tracksuit and had a sports flask in his hand.

"Mr Brown. Come in," he said in perfect English with only a hint of a Chinese accent," and who might you be?" he asked me smiling. His tone was almost flirtatious which was a tad disconcerting.

"I'm Troy, nice to meet you," I replied.

"Like the wooden horse?"

For fuck's sake."Yes."

We walked into his flat which was, by Hong Kong standards, vast. His living-room was at least four times the size of mine and looked brand new. It smelt new. The flat was Western style which surprised me given the decorated door, with a cream three-piece-suite and huge plasma TV on the wall in one half of it and a dining-table and bookshelf full of mostly Chinese textbooks, and bafflingly, a 2004 edition of the *Guinness Book of Records*.

There was also a floor-to-ceiling window which I assumed would have good views, but the curtains were drawn. He also had something that I've always wanted; a massive fish tank built in to the wall, with about twenty technicolour tropical fish gliding around dozily. I remembered reading a story saying that Thierry Henry was planning on having a three-story fish tank in his house. I was considering whether he had gone through with it when Raymond offered the two of us a seat and, without asking, gave us a cup of freshly brewed Chinese tea. The three of us sat down on the cream sofa which was sadly less comfortable than it looked and began to small talk.

"So what brings you to Hong Kong?" Raymond asked.

I told him the story and he seemed genuinely interested. This was surprising. Most people stopped listening halfway through, but Raymond was attentive, asking relevant follow-up questions about my work and how I was settling into Hong Kong life. He told me that he had moved into the flat two months ago and it was nearly finished. I complimented him on the fish tank before the pleasantries were interrupted, when Browny, who had not said much so far, asked.

"So, can we sort this out, Raymond?"

"Of course, relax," he said smiling. His tone remained friendly as he said to me.

"You can tell Mr Brown has been in Hong Kong for too long. He's always in a rush."

I decided not to tell Raymond that, due to my own experiences of the alarmingly slow speed that Hong Kong people walk, I am against this notion of Hong Kong as a fast-paced city.

"Wait here," Browny instructed me and the two of them headed down a corridor, and out of the room. I played a game of Snake on my phone to avoid a foolish, but strong temptation to snoop around the flat, and before I'd even got past a thousand points, the two men were back and the transaction was, it seemed, done.

"It's been a great pleasure meeting you, Troy," Raymond said, shaking my hand. On first impressions, I liked Raymond. He seemed to be an amiable man, one of the nicer drug-dealers.

After we had left, Browny said, "He liked you."

"He seems cool. How did you meet him?"

"Yeah, he is. Just don't get on his wrong side."

I noticed Browny had only responded to the first part, but didn't ask again, and decided not to pry by asking what this "wrong side" was.

Browny and I walked back to Wan Chai despite taxi services being back to normal. We stopped off to sit on some steep steps behind the Hopewell Centre and Browny gave me the cocaine that I didn't want in exchange for two thousand dollars. He pulled out a large bag of cannabis that he had presumably picked up at the same time. I declined the offer of a joint but sat with Browny as he rolled and smoked.

"Do you get everything off Raymond then?" I asked trying again to get more information.

"Yeah. We are colleagues really. We sort each other out."

"Does he have a job, or is this his job?"

"What do you think?" Browny replied, sarcastically.

I honestly didn't know, so his sarcasm was irritating. Unfortunately, if someone answers sarcastically and you still don't understand, you can't ask again unless you want to sound like a moron, so I remained ignorant as to the details of Raymond's employment.

"Are you sure you don't mind if I buy my cocaine off him sometimes?" I asked. "It's a lot more convenient than traipsing to Tuen Mun every time."

Browny scowled before saying, "As I said, we work together, so I don't really mind either way. I expect you to give me a couple of lines when you come round though."

We talked about our plans for the following weekend. I had to make up details of the fake party that I had now bought five grams of cocaine for. I went with the story of a football team-mate's stag do in Macau – I was pleased with this lie. I didn't play for a football team so the lie was strong on two counts. I was relieved that Browny didn't ask if he could come. He told me he was planning on "chilling" over the weekend which was ambiguous. Did this mean heavy drug use, or was he actually planning on going to a beach with a good book?

We walked back through Southorn Playground, where Browny shook hands with a toothless Chinese man. I thanked him for helping me to buy the cocaine, then just before he left, he pointed at a large restaurant that looked nothing like the café we had been to earlier and said.

"Ah bollocks, that's the dim sum place I was on about before. We went to the wrong place!"

CHAPTER SIXTEEN

I called Liu when I got home telling her that I'd got the seal of approval from a new, potentially more prominent dealer. It's startling how easily you can find a new dealer if you are looking for one. Now things had started, they were moving rapidly. Liu was complimentary, told me to "keep up the good work" and that she would contact me soon.

For the rest of the week, I tried to forget about my new, covert, double life and got on with things as normally as I could. Work was becoming troublesome as the energy that I'd previously spent teaching was now spent worrying about having delved into a drugs underworld. There were moments when I would forget everything for a few minutes, living in the moment as I discussed shopping habits with Korean women, but when fear of my situation crept, suddenly and unwelcome, back into my head, I found it extremely difficult to keep up my smiling façade. There had been two incidents where, mid-class, I'd got caught up in my thoughts and stared dozily into space, entirely forgetting that I was supposed to be teaching.

"Are you OK, teacher?"

"Yes, sorry. I have a migraine."

On one of the occasions, this had caused a kindly student to ferret through her handbag and pull out some suspect looking herbal remedy which I politely declined.

In a bid to regain a degree of normality, I met Dom to watch a film on Saturday evening. When I arrived at Pacific Place's lavish, and costly cinema, I was surprised to see Sander, clad in a well-fitting navy-blue suit, standing beside Dom in the ticket queue. I felt my heart noticeably sink at the sight of him which is not what you're after when you see your friend. I'd been semi-deliberately avoiding him since the fateful evening in Azure which was nearly three weeks ago now. I wasn't sure whether he'd noticed my ignoring him. By the way he greeted me, with a firm hug and hair ruffle, ostensibly not.

"Hey man, how you doing?"

"Yeah, been boring recently mate. I've been low on cash-flow so taking it easy," I said, trying to act normally, despite feeling a sharp stab of anger towards him and his stupid blue suit. "How's everything with you?"

"I'm good, man. Same old Sander. Too many ladies, too little time!"

This referring to himself in the third person was new to me and I sincerely hoped it was a one-off. The three of us chatted inanely as we queued then watched the film, which didn't need to be in 3D and was by all accounts, very average. I struggled to keep up with the wafer-thin plot because I was weighing up whether to ask Sander about what happened with Sophie. I was also finding his loud crunching of toffee popcorn to be distracting and irritating. When we left at eleven o'clock, Dom, who is easily pleased, was in high spirits claiming that it was "the best film of the year," which it definitely wasn't.

As we sauntered down a strangely quiet Hennessy Road, I decided against mentioning Sophie, preferring instead to try to blank it out and listen to Dom's contentious claims that, "there has to be a sequel!" Following a brief lull in conversation, Sander skillfully flicked the cigarette he'd been smoking into a nearby bin and addressed us with enthusiasm.

"Kris is hiring out a junk boat for his thirtieth. Do you guys fancy it?"

"Isn't Kris the dickhead?" Dom asked, blatantly.

Sander laughed and continued.

"I don't think Troy is a huge fan of his, but when you get to know him, he's an awesome guy. Anyway it should be a good do. What do you say?"

"Possibly, when is it?" I asked, unenthusiastically.

"Two weeks from now. It will be a cracking day out. (It sounded annoyingly unnatural for Sander to use the word "cracking.") There will be plenty of booze, women and cocaine."

"What?"

I would usually have turned down an offer to spend my only day off with Kris and his idiot friends but I was intrigued by Sander's comment about drugs. As far as I knew, Sander was strictly a beer and cigarettes man, so I was surprised that he was openly showing his excitement for narcotics. Given that I was supposed to be searching for drug-dealers, a cocaine-fuelled boat party was something that could feasibly result in finding more worthwhile information.

"Deal me in," I said and Dom agreed.

*

Sander and Dom decided to stay out for a drink but I declined as I was tired and looking forward to a night in, watching the football. After getting home, opening a Corona and sitting on the sofa, I felt relatively worry-free for the first time in a while. Having an ordinary evening with my friends had been an appreciated distraction. Sadly my intentions for a night of viewing stalling internet streams were shattered when a call from Detective Liu ended my five-day oasis of normal living.

"We want you to find out more about this man, Raymond," she said with no explanation as to the lack of contact.

"OK. What do you suggest?"

"He has let you into his house before so there is no reason that he won't do it again. Go and buy some more cocaine. Look around the house and find out anything you can," Liu replied.

"And that's it?"

"For now. Report back to us when you have met him."

As I wasn't actually taking copious amounts of cocaine in a pool party in Macau with a fictional pal, I decided in a "no time like the present" wave of adrenaline that I would try to meet Raymond tonight. In a similar vein to waiting to ride your bike down a dangerously steep hill in a quarry (which was a key part of my formative years), I knew that it was better to do things before you thought about the consequences too much.

I called him.

"Hello," he answered.

"Hi Raymond, how're things? It's Troy. We met the other day."

"I remember."

"Have you got any cocaine?"

"Yes, I'm at home now. Come over."

I got changed into my chinos and wore a Barcelona football shirt, hoping that it might act as an easy conversation starter should there be a tense atmosphere. The walk to Star Street wasn't far and I arrived at his front door ten minutes later, making me seem too keen and / or worryingly desperate to get hold of drugs.

"Good evening, Troy. Please come in," greeted Raymond. He was wearing a smart black shirt with tight corduroy trousers and looked sharp, minus a pair of bright white pointy shoes which I

110

didn't rate. I entered his luxury abode and was surprised to see five other Chinese men wearing suits sitting in the living-room.

"Gentlemen, this is Troy," Raymond said.

I stood at the entrance to the door while the businessmen, who all looked of similar age to Raymond, stared at me, scrutinizing my existence. Three of the five were smoking and there was the detritus from a finished game of mahjong strewn across the large glass coffee table.

"Hi."

They grumbled a few "hellos" then swiftly lost interest in me and resumed talking to each other in Cantonese.

"My workmates," Raymond explained. "Follow me."

I was glad to get out of the – possibly imaginary, due to my paranoia – hostility of the living-room as we trawled to Raymond's bedroom which had a huge bed and drawn curtains revealing a first-class view of Wan Chai's bright lights which were illuminating the dusk evening.

"So, how much do you want?" Raymond asked.

He didn't seem as friendly as the last time I had seen him.

"Could I get five grams?" I asked.

"I don't have that much now. Call me next week."

I was unsure as to what "next week" actually meant. I would have much preferred an actual day but nodded eagerly.

The exchange had been brief and largely futile. I'd felt relaxed at his house the last time but the introduction of five suited Chinese men and a change in Raymond's demeanour had made me anxious. Who were the men?

I called Liu and reported that I had tentative future plans to buy five grams of cocaine from Raymond.

"OK. Good work. Meet Raymond next weekend and buy the cocaine, then we can check if it comes from the same supplier."

*

After an uneventful week at work, I called Raymond the following Saturday afternoon. Surely exactly a week later qualifies as next week?

"Do you have the y'know?" I asked him, clumsily and probably too bluntly.

"Yes. I'm not at home right now though. Can you meet me at Neway karaoke in Causeway Bay later?"

"Yes. See you there."

Neway is a chain of karaoke bars that due to the Asian obsession with singing must be making a small fortune. I wasn't sure whether Raymond was using it as a meeting spot, or if he was actually partaking in some singing. He seemed like the sort of man who would like karaoke.

I changed into some jeans and a T-shirt and put on some flip-flops before heading out. I'm not convinced by jeans and flip-flops but it was a warm, balmy evening so I excused myself on this occasion. It was a fifteen minute stroll down Gloucester Road to get to the bar. I had been there once before, a few months ago, and had fond memories of doing a heartfelt performance of Elton John's 'Yellow Brick Road' with Dom.

I went into the main foyer; it was a big place with a circular reception area illuminated by flashing purple lights. Behind were two long, narrow corridors full of karaoke rooms with muffled voices and poppy baselines seeping under the doors. I asked the lady behind the desk, where Raymond was. I realized after asking that it was an ambitious question and was fully deserving of the blank look that she gave me, through squinting eyes that were quite probably irreversibly damaged by the purple lights. I was just about to call Raymond when he bounded down the hallway, wearing a classy-looking black suit and tie.

"Good evening. How are you doing?" he said and shook my hand firmly. "Let's go for a smoke."

We stood just outside and Raymond, who smelt of whisky, pulled out a pack of Marlboro' Lights and offered me one. Apparently there's quite a lot of cultural etiquette associated with cigarettes in Asia so I duly accepted. Raymond lit my cigarette first, then his own.

"Good to see you again. So you want five grams?"

"Yes, please. Will that be OK?"

"No problem. It's in my car, so I'll get it for you later. You must sing first! Come in and meet my friends."

I didn't want to sing – not at all.

"Yes, that sounds excellent," I replied enthusiastically. I have a bad habit of overusing the word excellent. In this case, I definitely didn't mean it.

I got through the cigarette without any embarrassing coughing or smoke in the eyes, which I was pleased about. Raymond smoked two cigarettes in the time I had one, then he opened the door for me and we headed back in. I followed Raymond down the corridor and must have walked past about fifteen similar sized rooms before we arrived at a room with a much grander entrance.

"This is the best room," Raymond announced proudly and opened the door.

Before I could take in the surroundings, I was nearly deafened by the sound of three men screaming along to a Cantonese ballad by Eason Chan. I'd heard the song before in Kwan's barbers, and thought it was quite good. Not so much now. The men had terrible voices. I scrunched my eyes and tried to adjust my ears to the noise. It was a massive room, five times the size of the booth I'd been to on Elton John night. The room was dimly lit apart from some neon blue and white tube lighting. There was a huge flat screen TV on the wall, playing a video of an attractive Chinese lady walking through a field of tulips while providing words to the song at the bottom of the screen.

In one half of the room, there was leather seating all around the perimeter and tables in the middle full of bottles of Southern Comfort, Johnny Walker and Chivas Regal whisky and a selection of exotic fruit snacks on large plates. In the other half of the room was an electronic darts board with two men playing very seriously, then in the far corner was a smaller TV and a sofa with four men sitting playing a low quality, multi-player game of FIFA. Besides that were two unfrequented square tables for mahjong or chess. The room was occupied by about twenty Chinese men, all in smart suits. They were visibly drunk, and all but two of them were smoking. What a room; a grown man's playground.

Raymond put his arm on my shoulder and took me round the room, introducing me to his friends. I didn't even try to remember the names of anyone. A room full of twenty similarly dressed Chinese men – not a chance. Most of them seemed friendly, shaking my hand sincerely (albeit with limp wrists) and patting my back. I was instantly given a glass of whisky and offered a cigarette by a man who introduced himself as Wan. An older man, who was swaying and trying to sing along to the music, offered me a slice of watermelon but it was covered in whisky so I skillfully managed to drop it in a bin when he wasn't looking. Most of the men looked a similar age to Raymond, with three notably older-looking men who were sitting near the dart-board locked in deep conversation.

The disturbance caused by my entrance lasted until the end of the Eason Chan number, when it subsided, and Raymond beckoned me to sit with him.

"This is a great room," I told him, in the quiet spell while a new singer was selecting his track. "How do you know all these guys?" I asked.

"Work colleagues. They are good men, my brothers," Raymond said, smiling and showing his bright white front teeth that were apparently invincible to his constant smoking. I wanted to ask Raymond what his job was but remembered Browny's comments and stopped myself.

"Let's sing. Who do you like?" he asked me, in between bites of a durian fruit.

I had to consider at this point that I was sober, and a terrible singer. What song would be appropriate? In the event I didn't have to make a decision as the man setting up the new song had put on 'Uptown Girl' – the Westlife version – and handed me the microphone. Shit. A video featuring a handsome Italian-looking man kissing a woman on a yacht started, and the opening bars of the track kicked in. Due to my nervousness, I missed the start of the song, causing a few chuckles.

"Whoa-oa-oa-oa-oa-oa-oa-oa-oa-oa-oa-oa-oa-oa," I started to sing, out of sync and drastically out of tune and luckily a few of the drunker men joined in with me. Now I was enjoying the attention I was getting. Karaoke is serious business in Asia. It has to be heartfelt. After my stirring / woeful rendition, I sat down feeling pleased with myself and was presented with another glass of whisky by Wan.

"Good sing!" he said, delighted.

"Thanks Wan. Your turn next," I replied and eased into idle conversation.

Wan reaffirmed what Raymond had told me, telling me that the men were his work colleagues who were letting their hair down for the weekend. Again there was no detail of what the nature of the "work" was. Wan's English was pretty good and we spoke about housing prices in Hong Kong and a recent scandal in China involving a philandering politician. As we were getting on well, I chanced my arm and tried to find out some information about Raymond.

"How long have you known Raymond?" I asked.

"Five years. He's my boss. He's a good man and a good boss."

"It seems like you guys have a good working relationship?"

"Yes, we do. Now is our relaxing time. The next few months will be crazy though. So busy!" Wan said, exaggeratedly widening his eyes. (Hong Kong people always tell you how busy they are although being busy doesn't necessarily mean being productive. The odd preference seems to be dragging out a day's work over twelve hours rather than working quicker and getting out on time.)

"We have very big deal coming soon, so no rest."

I nodded sympathetically at Wan's upcoming workload, becoming more intrigued as to what job these men actually did.

After a few minutes, Raymond stumbled over, interrupted our conversation and put a hand on my shoulder.

"Let's go," he said.

I bid farewell to the suited men and we left. I would have been keen to stay and talk with Wan for longer but didn't want to get side-tracked from the matter in hand. I followed Raymond out of the building and into a nearby multi-story car park.

"You're a good singer," Raymond said but his compliment was rendered useless when he burst out laughing immediately after saying it. We arrived at his car. Although not interested in cars, I could appreciate that his shiny, brand new Audi was probably worth loads of money.

"Get in and we'll take a ride around the block." Raymond was clearly in no fit state to drive and it took him a good few attempts to reverse his car out of the space and out of the car park. It was quite embarrassing, but as a man without a driving license, I wasn't really in a position to criticize. Bad driving in good cars is something that is common in Hong Kong. You frequently see Ferraris and Porsches parked at horrible angles (with even more horrible number plates), three metres away from the curb.

Raymond drove the car – which was definitely the nicest car I'd ever been in – to a quiet side street and pulled up just behind the Hong Kong Central Library.

"Five grams, yes?" he asked me.

"Please."

"Sure thing," he said and opened up his glove compartment revealing a chaotic mix of magazines, cigarettes and packets of drugs. He handed over a cloudy packet and I gave him five thousand dollars in exchange. Cocaine is so overpriced it's ridiculous.

"Thanks, Raymond. I appreciate it."

"No problem."

I wondered just how big time a dealer Raymond was, and felt excitement that turning him in would surely see me freed from my drug charges. The excitement was swiftly overtaken by my returning guilt when I considered that I quite liked Raymond. This would have been much easier if he were a complete dickhead. Guilt is just so shit.

I politely declined his offer of a lift – given Raymond's state there would have been a very real chance of him crashing the car – and walked home, contemplating the night's events. It had been an interesting evening. I was wondering what the deal was with Raymond and his friends. The last twice I'd seen him he was with an entourage of suited men. Were they all drug-dealers? They seemed like a wealthy bunch of men. Suddenly, my brain clicked into gear and my heart started beating faster.

Shit. Had I been really thick? Chinese men dealing drugs, wearing expensive suits and driving flash cars. Now I thought about it, it was obvious.

They were Triads.

CHAPTER SEVENTEEN

My only knowledge about Triads had come from watching *Internal Affairs*, starring Hong Kong's ageing poster-boy Andy Lau as a bent cop on the payroll of the gangsters and his battle with a straight cop, working as an informant with the gangsters. I remembered how the informant in the film ended up getting shot dead in a lift and decided to stop comparing myself to fictitious action heroes. I thought about my next move. "The big deal" that Wan had mentioned was surely relevant? It must have been related to drugs. Were Raymond and his gang picking up cocaine from the top dogs? If I could get the police there to intercept their deal, would this ordeal be over?

I just needed to find out when and where the deal was going to happen, which – granted – was quite a lot. I tried hard to convince myself that drug-dealers deserved to be arrested, whether they were cordial men like Raymond or not; what they were doing was still pretty shitty and, with the exception of people who enjoy longevity on nights out, Hong Kong would be a better place if I could help the police to cut out a major source of cocaine importation. I kept telling myself this but found it difficult to think of myself as anything other than a spineless bastard.

Back home, feeling awakened and seeing a light to the end of my Hong Kong drug-troubled tunnel, I called Liu telling her the evening's events.

"Come to the station now," she instructed.

It was nearly midnight by the time I arrived. Hong Kong police didn't seem to get much time off. In fairness, most people in Hong Kong spend loads of time in work – there is a strange contradiction in how the locals pride themselves on a strong work ethic yet constantly moan about working overtime. Liu met me at the entrance looking tired but still suitably glamorous. Her hair was straightened and she was wearing thick-rimmed glasses which took the attention away from her large-toothed mouth. She led me through to her office, which I hadn't been in before. It was slightly smaller than Dixon's with a filing cabinet in the corner and a large cheese plant adding colour to an otherwise entirely grey office. Her desk was cluttered with stacks of paper and there was a photo of two smiling toddlers kitted out in dubious Disneyland attire. I sat down opposite her and she said Dixon was going to be joining us soon.

"So what have you got for us?" she asked, making a half-hearted attempt to tidy her papers up.

"Quite a lot, I think Raymond is a Triad."

"What makes you think that?"

I told her about the suited men and the karaoke night.

"That doesn't mean anything," she said dismissively. "That is completely normal behaviour for Chinese businessmen."

Feeling slightly deflated, I pressed on.

"Well, I think Raymond is buying a large quantity of drugs soon," I said. "His friend told me that they are meeting some associates for a big deal. I think he may be meeting the foreign suppliers that you are after."

Liu looked contemplative as Dixon entered the room, looking like he'd just woken up. The two police officers began to chat animatedly in Cantonese for a long few minutes, leaving me feeling useless and awkward. I stared at the cheese plant.

"What exactly do you know?" Dixon eventually asked me.

"I'm pretty sure that they are Triads and that they have a big deal coming up soon," I said.

"This isn't enough to go on, Troy. It's just a hunch. And no offence, but you're not a policeman," Liu said.

"Well, what should I do? You've asked me to find out as much as I can. I've got information about what I think is a drug deal and you are telling me it's not enough?" I said, agitatedly.

"We need actual evidence of any cocaine-dealing activity. All we have is your word, which is not enough," Dixon replied.

"So what's next?"

"If you are really convinced about Raymond being a Triad, we would need proof of the deal," Liu said.

"How can I get you proof?"

"Well it wouldn't be easy and there would be some risk involved. He would need to be put under surveillance."

I felt my heartbeat accelerate.

"If you hear him talking about the deal, you would go and intercept it?"

"We'd certainly weigh up the evidence, and if it sounded like it was going to happen, we would try, yes," Liu said.

"OK, deal me in then. What happens next?"

"Arrange to meet him, then come to the station tomorrow and we will brief you fully and give you the equipment you need.

*

I sent Raymond a text at eleven on Sunday morning to arrange yet another meeting. I told him that some imaginary friends had asked if I could get a gram for them. Karaoke the previous night had ostensibly solidified our relationship and Raymond promptly replied, inviting me to go to his house at any time after four o'clock because he was still suffering from a hangover. I called Liu confirming that I'd arranged to go to his house and she told me to get to the police station at three o'clock.

After clock-watching and fretting for a few uncomfortable hours, I got changed into some freshly-laundered jeans and white T-shirt that had a picture of a woman with a rose in her mouth on the front. I didn't particularly like the T-shirt and was puzzled as to what was going through my mind when I'd decided to buy it. I hoped I hadn't been influenced by Sander. It was starting to drizzle slightly as I left my house and set off to the police station, causing the locals to open their umbrellas aggressively with little to no awareness of those around them. I fought through the crowds wielding their devices threateningly near my eyes and managed to arrive at the police station with my vision intact but my clothes drenched. Dixon and Liu were waiting for me.

"No umbrella?" Dixon asked.

It was clear that I didn't have one so I left the question unanswered.

I followed them through to Liu's office which was considerably tidier now, although there was a large red file teetering precariously on the edge of her desk.

"All we need you to do is hide some small recording devices in his living-room," Liu said matter-of-factly, impressively glossing over the sizeable risk factor.

"So you want me to bug his house?" I asked; just to clarify that my life had now led to my being asked to sneak around putting wire taps in a Chinese gangster's house.

"Exactly. Just be discreet. They are good recording devices but the more you place in his house, the more chance we have of hearing something that will help us," she said before pausing, "And you."

Dixon displayed the wiretap devices that I would be using. They were tiny black squares, similar in size to fifty pence coins. I examined them and had no idea how these dainty, little things had the ability to record sound. They had suction pads on the back and Dixon proudly informed me that they would stick to any surface so it would be "easy" for me to hide them.

We then went through a long, mundane instructions briefing from a police technology expert (Is that a job title?), who had done nothing to avoid succumbing to the stereotype of a technology man and was small and thin with greasy floppy hair and over-sized glasses. The briefing reminded me of when you are being told the rules of paint-balling by some humourless worker. Although probably quite important, you become impatient and irritable and just want to start as soon as possible. Just give me the gun. I'll figure it out.

"All set to go," Liu said after twenty long minutes.

"Do you have any more advice?" I asked.

"Just act natural. He's been friendly with you so far. If and when the chance arises, stick the devices in places where he will never look."

"It's as simple as that?" I asked, my attempt at sarcasm not recognized.

"Yes it is. Don't worry about anything," Liu said with a confidence that suited her Canadian accent. (It had been confirmed that she was Canadian after I noticed that her handbag had a large maple leaf badge sewn on the side; every Canadian I've ever met has had a Canadian flag somewhere on their belongings.) We left the station and got into a black Honda civic. I got in the back, the two of them got in the front.

"Let's do a quick test," Dixon said. "Speak into one of the microphones."

I hate any sort of microphone / sound test. What are you supposed to say?

"Hello. Does it work?" was the best I could think of.

I heard my voice reverberate throughout the car. I, like everyone else in the world, despise the sound of my own voice. It always sounds higher pitched than I like to think of it and there is a hint of a lisp which I definitely can't hear from inside my head. The sound was coming out of a radio system fitted inside the glove compartment. The wire was working. We were set to go.

In the post-rush-hour traffic, the roads were relatively quiet, and after five minutes, Dixon pulled up and parked besides a large skip full of stinking detritus just beside Southorn Playground.

"Good luck," Liu said. "We will be waiting here for you."

I got out of the car. The drizzle had completely blown over but most civilians still had their umbrellas up – just to be sure. It was five minutes until I was due to meet Raymond, so I killed a bit of time by walking the long way round Southorn Playground to get to his flat. I arrived outside the building at exactly four o'clock, then decided to do another lap of the waterlogged football pitch so that I would arrive casually late.

Raymond answered the door clad in blue jeans and wearing an un-tucked baby-blue shirt. "Troy. Good to see you again. We are seeing a lot of each other! Come in."

I followed him and sat down on the cream sofa which to my relief was not frequented by potential gangsters this time. The house was empty. He remained standing.

"How's it going?" I asked him.

"I'm OK. And you?"

I was feeling jittery.

"How's work?"

"Fine but we have a busy period coming up," he said, in a way that killed the conversation instantly.

"So what can I do for you?"

"I just want to buy another gram if that's OK. My friends are so annoying. I wish they'd just told me last night so I didn't have to bother you again."

Raymond was totally uninterested in my boring tale and although smiling, seemed impatient.

"Yes. No problem. Wait a moment."

He stood up and disappeared down the corridor.

This was my chance.

I reached into my trouser pocket and pulled out the tiny devices that I had been given. I scanned the living-room looking for suitable places to put them where Raymond would never find them. I entered stealth mode, got up and attached one to the back of his TV. Nobody looks behind a TV do they?

I jammed a second device underneath his sofa which I thought was a solid location. I scoured for any other places and settled on putting one inside the sleeve of the dated Guinness Book of records, causing Kris Akabusi's face on the inner sleeve to distort slightly but not noticeably, which he would surely not read. I lowered myself down until I was lying flat on the cold marble floor and pressed my hand under the cupboard, scratching my thumb on its splintered edge. I fiddled about and finally attached the wiretap.

Raymond returned to the living-room approximately two seconds too early. I was still lying on my stomach. How do you explain that?

"Is everything OK?" he asked.

"Yeah, fine. Just a bit of back trouble," I responded; by no means an explanation, but for some reason deemed passable by Raymond. Chinese people obtain inexplicably odd poses at times; crouching, bending knees and doing thrusting stretches in public etc. so Hong Kong was probably a good city to be able to talk myself out of my peculiar positioning. I stood up and brushed myself down and to my relief the subject wasn't mentioned again.

Close.

"Here you go!" said Raymond and pressed a small packet of cocaine into my sweat-sticky palm. Despite us being the only people in the room we still did the transaction as if people might see, which was odd. I parted with another thousand dollars, said my thanks and left the flat. I'd done it.

Exhilarated by my success, I bounded out of his building and back to the stationary police car. Liu and Dixon were sitting in silence when I arrived. I wondered if they actually liked each other. It must happen in the police that you get partnered up with someone whom you don't like. That would be really shit. I got back in the car and told them what I had done.

"Good job," Dixon said. "You have done all you can for now. We will be listening to Raymond's activities and hopefully this will lead us to some important information."

I was dropped off at my house and instructed by Liu to get on with my life as normal until I heard from the police. I felt a huge level of relief. I could actually, sort of, relax for the first time since this ordeal had begun. It was a tainted freedom, however. It wasn't over; I just had a temporary reprieve. It was a similar situation to when you go to an STI clinic. You are happy with yourself for going and relieved when the indignities and discomfort are over, but you then have the worry of the results constantly on the back of your mind to contend with.

CHAPTER EIGHTEEN

The next morning I went back to work, trying hard not to think about my eventful weekend, cocaine or prison sentences. Until I heard from Dixon, there was nothing I could do, and to state the stupidly obvious, worrying about things was not going to make them go away. I had a class with the two Brazilian beauties, which successfully diverted my mind for an hour, before a class with an intelligent and therefore difficult-to-teach, gay German man called Lars. I went to McDonalds for lunch, but unfortunately, Aiden had also sought refuge in fast food and was sitting, furiously typing with mayonnaise-smeared fingers on his laptop in the corner. After making eye-contact with him, it would have been socially unacceptable to sit alone and he made a weak effort to feign happiness, as I trudged sadly towards his table. In the quickest time possible without getting indigestion, I guzzled down a cold, badly arranged Big Mac while having a strained conversation about how Undercover Boss doesn't work anymore because the staff must know what's going on by now. My final class was a mind-numbing hour with a teenage girl, whose only input into a class about hobbies was that she liked sleeping and shopping. When pressed for more she responded, "Nothing to do," which did little to open up conversation, and left me wanting to smash my head repeatedly against the wall.

The day had been a slog so I was relieved to get home and put my feet up. After removing my trousers (an after work treat that had surprisingly survived despite my current circumstances), I sat on the sofa, making an exaggerated "Ah" noise in a subconscious yet futile attempt to convince myself that I could relax. After the eight hour break (of sorts) that work provided, my mind had begun spiraling back into a pit of worry, when I received a text. Expecting it to be from a drug-dealer or a police officer, I was taken aback to see that it was from Sophie.

"Hi. Why haven't you replied to me? Is everything OK? x."

How the tables had turned. Back in school, I had been the one texting her innumerous times without reply. I knew it was childish to totally blank her but I genuinely didn't want to see her after what had happened with Sander. Although I had bigger problems to worry about now, it still hurt immensely. I still didn't know whether they had slept together and still hadn't decided if I wanted to know the full story or not.

Continuing to act with sterling maturity, I didn't reply again. About an hour later, she rang me. I waited for a couple of rings, took a breath and answered in a voice that came out much deeper than I'd intended.

"Hello."

"Ah, so you're still alive?" Sophie said, her attempt at breezy light-heartedness not convincing. "Why have you been ignoring me?"

"It wasn't deliberate. Just been busy, you know. I've had a lot on." This was a shit excuse. Nobody is too busy to send a text. It takes less than ten seconds.

"Oh, OK." She sounded confused. "Do you want to go for a few drinks on Wednesday?"

I thought about it, decided to stop being a dick and agreed.

*

I heard nothing from Dixon or Liu over the next two days and was pleased to spend a pleasant afternoon with Carmella on Wednesday. We hadn't done it for the last few weeks so I was happy to find her sitting on my sofa with a redolence of onions and spices coming from the kitchen where she had made us her self-christened "famous" Filipino stew.

"How's everything with you Mr Troy?" she asked after we had both eaten a large bowl of the hearty dish. "Why haven't you been here recently?"

It struck me at that point that I'd been so caught up in my own adventure that I hadn't been home for the last three Wednesdays. I hadn't even had the courtesy to let her know.

"Sorry. Have you been here the last few weeks?"

"I have. I've missed seeing you. It's a highlight of my week!" she said, semi-sarcastically.

"Shit. Sorry Carmella. I should've told you. Why didn't you let me know?"

"You're a busy man. I didn't want to bother you," she said, smiling. "It's no problem."

I felt like a bit of a bastard. We talked for a while and she told me about the last few Sundays. Her friend Nerissa had thrown a drink in a man's face because he asked her, "How much?"

"But you told me that Nerissa is a prostitute!"

"She is, but this man was so ugly!" she said and burst out laughing. Her laugh was infectious and I couldn't help joining in. Carmella had told me before that she'd never had sex for money but was very open about the fact that some of her friends were strippers and prostitutes and enjoyed recounting funny and entertaining stories about their adventures, usually at the expense of the impotent, incompetent, and in some cases, incontinent punters. When her laughter subsided, she asked me if I wanted a game of FIFA. I'd patiently taught her how to play it several times but she was hopeless. Despite her sizeable shortcomings, she enjoyed it and always giddily asked me for a game. We always played on the same team but she was so bad that we lost every game heavily. It was fun though and the afternoon flew by quickly until I realized that it was six o'clock. I was meeting Sophie in half an hour.

"I've got to go, Carmella," I said, after she had just run the ball into her own net and started laughing.

"Where you going? Hot date?" she asked.

"Not really. I'm meeting a friend," I told her.

"Girl?"

"Yes, but not like that," I replied.

For the first time all afternoon, I noticed that Carmella wasn't smiling anymore. Her face had dropped and she looked slightly hurt. I wasn't sure if I was imagining it so didn't comment.

"I'm sorry, I've been a shit friend recently," I told her and promised that we would continue our Wednesday afternoon festivities next week.

"No problem. Have a good week," she said and the familiar grin was back on her face as she left.

*

Whereas previously I would have made an intensive effort to look my best to meet Sophie, I couldn't be bothered now and just splashed some water on my face, sprayed a bit of Lynx Inca under my arms and headed out wearing a plain white T-shirt and some ill-fitting basketball shorts, which I'd obtained erroneously after a mix-up at the launderette. She'd suggested going to Trafalgar, a fourth-floor bar on Lockhart Road with a balcony sitting-area offering good views of the debauchery on the streets below. On the short walk to the pub, I decided that I would ask her straight up about Sander. There was nothing to be gained from skirting around the subject.

I arrived promptly to find Sophie already at the completely empty bar. She'd bought a large glass of white wine for herself and a pint of Kronenbourg for me. As always, she looked sparkling. She was wearing a short denim skirt with a tight black T-shirt and had large sunglasses perched on her head.

"Hello, stranger," she said, and leaving the drinks on the bar, came and gave me a fervent hug, pressing her excellent breasts into my chest. It was a warm, muggy evening so we sat outside. "Why have you been ignoring me, then?" she asked, sounding genuinely upset as we sat down.

"I haven't. I told you I've been…"

"Bullshit!" she said, teasingly.

"OK. You're right. Do you really want to know?" I asked.

"I really do, yes. I don't understand. Have I done something wrong?"

"Not exactly, I don't have a right to be annoyed. I'm being a bit of a dick. It's just that I was so excited to see you out here and that afternoon in my flat I really thought that there was a spark between us." I shuddered at myself saying this – it sounded horribly cheesy. I should have planned this speech a bit better. "And then the next night, you were all over Sander. I couldn't believe it."

"Oh god!" she said and put her head in her hands, looking crestfallen, before grimacing and asking, "Did you see that?"

"Unfortunately," I replied.

"Shit! Troy, that was absolutely nothing, I promise. I was totally drunk and you know what he's like better than anyone, I expect. He's a creep. He kept trying it on. At first I rejected him but he kept trying. Eventually I thought that if I kissed him, he would give up and leave me alone."

"Do you not realize the flawed logic in that? You think that kissing a sleazy man will put him off?" I said, incensed by her poor explanation.

"For fuck's sake, I kissed him for about two seconds then stopped and told him that I couldn't do it," she said, looking upset now. "Do you know why I said that?" she asked, looking at me with her chocolate brown eyes," because of you, you idiot."

My feelings were muddled now. She had admitted to kissing Sander, ending any faint hopes that there might have been another unlikely explanation, involving a look-alike. But she stopped kissing him because of me? This wasn't the ideal way to hear that a girl shared your feelings for her but nonetheless it was flattering and undoubtedly marvelous.

"What?" I asked, struggling to think of a response.

"I made a mistake Troy, a stupid, drunken, childish mistake. The truth is I felt that spark in the chemist too." (Why does it sound fine when girls use cheesy lines? Unfair!)

"Honestly?" – Why do I keep questioning her? Am I trying to make her change her mind? – "Do you know how I felt about you in school?" I asked.

"I had some idea but I was a bit of an idiot in school. In my defense, what teenager isn't an idiot? Anyway, why don't we forget about the past and think about now?"

With that she looked straight into my eyes, leant over the table, and kissed me. This should have been delightful but in my limited experience, first kisses are rarely perfect. The distance between us was slightly too far, we tilted our heads the same way, tried to laugh it off, then did it again. When our mouths finally connected, we banged our teeth together, then were out of sync with one another and I nearly bit her bottom lip. Feeling flustered, resenting myself and thinking, "I bet Sander didn't have these problems," I was relieved when Sophie stood up, walked round the table, sat on my knee and we tried again.

This time, it was infinitely better. It was wonderful.

"Let's go back to mine," she said.

CHAPTER NINETEEN

Sophie lived in Sheung Wan, just outside of Central. A horribly busy, rush hour MTR ride would have ruined the mood somewhat so we hopped in a taxi. We didn't talk during the ride and it became slightly awkward when the taxi got caught up in a turgid traffic jam.

My heart was pounding and I was too excited to think of anything to say. Small talk wouldn't have been appropriate and talking about the near certain fact that we were imminently going to sleep together would have been difficult to put into words. Surely I couldn't manage to ruin my romantic chances in a fifteen minute taxi ride? As we got to her apartment block, she squeezed my hand tighter and smiled. I fumbled around trying to get money out of my pockets to pay the taxi driver, while also skillfully hiding my erection by doing the belt trick. In a turn of good fortune, the lift was there so the painful wait wasn't extended by much longer. I was extremely anxious, which was all the clearer when I started to sweat uncontrollably. I'd quite literally dreamt about this moment before and although overjoyed and excited, I was worried about the practicalities. The reality was that I'm not, and never have been a ladies' man.

On a drunken one-night stand, things tend to work themselves out fine. I don't worry so much and inhibitions are loosened. Sober, with a girl I really like – a totally different matter. I tried to cast my mind to what handsome men do in films. What would Ryan Gosling do in this situation? This then led to an unwelcome feeling of inadequacy as I wasn't quite in his league. I wondered if Sophie was sharing my angst.

She seemed fine, and unlocked the door with no problem – I would have had trouble with such an intricate task at this point – and we went in to her flat. It was a similar layout to mine only it was clear that a woman lived there, owing to it being clean and smelling like coconut shampoo. There was also a fair bit of girl-related nonsense knocking around; the wall above her TV was dominated by a photo montage of family and friends and there were a couple of pink cushions, some unseasonal fairy-lights hanging above the door to her room and a black and white poster of a man and woman kissing under the Eiffel Tower on the bathroom door.

Fortunately, Sophie took the lead and started to kiss me passionately while managing to take her top off at the same time, which was an impressive piece of multi-tasking. She took my perspiring palm and led me to her room, then possibly in a subtle attempt to remove my sweat from her own hands, placed them on my chest then shoved me surprisingly aggressively on to the bed. I now had a full blown erection, which had come unstuck and was idiotically sticking out of my trousers, with the belt that had previously acted as a hiding place, now throttling my shaft, causing a sharp searing pain. As I fought not to grimace, Sophie hurriedly pulled off my T-shirt and kissed my nipples, which I doubt she enjoyed, before removing my trousers and shapeless, faded boxers, gladly freeing my chafed penis from the clutches of the belt. I got the impression that Sophie considered giving me a blow-job but thought better of it, then without removing her skirt, she pulled her knickers to the side and straddled me. After a slight fumble, and the guidance of her left hand, I felt myself slide inside her.

It's funny how men, well me anyway, spend so much time thinking about sex, but when it is actually happening, it's one of the few occasions where you think about anything but sex. As I sat on the bed of the first girl I've ever loved, while she kissed my neck and rhythmically, expertly rode up and down, I was thinking about how many goals Tony Yeboah had scored during his debut season at Leeds. An untimely, but ultimately helpful digression, as we had sex for at least three or four minutes (exonerating total embarrassment) before I finally walked in on myself. At the moment I realized what was actually happening, my whole body clenched up, before – unable to restrain an ugly, raucous grunt of ecstasy – I came inside her, then toppled helplessly backwards, as Sophie collapsed on to my sweat-drenched chest.

She ran a hand through her ruffled hair then looked deep into my eyes and smiled.

"I enjoyed that," she said.

Momentarily unable to find my voice, I gulped, exhaled deeply and finally managed to respond, "Yep, I think I did too."

"Good," she said, then picked up an oversized pillow and playfully whacked me round the head, before pointing at my gradually shriveling nob. "I might want to do it again soon if he's up to it."

Later, as we lay down together after a second round of sex, I considered that this was possibly the first time I'd slept with a girl that I, maybe, loved. There arguably was a point when I felt like that with Imogen, but I couldn't remember it.

The awkwardness and worry of the taxi journey had completely evaporated and we happily chattered about nothing for a good while. Sophie made a pair of weak coffees and lit up a cigarette in the bed which I found incredibly sexy despite not being a smoker. (In all fairness at this moment, she could have picked wax out of her ear and flicked it in my face and I would have found it incredibly sexy.) The whole scene was reminiscent of a film and for a few seconds at least, I felt that maybe Gosling and I weren't so dissimilar after all. Sophie rested her head on my chest and fell asleep within a few minutes. I stroked her hair and lay blissfully, staring at the ceiling for an undetermined amount of time, feeling all my stresses and problems temporarily drift away. I felt a sweeping sentimentality that now, some ten years after first pining for Sophie, we had finally got together. My sixteen-year-old self wouldn't have believed this outcome.

*

I was unsure whether I'd slept at all when the morning sunlight started to creep through the cracks in the curtains, flooding the room in a luminous orange glow. Outside, Hong Kong was starting to wake up. I could hear the low buzz of the earliest morning traffic commencing. I looked at Sophie's clock to see it was five-thirty a.m. I have always seen the hour between five and six to be the worst time of the day, whether it's a.m. or p.m. If you're getting in from a night out at five a.m., you are tired and dry-mouthed, knowing that the next day will be a total write-off. If you are waking up during this hour, for anything other than a holiday, you are in a foul mood. P.m. is no better. You never arrange to meet someone at five p.m. If you are at home, it's too early to have tea and there is nothing watchable on TV. (*Neighbours* never recovered after its move to Channel 5.) Today, my opinion of five o'clock was different. Today, my opinion of life was different.

Just after six o'clock Sophie began to stir, making those "mmm" noises that girls do in the morning. A much more pleasant sound than the "urgh" noises that men make. I was, perhaps creepily, staring at her in anticipation of her eyes opening, which they did suddenly about ten seconds before the alarm on her phone played, 'Good Morning' by Kanye West. She blinked rapidly a few times and seemed to take a second to comprehend why a man was staring at her, before her mouth curled into a smile and she said.

"Good morning, mister."

She sat upright, arched her back, revealing her slender body to be impressively flexible, and stretched her arms, then leant over to give me a kiss before getting in the shower. I was glad it wasn't a long kiss as my breath in the morning is tragic and I didn't want her to have to realize what she was dealing with.

I wasn't starting work until ten so I lay there acquiescently, sprawled in her bed, while she banged about getting ready. I like watching a woman's morning routine; there is something enjoyably calming about it. She returned from the shower with steam rising from her and smelling delightfully of a fruit that I couldn't place, then stood with the towel deftly wrapped round her head while applying her make-up. She fumbled through a disorganized cupboard, muttered under her breath, then found hair straighteners and spent five minutes aligning her hair with a rhythmic clapping noise. After a few minutes of deliberation, she opted to wear a black dress instead of a dark gray one that was almost identical.

"So," she said, after finally being satisfied with her appearance, "What happens next?"

"That's a good question. What do you think?" I replied.

"Well. I think it's only fair that I stay at yours tonight, given that I put you up last night?" she replied, with exaggerated wide eyes.

"I think that's probably something I can arrange," I said, trying to match her flirty tone but not quite being able to.

"Well that's settled, then. I have to go to work now but feel free to stay here until you go to work. I think I can trust you not to steal anything."

And with that she gave me another kiss and left.

That morning my head was in the clouds; a sleep-deprived state of delirious euphoria. I bounced from the MTR station to work with a heightened sense of my surroundings and a love of mankind. I was being much nicer to people than I needed to be. During the walk, I smiled and said hello to a topless man who was dragging a cart of piled cardboard. He looked at me suspiciously. On arriving at work I made a special effort to compliment the receptionist on a new haircut which she informed me she'd had done two weeks ago, and even attempted to make small talk with Vicky.

"You got any plans for the weekend?"

"I'm just preparing for next week's classes," she said, looking at the floor.

"Oh. All weekend?"

"Yes. Can you make sure that you replace the teabags when you have the last one?"

End. It was the most we had conversed in the last month. I put in a special effort to be a good teacher, drinking enough coffee to combine energy with my joyous mood. At two forty-five, I received a message from Sophie saying:

"I had a great time last night. Looking forward to seeing you tonight. Xxxx."

As a result, my class at three until four was probably the best, most passionate, energetic class I have ever taught.

*

My relationship with Sophie gathered pace rapidly. In part, this was due to the fact that we already knew each other well, so we a head start, but also due to the increased reliance you immediately instill in someone when you get together in a foreign country that lacks familiarity. Anywhere in the world, the beginning of a relationship is always excellent. You really like each other and have improbable amounts of sex, only stopping when it becomes physically impractical. For the next three evenings, we stayed at mine and went to bed within an hour of Sophie getting back from work, only getting up to pick up takeaways or grab drinks from the fridge. After sleeping with someone, you feel incredibly open. You have seen each other naked so there is nothing left to hide; you talk brazenly and honestly about anything and everything (police informant work excepted of course). We also had the best part of a decade of catching up to do.

I talked frankly about the breakdown of my relationship with Imogen and Sophie told me about an ex-boyfriend called Richie who was a semi-successful photographer in London. Surprisingly, I wasn't jealous of tales of her past and listened with interest as she told me how he was a lovely man but they wanted different things. I decided that I'd probably like him if I met him. Since leaving England, I hadn't suffered from jealousy anywhere near as much as I used to. In high school and university, I was shamefully jealous of the boys who had the confidence to talk to, and sleep with lots of women, trying to cover it up with what I thought was a witty cynicism but was really just startling insecurity. In my directionless early twenties, I was envious of people who had good, well-paid jobs. Since arriving in Hong Kong, rather than wasting energy on such negativity, I'd begun to find myself glad at others' happiness and had become more realistic about my own capabilities. (That said, if I see a good-looking man driving a nice car, or accosted by a stunner, my knee-jerk reaction is still, "What a dickhead!")

Over the course of the weekend's conversations, I discovered that Sophie was, without question, considerably cleverer than me. Although this was slightly intimidating, I didn't mind. It was impressive. Whereas men have vast quantities of knowledge of certain subjects (such as football or films) girls seem to have a much better, more balanced knowledge of things. Sophie seemed to know something about everything. She could hold down a conversation about most topics: history, politics, films, books, art, music, cooking, etc. Hell, she even knew a reasonable amount about the financial turmoil at Leeds United.

Sophie and I did the typical thing that all new couples do, and totally sacked off our friends, turning down offers of pub trips and restaurants, citing being "busy at work" and "a bad stomach" as our transparent excuses. It's easy to moan about your friends selling you out when they get a new girlfriend, but when you are the one with the new girlfriend you start to understand and become a terrible hypocrite. After a week of making excuses, not picking up our phones and generally just being shit, I called Dom and told him about Sophie.

"Congratulations, mate. How did you manage that? She's definitely out of your league."

We chatted for a while and arranged to get everyone together for a few drinks on the Friday night at Red Bar, in the IFC – more specifically, the public seating area outside Red Bar where you are allowed to take your own drinks and can enjoy majestic views of Kowloon's bright lights. Sophie was initially reluctant to go out. Are girls even worse than men when they embark on a new romance?

Dom, Anna, Sander and a girl, whom I was ninety per cent sure I'd met before, were already waiting, when Sophie and I arrived casually / offensively late. Dom, pleased with his wit and drunker than was necessary, greeted us with a loud and dreadful rendition of a JLS number. Feeling partly like a celebrity, and partly like a dickhead, I couldn't help grinning and we did the rounds talking to our friends who seemed genuinely happy for us.

I was pleased; basking in the smug pleasantness of the evening, drinking beer and eating an average pizza that we'd bought from the bar. (I'd reached an agreement with a bouncer that if we bought one pizza we'd be able to use the bar's toilet facilities – shrewd negotiation skills and a far cry from my previous encounter with a doorman.)

As is customary on a night out with mixed company – the school disco routine never ends – the men and women disbanded and formed small sub-groups. Sander idled up and stood next to me.

"Hey man. I'm so happy for you!" he said, fortunately wiping some tomato puree from one of his front teeth before facing the indignity of my telling him about it. (I can continue having a conversation with someone if they have food on their face but on a tooth is too much.)

"Thanks mate, I appreciate it."

"I've got to tell you something though," he said. I'd noticed that he was chain-smoking and seemed uncharacteristically on edge. "I got together with Sophie a few weeks ago."

I wasn't sure how to take this. Was it good of him to tell me about it? I couldn't work out whether he was being noble or being a prick, so it was difficult to know how to respond. I opted for neutral.

"I know."

"What? Really man? Why have you never mentioned it?"

"It's fine. I know it meant nothing so don't worry about it."

"You sure you're alright with it?"

"Forget about it. I appreciate you telling me though," I said, still unconvinced whether I did.

We shook hands firmly and he patted my back. I seemed to be constantly shaking hands with men in Hong Kong. My bubble slightly burst and my mood knocked down roughly three notches – from a solid nine to a six, I strolled over to Dom who was debating with Anna about whether Birmingham or Manchester is better for a night out – a poor conversation that was going to have no satisfying conclusion. The night took a fairly predictable route afterwards with dubious watered-down shots in an overpriced bar,

Sander having a very public row with the girl he'd brought in a taxi, and inept dancing to bad music.

Sophie and I arrived back at mine just after one a.m. We'd snuck off without saying goodbye, when Dragon Eye – an expensive club frequented by idiots – was mentioned.

"Wasn't that great?" Sophie said, slurring her words but maintaining a degree of class by making me an expertly brewed cup of tea.

"It was. How do you feel about going public then?" I asked when we'd got into bed.

"Really good. I know we've not been together for long at all but it feels so right. I'm so happy. I'm so ha…" She trailed off.

"So am I," I replied, and started to consider that I might have a girlfriend.

CHAPTER TWENTY

The start of my relationship with Sophie had, by barely believable convenience, coincided with my hiatus from the police work. I hadn't heard anything from them in the past ten days – not a word. Sadly, this timely twilight-zone phase came to an abrupt end.

On Tuesday evening, when I was still floating around in an ethereal place, I received a call from a withheld number. (This happens a lot in Hong Kong – it's usually someone trying to flog a credit card or entice you into getting a high interest loan. Fortunately, as I speak no Cantonese, the callers usually give up and hang up on me. It's wonderfully unflattering having cold callers hanging up on you.) It was Dixon.

"We have new information. You need to meet me tonight."

The momentous crash back to my skewed reality was comparable to the alarm going off for work on Monday morning after spending the weekend taking good ecstasy. Wishing I hadn't picked up the phone, I agreed to meet him at nine o'clock. My first thought after Dixon called was that I was going to have to start lying to Sophie, less than a fortnight into our relationship. I racked my brains as to what I could feasibly be doing on a Tuesday evening that could last an indeterminate amount of time. I texted her saying I had to see Dom.

"We have been tracing Raymond's activity for the last two weeks," Liu told me, after I had sat down in her office. "Initially there was not much of interest but he had visitors yesterday."

"What happened?" I asked.

"They talked in detail about a 'big meeting' this Friday night at a bar in Sheung Wan. It matches what you mentioned. We think it's possibly a lucrative drug deal."

"So what are you going to do?"

"Hopefully we are going to intercept the deal and make a lot of important arrests."

I felt a surge of excitement and pride; I was right, they were Triads. This was nearly over. "And if it goes to plan, what will happen to me?"

"You will be free to go."

Work on Friday was grim. My mind all over the place, I put in a shoddy performance and abruptly stopped my last class fifteen minutes early as I needed the toilet due to nerves. It was simply a case of wait and see what the police had found out. Best case scenario – I would get a call from them saying that I was a free man.

Of course things wouldn't work out like that.

I heard nothing from Dixon or Liu all evening. I tried to call them four times to no avail. I reassured myself that they must be too busy to talk in the midst of their arresting an entire gang of Triad drug-dealers. I couldn't remember so eagerly anticipating phone action to this extent since the days of my teenage obsession with Sophie. I tried to watch a film but couldn't focus and found myself sitting, staring at my dormant phone.

At one thirty a.m., I finally got a call. It was Liu.

"Hello," I answered, giddy with nerves.

"Troy," she said sternly, then paused; which I hoped was to add effect before giving me the good news.

"Yes. Go on what happened?" I asked. The wait was torture.

"It was a total false alarm. You – we – got it completely wrong," she said, sounding gutted.

"What happened? Didn't you arrest anyone? Why not? I thought you overheard them talking about the deal?" I began to ramble hopelessly.

"Listen to me," she interrupted firmly. "It was nothing to do with drugs. It was just a business meeting. We went in and found nothing. We have embarrassed ourselves."

"No, that can't be right. They were the guys you wanted. They were Triads!" I continued, clinging on to the merest of chances that I had either misheard or Liu was joking for some inexplicable reason.

"We just did a police bust on a perfectly legitimate business meeting between two construction companies. They were discussing their respective bids for a new project next year. There were no drugs."

I couldn't believe how completely stupid I had been. After hearing the full version of events, I discovered that Raymond was a Quantity Surveyor; apparently just one that happened to enjoy sociable drug use. He was a casual, small-time dealer, not a Triad kingpin. The other men whom I'd met were not gangsters in any way, shape or form. My judgement had been so unbelievably bad that I was starting to question my mental health.

*

Early on Saturday morning, I walked the now familiar road to the police station preparing how to discuss my spectacular miscalculation and fearing what was next. Dixon was waiting for me when I arrived and suggested going for a sandwich. He didn't seem to take days off work. We walked in silence for five minutes before stopping in a local café.

"Some of the men we harassed and searched on Friday are threatening to press charges against us. If the media gets hold of this, there could be lots of bad publicity. We could be humiliated," he said, gravely, not looking at me.

"I'm sorry, Dixon," I said. "I honestly thought that I was on to something. I got it wrong."

"You really did – badly wrong. Aside from public embarrassment, do you know what this means?"

"What?"

"You are back to square one. You need to start again."

"Well, you've hardly given me much help have you?" I asked, annoyed.

"If I could give you any more information, I would. Don't you dare blame me. If it wasn't for me, you'd be facing prison."

The two of us sat, not talking for the duration of our egg sandwiches, which had far too much butter on them. I had done everything that was asked of me, and possibly more, so it seemed unjust that Dixon was annoyed with me. I'd really tried to help him to find the right people. Unfortunately it had been totally pointless; Tuen Mun, Browny, Raymond, the "Triads"– the whole thing. I was no closer to getting out of the trouble I was in.

*

After Dixon said he'd call me once he'd decided what to do next, I left him sitting in the café, staring at his stained coffee cup, and trudged home. I was utterly demoralized. I had spent a lot of time and energy on this lead. Not to mention putting myself in some ridiculous situations with potentially dangerous people. Although Browny had seemed harmless enough, I appreciated that he was still a long-term drug-dealer who possibly had psychotic issues. Similarly, Raymond came across as a nice bloke, but I'd thought I was dealing with a Triad leader.

138

The fact that Dixon and Liu seemed angry about the whole thing had made me feel even worse. I had found two drug-dealers. I knew they weren't the men (drug-dealers are always men) that they were desperate to catch but I had done a good job and, in my opinion, deserved at least a bit of credit. Moreover, the police instructions had been incredibly vague, "Try to build up a rapport with the drug-dealers," and "Find out as much as you can." Not exactly a detailed, step by step, "Don't worry, we've got your back" set of instructions. I was beginning to wonder whether they actually had my best interests at heart after all. Maybe my arrest had just opened up an opportunity for them.

*

I decided that seeing Dom would cheer me up. Sophie was very receptive of my moods and on the occasions where I'd fallen into silent fretting about my informant work, she'd been straight in there, asking, "Are you OK?" "What's wrong?" etc. and I couldn't face that now.

I arrived at Dom's building and was buzzed in by Hung, his elderly security-guard, with whom I had built up some level of acquaintance despite the language barrier. We nodded at each other, then I strolled past to the lift and went up to the fourth floor where Dom's tiny – but slightly bigger than mine – flat was located. We had mentioned a few times that moving in together would be a good idea but one of us needed to take the initiative and actually do something about it. So far this hadn't happened. I knocked on the door and Dom called out.

"Come in."

I entered the flat and was greeted by a sweating, topless, red-faced man.

"Alright, mate," he said, smiling and seemingly thinking an explanation was not necessary. "How're things?"

"Not bad. Bit of a shit morning. How about you? And why are you topless and sweating?"

"Oh yeah, that. I've just been doing some weights," he said.

I looked around the living-room and saw no sign of dumbbells.

"I don't have any weights so I've been improvising," Dom said, nodding towards three chairs that were stacked on top of one another." I've been benching the chairs."

"Do you always use your chairs as weights?" I asked him, puzzled, but quietly impressed by his ingenuity.

"My neighbours stole my weights."

"I'm sorry, what?" I asked. This was not a normal thing to happen.

"Yeah, they are bastards. I left them outside when I was cleaning my house and they stole them. They took a pair of trainers as well."

"Aren't you going to do anything about it?"

"Nah. It doesn't matter. Forget it."

Dom was incredibly casual about his neighbours stealing his belongings and I noticed that he was grinning. He seemed extremely happy to see me – worryingly so – and I wondered why he was in such a jubilant mood. Was it just the post-weights endorphins? He bound into his bedroom, stuck on a Toronto Raptors vest, then walk-danced to the fridge, pulled out a pair of Gatorades and came and sat down next to me on his Ikea sofa. I was unsure why he had given me a Gatorade.

"How's things with the lady?" he asked.

I told him she was good but he'd probably heard enough of my talking about Sophie recently so I didn't want to risk boring him with even more details of my blissful new relationship. I was aware that when I spoke about her I found it difficult not to smile which probably made people want to punch my stupid, smug, grinning face. Besides, I was keen to discover why he was so happy.

"How're things with you? What did you get up to last night?"

The exact second I finished the question, Dom replied, "I had a very good night!" Then he looked straight at me, smiling. "She left about an hour ago – Australian beach-volleyball player. Beautiful," he said, his eyes widening with satisfaction.

This explained his uncharacteristically good mood for early afternoon on a Sunday.

"Let's go play squash!" Dom said. This was also another sign of a man who has recently had sex – spontaneous ideas and too much energy.

"Not sure I can be bothered now," I replied. Then, after a pang of shame for finding his good mood annoying, decided to ask follow-up questions and humour him. "Where did you meet her then?" I asked him.

He told me the tale of how he had been sunbathing at Repulse Bay beach on Saturday morning when a girl, called Lorna, asked him if he would make up the numbers for a beach-volleyball game she was having with some friends. After impressing her by being quite able with the ball, they had exchanged numbers.

This was what Dom had called "sowing the seed" and apparently it was "nailed on" after he had hit a big serve to win their team the match. After texting her throughout the afternoon, they had met up in Carnegies in Wan Chai in the evening, then evidently made the short walk back to Dom's apartment together. "She's so nice. I think she's the one!" Dom said, and took slightly too long to laugh at what he had just said, making me think that he might not have been joking.

We continued to chat (more accurately, I continued to listen), for the next half an hour before he forgot about squash and decided that it was a perfect day for us to go for a jog along Bowen Road. I didn't really fancy doing any kind of physical exertion but running is a good way to make you stop thinking, so it was probably not a bad shout. Also, Dom's mood was the antithesis of mine and his positivity was helping to cheer me up and forget about my wider predicaments.

I borrowed a musty-smelling pair of shorts and some huge, uncomfortable Nike trainers and we jumped in a taxi and headed up the steep and winding Stubbs Road that led to the start of the trail.

"She's just moved to Hong Kong and is looking for a job as a teacher. Do you think you could get her one?" Dom was asking me as we did some token stretches before starting the run.

I don't generally like any exercise that doesn't involve a ball, but I do enjoy running along Bowen Road which is a brilliant trail; a five kilometer, totally flat, car-less road carved into the hillside, taking you from Happy Valley to Central, running behind all the skyscrapers. It feels like you are behind the scenes of Hong Kong. A strange trail of thought had led me to a cheat you could do on Super Mario 3 where you ended up behind the scenery so you could avoid all of the enemies and jumps. It was like this, you could see and hear the chaos of Hong Kong, but you were on the outside looking in. The first time I had found the track, by accident, I was blown away by just how good the views were. With little else to compare it with, I decided that it was probably the best running track in the world.

Given the Gatorade and Dom's already worryingly high energy levels, we decided that we would try to do there and back. We started off at a steady pace with Dom still yet to have talked about anything other than Lorna. "She's from Melbourne originally but moved to Brisbane when she was in high school," he was telling me as I puffed and panted my way around the first

141

bend pretending to care about a stranger's educational background.

We made the first leg in a decent time, did a few more stretches then headed back. Dom had finally quieted down which had led me to start thinking about my problems.

Then, possibly inspired by the fresh-ish air, I had a revelation; maybe I'll just tell Dom about it? The police would never know and Dom might be able to offer some good advice. The old "problem shared is a problem halved theory" might be exactly what I need. We ran in silence for a few minutes as I started to think about how I would tell my barely believable story to my sweaty, hyperactive friend.

I was actually feeling surprisingly healthy and could have continued to run, but told Dom that I needed a rest at the half way point of the run, where there was a small park, usually frequented by smatterings of local nutcases, but presently uninhabited. I figured that if I thought about it more, I might not tell him. I needed to tell him now, while the idea seemed good in my head.

"Shit, I'm knackered," I said, overdoing my heavy breathing.

"Me too," said Dom, clearly lying. He was stupidly fit and had barely broken sweat. "I need to keep in shape if I'm going to keep Lorna happy. She was wild last night!"

"Dom, I need to tell you something," I said, after we had regained a regular breathing pattern.

"I knew it. You're gay!" he replied, pleased with his white-hot wit.

"No. Not that I'm aware of. I'm in a bit of trouble. I need to tell someone about it because it's doing my head in."

I poured out everything that had happened over the past month. From getting caught in the toilets of Azure, right up to this morning, when, after thinking I was almost out of the mess, I was back to the drawing board.

"Bullshit. I don't believe you. You've been watching too many episodes of *The Wire*," Dom finally replied after I'd finished.

"I swear I'm telling you the truth. You can't tell anyone. The police said if I tell anyone, the deal is off and I will have to face the Hong Kong courts."

After a while, he started to consider that I was, in fact, telling the truth. Clearly still thinking about *The Wire*, he did a realistic impression of Clay Davis' "Shiiiiiiit!", which was entirely unhelpful. Gradually he calmed down and became more serious.

"Fucking hell, mate, that's ridiculous. What are you gonna do?"

"I can't do anything now. I've got to wait for them to tell me what to do."

"What would actually happen if you just accepted the charges? Prison?"

"They told me I would almost definitely face a prison sentence, and a hefty fine. It would be an absolute life-ruiner. My family would disown me, I'd be financially crippled and it would be impossible to get a job. I need to make it go away."

"Mate, if you're messing with the bloody Triads, you could get into more trouble than that."

"What would you do?" I asked.

"Well for starters, I wouldn't have been stupid enough to get caught taking cocaine abroad."

"Cheers."

"But if I was in your situation, I honestly don't know," he said.

It had been a big decision to tell Dom and while not sure what I was expecting from him, I hadn't envisioned that he might be totally useless. It did, at least, feel like a sizeable weight off my shoulders just to have told someone about it. The whole situation now actually started to seem like it was real. There had been times over the last few weeks when it had felt like I was in some bizarre lucid dream.

Dom and I decided not to complete the jog and precariously made our way down the perilously steep Wan Chai Gap Road and back home, talking more about my predicament.

"I've got to go home, mate," he said when we arrived back in Wan Chai. "I'm meeting a couple of the basketball lads for Sunday lunch in an hour. Listen, I'll think about what you've told me and try to muster some advice to give you. It's not a situation I've known anyone to be in before, so my apologies for not really knowing what to say."

"Thanks Dom, I appreciate it," I said." Please don't tell anyone about this."

"You can trust me, mate," he replied and we went our separate ways.

CHAPTER TWENTY-ONE

W hen Sander called me on Wednesday evening asking if I still wanted to go to Kris's junk boat party, it was a surprise. With so much going on recently, I'd totally forgotten about it. After initial reluctance, I remembered Sander's mention of drugs at the party. With the Raymond lead hitting an emphatic dead-end, I was running low on ideas, so any mention of cocaine was something I had to follow up.

Sophie had a compulsory team-building trip to Macau which sounded dreadful and she was quite rightly annoyed about it. It sometimes feels like Hong Kong companies will do all they can to stop the existence of the weekend. This was, however, a stroke of luck for me as, without Sophie there, I could attempt to forage for drug-related information without her suspicion.

After confirming that I'd go, the now all too familiar ache of guilt started brewing when I considered that I was only going on this man's birthday boat-trip to try to find out information to tell the police. I'd already tried to get myself out of trouble at Raymond's expense and although the police were no longer pursuing him, a dull ache of remorse remained lingering in my stomach. And now I was at it again – trying to fuck people over to save myself. Kris was undeniably a smarmy idiot but what I was doing still made me feel suitably despicable.

We were meeting at Central Ferry Piers at nine a.m. Sander came to mine beforehand and we shared a cab. He was clad in a Singha beer vest and boardshorts and was visibly excited about the day ahead, tapping his foot and badly humming along to a Chris Brown number that was crackling on the radio. I wondered if he was more excited by the thought of cocaine, or women, or maybe he was simply looking forward to doing swan dives from the top deck of the boat. He was a good diver – aesthetically very pleasing.

We got to the ferry-pier bang on nine o'clock to find twenty or so people standing around in small clusters of twos and threes.

The start of a junk boat trip is always excruciatingly awkward. Although some people know each other, there are lots of introductions, small talk and uncomfortable pauses – the type that isn't a problem in the evening, but which people struggle with when in broad daylight and sober. I stood on the outskirts of the group as Sander immediately muscled into a group of women, picked up a small Indian-looking girl whom I assumed he'd slept with, and spun around with her in his arms. How did this guy have the energy? He was constant – a constant menace.

I was relieved when Dom arrived, a minute or so later. As a man who struggles with mornings, he was tired but in good spirits.

"Alright, mate. How're we doing?"

Dom and I were good enough friends to appreciate that free-flowing conversation wasn't a necessity at this time of day so we stood around not talking much for the next couple of minutes. After ten arduous minutes, a taxi pulled up and I heard the Black Eyed Peas' 'I've Got a Feeling' blaring. The doors to the taxi were flung open and Kris stepped out, with an old school ghetto-blaster held on his right shoulder. He was wearing bright yellow ray-bans, which looked identical to the fakes that I'd bought from Mong Kok (but I was certain his were real), a white linen shirt, and very short denim shorts.

"Let's get this party started, warriors!" Kris shouted over the top of Will. i. am and then went through the ritual of shaking hands and body-bouncing every man, which is something I've always deplored, and having elaborate hugs and kisses with all of the women present.

Kris swaggered over to Sander, put his arm round him and the two of them led the way to the boat which was bobbing around at the pier. As soon as we got on, every one of the now fifty or sixty revelers was greeted with a champagne flute. Despite the time of day, I noticed most people were glugging their drinks quickly. Dom and I headed up to the top deck and managed to get a good spot, sitting down towards the back. From here I could scour the crowd of mostly twenty and thirty somethings in more detail.

When satisfied that everyone was on, the captain put the boat into action and it veered right towards East Kowloon. It was fortunately a perfectly clear day, so within a few minutes of the boat heading out, there were brilliant views looking back to Victoria Harbour, with the sunlight catching beautifully off the Bank of China building and the reflection shimmering on the turquoise sea. Days on junks are when you get an arrogant smugness about living in Hong Kong. You can rest assured that someone will say, "You can't do this in England!" and you then both talk about how amazing Hong Kong is with a sickly sense of self-satisfaction.

For some reason I didn't gather, there was an eight-story-high rubber duck floating around near Tsim Tsa Tsui, which a Dutch artist had put there; it was seen as an early photo opportunity for most females on the boat. I saw not one but two men pretending to be a duck when snapped and considered if I would have done the same if asked to be in the photo. The early champagne was taking effect and the volume of awkward small talk shifted towards a louder, more comfortable level.

"Do you know what you're going to do about your police stuff?" Dom asked me, loud enough for most of the boat to hear. I didn't want to talk about it with him on the boat, as he would potentially attempt to help me, and unwittingly sabotage my subtle detective work. He appeared relieved that I didn't want to discuss it. Besides, his pressing concern seemed to be his ill-fated search for a girlfriend. Lorna had texted him saying that she had a boyfriend back home and couldn't see him again.

"There was no mention of a boyfriend at my apartment," he said, angrily, "Or when I was buying her expensive cocktails all night. Seriously, women should wear a badge to say that they have a boyfriend and then I wouldn't waste my charm and money chasing them!"

The natural progression of the conversation was to talk about traffic-light nights at nightclubs. The pair of us ridiculed the idea and anyone who had been to the nights, before both admitting to having un-ironically worn amber T-shirts at said events in the past, despite being emphatically single.

We moved on to discuss "The boyfriend," who always stirs a negative image of a man in your mind when a girl mentions him. Unless "the boyfriend" is a pal, I never like the sound of him. I always picture a muscular man wearing a vest, having a non-specific regional accent and treating his girlfriend badly. Of course this image is worsened depending on how attractive the girl is. It always feels like a small punch in the gut when a girl whom you assumed was single says, "My boyfriend is picking me up." He is always picking her up. "The boyfriend" always drives.

Dom and I continued to chat, mostly nonsense, and in the process isolated ourselves from the rest of the group until a second round of champagne came and we decided we should "mingle" – a word I don't like. I like it even less when someone comes and asks me, "Why aren't you mingling?" I feel like saying, "Because I would have to speak to people like you who ask questions like that," but always say, "I will later," thus putting myself under pressure to be a good mingler when I feel it's my time to impress.

We approached a couple of friendly-looking, thirty-something women and had a pleasant enough conversation about summer in Hong Kong and the purpose of the rubber duck. One of them, Lucy, was clearly interested in Dom and giggled at everything he said whether it was a joke or not. Over the next hour I nursed a couple of chilled Coronas and spoke to an extremely boring recruitment consultant whose only question in a twenty minute conversation was, "What's your name?" before he barraged me with a tirade about how he had "smashed" his targets this year. Jesus.

Despite his best efforts, I was enjoying the day out. I'd decided that I'd simply have a good day, then if and when someone mentioned cocaine, I would tactfully try to find out who they bought it from. Momentarily forgetting about my secretive reasons for being at the party, when the boat stopped and chucked the anchor out near Clear Water Bay in Sai Kung, I decided I was going to be the first to jump in. This was an excellent opportunity to show off and beer bravado was starting to kick in. I was well situated to be first in line and jog/walked over to the highest point of the deck. On arriving at the edge, I decided a jump wouldn't be enough and opted for a swan dive. It started well. I spread my arms wide, got decent air and felt it was going to be spectacular. Unfortunately the landing was torrid and I managed to both wind myself and bust my nose when smacking into the water.

I looked back up to the deck, hoping to see the whole boat applauding my bravery but sadly nobody had even watched me. Wiping the blood from my nose, I clambered back on the boat in time to see Sander and Kris do a highly impressive, tandem back flip. We stayed by Clearwater Bay for a good while, with people swimming around and a banana boat being sent out. Banana boats are one of those things where the idea is always better than the reality, so I didn't bother.

Kris tried his hand at kite surfing and – excellent news – he was bad at it. Not quite bad enough to laugh it off. While he was quietly fuming and looking entirely unapproachable, I spoke to a teacher called Aaron who was by all accounts a nice bloke, but had a really annoying habit of speaking to me like I was one of his Chinese students. He spoke far too slowly with an irritating inflection which made everything sound like a question. He was not the first teacher I met who had developed this extremely annoying way of talking. I had made a conscious effort not to start and would like it if someone punched me in the stomach at any sign of it.

By three o'clock, the majority of the party had moved into an extremely sociable mood, chattering and dancing so I decided now was the time to try to find out anything I could about cocaine dealers in Hong Kong. I reassured myself that nobody whom I was going to talk to would get into any trouble and it would only be the serious dealers at the top who would get into trouble. I'd managed to get it into my brain that these dealers were definitely bad men who deserved to be caught. My first move was to sew the seed of the conversation with Sander.

"Hey San, you know that thing you mentioned the other week?"

"What?" he replied, clearly not remembering.

"You said that you were going to have some cocaine?" I asked timidly.

"Oh yeah. Ask Kris. He'll sort you out," Sander replied casually, taking a drag of a large, pricey-looking cigar which he'd bought specially for the occasion.

Kris had just returned from his humbling wake-boarding experience and was a bit pissed off. I decided to give him a few minutes to calm down, then went over.

"Hey Kris, I don't suppose you've got any spare coke? I'll pay you."

"Fucking hell, Troy my boy. Of course. Come with me," he replied and gave me a hard pat on the back which resurfaced the pain of my earlier winding. I followed him inside and down towards the wooden toilet cubicle near the front of the ship. Inside the cabin, I noticed a middle-aged woman kissing and straddling Marc (Kris's pal) in the corner. Kris said, "Lad!" then gave Marc a high five before opening the door to the toilet, and apparently not acknowledging the irony of two men going into a cubicle together, said, "Come in then you poof!"

I thought that, while we were in the process of doing it, it would be a suitable time to try to get some information, so after Kris had hoovered a chunky line up his left nostril, I asked him, "Who do you buy this from mate?"

"Just some guy I know from out and about, but I can't say who. He wouldn't be happy if I started dishing his name out," Kris replied.

I didn't ask any further questions and felt a spot of short term relief that not much more could be done. Gladly, Kris made a considerably smaller line for me and I gingerly snorted it, pretending to be happy at his generosity and making an unnecessary whooping noise to suggest as much.

I thanked Kris then we headed back to the rest of the party on the top deck. It was mid-afternoon now and a few women were sprawled out sunbathing and / or asleep. I found a sunburnt Dom sitting next to Lucy and was unsurprised to see her hand on his lap. The cocaine had acted as a good counter to the early beers and sunshine and I was happy to talk nonsense with anyone who would listen for the rest of the afternoon, as we sipped the seemingly endless, but now lukewarm, supply of Coronas and munched on gigantic slices of Paisano's pizza. Some rogue had clearly had more than their fair share, which caused controversy when an aggressively drunk woman, annoyed at not having eaten, started an embarrassing witch hunt by going round and asking everyone how many slices they'd had.

Just as the boat was getting back towards central ferry piers, Kris, who could now barely walk but was perfectly able in terms of talking – he was talking a lot – staggered over and put his arm around my neck.

"Give me your phone," he whispered in my ear; then after sneering at my Nokia and punching a few buttons, he returned it, then started singing 'Titanium' by David Guetta loudly and out of tune before dancing with an attractive girl to his own singing.

I looked through my phone-numbers and found a new contact and number. The contact name was, "Riley."

*

I awoke at eight a.m. the next day feeling the effects of a day's drinking in the sun, and when I looked in the mirror, noticed that my nose was badly sunburnt. I showered, had a coffee, then scrolled through my phone to "Riley's" number. I decided I would get in touch with the mystery man later in the day. Drug dealers were unlikely to be awake at this time of day. I couldn't imagine Monday morning being peak business hours.

Work was average. I had two classes in the morning, both of which were about holidays, or "vacations" as their irritating American book told me to teach. Holidays is arguably the most overused English teaching topic, run close by food and drink and hobbies. After nearly a year of teaching I was finding the topics infuriatingly repetitive and boring and I'd long lost count of how many times a student had told me about their dream holiday to Taiwan, "If you could go anywhere in the world, where would you go?" Ninety per cent of Hong Kong locals said Taiwan. I'm sure Taiwan is pleasant but is it really the best place in the world? I always tried to encourage students to suggest somewhere a bit further afield to which they usually replied "Macau".

At lunchtime, I decided it was a suitable time to contact Riley. I considered texting him but decided that there was a strong chance he wouldn't reply. This would leave me in limbo, and result in me having to call a few hours after sending the message that he hadn't replied to. It would both waste time, and make me look like a bit of a loser:

"Hi, I was just ringing to see if you got my text?" (If ever you find yourself calling a girl and asking her that question, you can definitely assume that any romantic intentions you had are now completely over.)

I headed outside to an allyway near my work, where at least some of the noise of traffic and people was blocked out. He picked up after one ring.

"Good afternoon," answered an English man, "Who's this?"

I opted not to give him my name and just go straight in: all-out attack.

"Hi. Could I meet you to buy some coke tonight?" I asked. Over the last few weeks my confidence in talking to potentially dangerous men was steadily improving.

"Yes, sure. When? Where?"

"How about Wan Chai?" I suggested.

"No, I can't do that tonight. How about TST? Meet me outside Chung King at six."

"OK. See you th..."

He hung up.

Well, that was easy enough, I thought, and treated myself to a Big Mac meal and extra chicken nuggets to congratulate myself. (An issue I have with McDonalds is that the Big Mac is not actually the biggest burger. The double quarter-pounder is. It's comparable to a darts board. Like the Big Mac, the Bull's-eye has the best name, the bravado and charisma, so it should by merit be worth the most points, but it's not.) McDonalds is one of the few things that are cheap in Hong Kong, so I found myself eating it on a prolifically regular basis. The afternoon dragged on. All three of my classes were very low level. A sample conversation being:

"What's your name?"

"I'm fine."

Depending on my mood this could be endearing, challenging or unbearably frustrating. Today was the latter. Three hours in a row of pulling teeth. No fun. I ended my last class ten minutes early and snuck out so that I didn't have to say goodbye to my colleagues and risk getting caught in conversation. One of the receptionists, an avid Avril Lavigne fan called Minnie, had a strange habit of locking me in conversation right at the end of the shift. She would barely speak to me all day, then just as I was leaving, ask a barrage of questions about how my classes had been and what I was doing that evening. During the day, I'd be content to chat, but at the end of the day, when I've finished work…no.

I didn't have time to go home before meeting Riley so I took the MTR to Tsim Tsa Tsui and walked the short distance to Nathan Road. It was a warm, muggy evening and was just starting to get dark as I arrived outside Chung King Mansion. I hadn't been here since the first few weeks of my Hong Kong adventure. It was exactly as I remembered it – a grubby, old, seventeen-story tower-block that looked rundown to the point of appearing derelict from the outside. Amongst the shiny new skyscrapers and designer shops, it stood out like a sore thumb with the usual buzz of people of all nationalities hanging around outside.

It was coming up to six and I headed to the main entrance of the building. It then struck me that, although a famed landmark, this was a stupid place to meet someone. The area was unbelievably busy. How was I supposed to meet a man whom I had never seen before? I had no idea what he looked like and all I had to go on was that he was a man. I wondered if I should have asked him to be reading a newspaper, or carrying a tulip. I waited outside the entrance for ten minutes or so and was starting to think that there was no chance that I'd meet him. I pulled my phone out and was about to give him a call when I was interrupted.

"Oi, Troy. How are you doing, mate?" It was Frank, the man whom I'd met in New Makati in Wan Chai many months ago. I was surprised that he recognized me. He was wearing wet-look hair gel and his shiny skin suggested he hadn't drawn the line at his hair and had smeared it all over his face as well. He was wearing long combat shorts, flip-flops and a baggy Ralph Lauren polo shirt.

"Hi Frank, nice to see you again. How're things?"

Frank had seemed like a nice enough feller and normally I would have been happy to chat with him. Given that I was waiting to meet a drug-dealer right now, this was wretched timing.

"I'm very well mate. Not seen you in the Wan Chai bars for ages. Where you been?"

"Oh, y'know how it is," I replied. This neither answered his question, nor made sense, but Frank nodded agreeably.

"What you doing out here, then?" he asked.

"I'm meeting a friend but he's running late," I said, looking at my watch for effect.

"You going out for a few beers?" he asked.

"Yep, just going for a couple," I lied. "What are you up to?"

"I'm meeting someone as well, but they're also running late. Just because the locals are always late doesn't mean we should copy their bad habits does it?" Frank said, smiling.

"What time were you meeting your friend?" I asked him.

"Ten minutes ago," he replied with a wry smile. "I'll give him another five then I'm going."

We chatted for a few more minutes. He asked me how Carmella was doing and recommended a new English pub in Wan Chai that apparently did an excellent roast.

"Sorry mate, I'm just going to ring this guy. He's taking the piss now."

As Frank pulled out a Samsung galaxy from his combat pockets, I suddenly got a very strange feeling. He punched a few buttons then put his phone to his ear.

My phone started to ring.

CHAPTER TWENTY-TWO

❝Well, fancy that!" said Frank, his tone lighthearted, and seemingly unsurprised by this considerable, unlikely coincidence. He was such a normal, if unhealthy-looking, middle-aged man that the revelation of his extra-curricular money-maker was fairly astonishing. I wouldn't have been shocked to know that he occasionally took recreational drugs, but I would never have put money on him being a dealer. He didn't fit the profile.

"What a coincidence. I had no idea that you were 'Riley'?" I said, feigning a forced laugh, "It's a small world, eh?" (Hong Kong really is a small world – seven million people crammed into Kowloon and a few small islands. Hong Kong Island has seventeen thousand people per square kilometre which is, if you think about it, fucking ridiculous.)

"I am, sir. Frank Riley. Pleased to be of service. I'm starving so fancy grabbing some food first and then I'll sort you out?"

"Sure," I said, aware that this was the second time in recent weeks that I'd met up with a hungry drug-dealer. Why was I always going for lunch with drug-dealers?

We set off walking up Nathan Road where we fought our way through the sea of people who were each fighting for a yard of space to make their next step. Nathan Road, like many areas in Hong Kong, is a place which I loved at times and despised at others. If in a good mood, the crowds, the shops, the smells, the traffic and the sheer bustle of the two-mile-long road running through the centre of Kowloon is interesting, invigorating and a great reflection of the cross-cultural aspects of Hong Kong. However, if in a bad mood or on a hot day, it's a horribly crowded, stinking and polluted main road which is far from pleasant. Given that it was the height of summer, I was leaning towards my latter opinion today and was pleased when, after a couple of minutes, Frank made a sharp right down a side street just after Kowloon Park and led us to a local café with outdoor, wooden seating.

"This place is good," he informed me. Besides, it's too hot to walk far." Then he made a drinking motion to the moustached waiter who promptly returned with two large Tsing Tao beers.

"Thanks," I said as Frank topped up my small cup.

"So, what's the story?" I asked him.

"Well, the real estate business went under a while back, so I needed to do something else to support myself," Frank replied, calmly, like we were talking about him doing part-time English tutoring rather than dealing cocaine.

"I've a few mates I know from Wan Chai who were making a bit of money on the side so I asked them if I could get involved. It was nothing big to start with; just shifting the odd gram to pay for my beer money," he continued.

"Fair enough!" (Is it?) "When did your business go bust?" I asked him, intrigued.

"About three years ago," he replied, "Which is why I now do a bit more than just the odd gram. It's easy money and beats sitting in an office all day."

"I can imagine," I replied. I was beginning to think that Frank might be of vital significance to Dixon, and my own escape route. The fact that I had met him before at least once – there was a good chance that our paths had crossed again through the haze of beer and smoke-machines on a Sunday afternoon, but I couldn't remember – meant I felt like I could probe a bit further.

"So how does it work? Do you just hang around Chung King and deal to anyone who wants it?" I asked him. (This seemed to be the general approach at Chung King. Indian and Nepalese men come up and whisper in your ear, "Suits, watches..." You reply, "No thanks," and they make the sizeable leap from timepiece to class-A drugs. "Cocaine, ecstasy?" Evidently not wanting to buy a watch or a suit is a prerequisite for actually wanting to buy drugs.)

"I used to do that," Frank replied, unnerved by my interrogation. "Not much money in it though, because there's too much competition. I've got a few regulars who buy in bulk now and that tides me over. It pays for my Sunday afternoons anyway!" He paused for a second and took a long pull on his beer, almost draining the glass.

"Come to think of it, who told you my number?" he asked.

"A friend of mine called Kris."

Frank's face turned.

"Who the fuck is Kris?"

"Tall, blond-haired banker. Bit of a prick," I offered.

"Oh, him. You're right. He is a bit of a prick. I sort him and his posh boys out for their weekend fix now and then," Frank said, calming down. "Prick shouldn't have dished out my number though. I'll have to have a word with him about that."

I quite enjoyed that Kris had been referred to as a prick three times within ten seconds but I didn't really know how to respond to that so sat silently and glanced through the broken English menu, doing that thing where you look at words but don't actually take in the information.

"I think I'll go for the sweet and sour pork. Good?" I asked Frank, changing the subject with the subtlety of a fridge falling over.

"Good shout. I'll get the same," he said, then beckoned the waiter back over and spoke in what sounded like decent Cantonese to order our dishes.

"Impressive, you fluent?" I asked him.

"Hiya," he replied, looking pleased. "I didn't know you were into the powder, Troy. How much are you after, then?

"I'm occasionally partial. Got a big party coming up, so was hoping to get four grams in." This fictional party had been pending for quite a while now but it always seemed to be the most reasonable explanation as to why I wanted to buy large amounts of drugs.

"OK. I don't actually have that much to hand; risk of possession and all that nonsense. Do you fancy coming to my house to pick it up? We'll go for a few beers as well?"

"Sure," I replied. "Where do you live?"

"Discovery Bay."

*

I arranged to meet Frank on Wednesday afternoon at Discovery Bay pier. Lying on the coast of Lantau Island, it's a half-hour ferry-ride from Central. I'd been to Discovery Bay twice before. It's an unusual place and doesn't feel like you're in Hong Kong at all. In the 1970s, local property developers had the idea of turning the area into a Costa-del-Sol-style holiday resort, with plush hotels and golf courses, to attract more tourists to Hong Kong. Midway through the construction, they had run out of cash, and after some issues with a Russian bank, the project was eventually bought out by another group who decided that, instead of being a holiday resort, they would turn it into an up-market residential area.

Nowadays it is mostly populated by expatriate families, with locals vastly outnumbered by a well-dressed, bronze-skinned, shiny-white-toothed breed of wealthy, middle-aged white folk and their public-schooled children.

I met a flip-flop-and-too-short-shorts-wearing Frank at Pacific Coffee where he ordered a pair of Frappuccinos and we sat outside to enjoy the sun. Frank did not come across as the Frappuccino type – I expected that, back in England, he was strictly a tea and biscuits man and had undergone a Hong Kong reinvention.

"How's things, mate?" he asked, slurping his frothy drink through a thick straw.

"I'm very well, thanks. How long have you lived out here, then?"

"I moved out about two years ago. I'd spent too long in pokey flats in Wan Chai. I needed a change."

"Nothing wrong with pokey flats in Wan Chai," I said, earning a chuckle from Frank. "Why did you pick here though? I bet it costs a few quid?"

"Well, I made the decision that I'll probably never return to England so sold my house back home and that has paid for my place here. I like it here. It's more like Tenerife than Hong Kong though, eh?"

Frank and I shared pleasantries for a while before he became less pleasant and made a few coarse comments about a middle-aged woman who had over-done the Botox and was breast-feeding her baby in the corner of the café. He then told me how he had signed up for golf lessons, wanted to buy a boat and had dreams of opening his own steak house. I nodded agreeably before he suggested that we "go for a walk."

Unsure if this was drug-dealer code or if he actually wanted to stretch his legs, I agreed, and we were soon strolling along the promenade and towards the beach.

"So, you said you were after four grams, right?" he said.

"Yep, will that be OK?"

"Sure. I live just here," Frank said and pointed at a newly-built, bright white, detached beach-house straight in front of us.

"Nice place," I complimented him, as we removed our flip-flops and he opened the large French windows for us to enter his living-room.

"It does the job. Give me two minutes, mate. I'll just pop upstairs and get it."

Frank's living-room had that expensive, yet ultimately tacky feel to it. He had wooden floors, three-quarter covered with a fake tiger-skin rug, a huge cream sofa and two guitars – a Fender Stratocaster and a Gibson Les Paul – sitting proudly next to it. He had his own spirits bar fixed up in the corner of the room. There were arty pictures of scantily clad women sporadically placed on the walls and a framed Watford football shirt above his huge Samsung TV. It looked like something out of an average Danny Dyer gangster film. I wouldn't be surprised if Dyer himself had a similar living-room.

"Fix up a couple of whisky and cokes, mate," Frank called down from upstairs where I could hear him banging around. I made Frank's drink and poured myself a coke. It was early in the day to have a stiff drink.

"Right, here you go," Frank said, after he'd returned, giving me three small plastic packets.

"Nice one. Thanks. Is that three grand?"

"Yes please, mate," he said and I handed him three big notes from my wallet.

"Let's go to the driving range," Frank said. "I need to work on my swing. I can get you in as a guest if you fancy it?"

"Sure, sounds good," I answered, worrying that the last time I'd been to a driving range was when I was eleven and the trip was cut short because one of my friends had accidentally swung, hit another pal in the mouth and knocked his front teeth out.

Apart from public transport, cars are banned in Discovery Bay. The only legal alternative is to drive a golf buggy that costs an obscene amount of money. Seeing businessmen in sharp suits dropping their kids off at school in these stupid vehicles is a ridiculous and strangely depressing sight. Needless to say, Frank owned one of these vehicles and proudly told me to hop on. I wondered if there were strict drunk-driving laws for these things, seeing as Frank seemed to be constantly oiled.

Frank proudly introduced a new set of golf clubs and told me that they were "the best in the business" and "weren't cheap." Frank, like Sander and many people in Hong Kong for that matter, enjoyed parading expensive things and unsubtly searching for compliments.

"They look sweet," I said, questioning my choice of adjective. Do people still say "sweet?" or has it been out-muscled by "sick"? I enjoyed the journey in the golf buggy. The openness of it gave the impression that you were going much quicker than you actually were. My initial cynicism about the vehicles had significantly dwindled after a thoroughly enjoyable ten minute ride snaking through the hills up Discovery Valley Road.

Frank had a bit of difficulty parking the thing before we went into the swank- looking foyer. I noticed I was carrying Frank's bag. Was I expected to caddy him? We went to reception where Frank flirted badly with a young Filipina employee then went through to some posh changing rooms with electrically operated lockers and flat screen TVs playing CCTV news on the walls. I had nothing to change into so stood, not knowing what to do with myself, while Frank had no qualms about taking off his clothes, took a five-minute social phone-call while completely naked, then changed into some serious-looking golf gear.

"Right, let's go ping some balls!" he said triumphantly, adjusting the peak of his Nike visor.

"Sure."

"That was Marcus on the phone," he informed me while feeding tokens into a machine to pick up balls to ping. "He's an excellent golfer. He's going to join us." I picked up the basket of fifty balls and we strolled out.

"Ah, he's beat us to it," Frank said, upon seeing a giant forty-something man with chiseled good looks and a well looked after, light brown side parting. He looked like he'd walked out of a Just for Men advert.

"Afternoon ladies," Marcus greeted, in an accent I guessed as South African but could have been Australian.

"How are you, Frank? And you must be Troy?" He came over shaking my hand firmly. The man oozed charm and had the character of a pilot who cheats on his wife.

"Are you a keen golfer?" he asked me. I appreciated that he had not judged my entirely inappropriate attire, or at least not commented on it.

"I'll be honest – no," I said, to which he laughed showing film-star, white teeth.

"Well. You've got to start somewhere. Old Frank was terrible a few weeks ago, and now he's just very bad. So everyone can improve."

Frank lined up his first ball, and although he lacked any kind of technique, got a good connection and hit it about two hundred yards. Marcus then stepped up and with the swing of a professional golfer, struck the ball beautifully and watched it soar into the distance. A tough act to follow, I found myself overcome with nerves as I stepped up. I placed a bright yellow ball on the tee and stepped back. I considered asking for advice but decided I would try to wing it. Maybe I'd fluke a good connection? I held Frank's "not cheap" driver and swung it behind my head then whipped it down and with thoughts of a Marcus-esque crisp connection, proceeded to smash the club straight into the floor about twenty centimetres away from the very visible ball, sending jolting vibrations coursing through my arms and badly jarring my back in the process. I turned round to see the two older men laughing hysterically.

Not fancying an entire afternoon of ridicule, I used the back injury as an excuse to sit out. In between the two men's swings, I became acquainted with Marcus. He was from Johannesburg and told me he worked for Welcome supermarkets. I presumed from his appearance that he wasn't a cashier and wasn't surprised when he informed me that he was the Financial Director. He was married with two young children and had lived in Discovery Bay for five years.

After I had watched the driving of a further two buckets of balls, I was relieved when Frank said he wanted to call it a day.

"Are we still on for tonight?" Marcus asked him as the two men stood naked in the changing rooms. Why was I in the changing rooms again? I wasn't getting changed. I should have learned from the first time.

"Of course, I've got the table booked for seven," Frank replied, toweling between his legs.

"Do you have plans tonight, Troy? You should come along," Marcus said.

"Where are you going?" I asked.

"We're going to the Marina Club for some dinner."

"Don't I have to be a member?" I asked naked Marcus, my eyes subconsciously drawn to his crotch. Why does that happen? I swiftly looked away hoping that he hadn't noticed.

"I know the guys pretty well. I'm sure something can be arranged," he said then thankfully put on some oversized boxer shorts.

We said our goodbyes to Marcus, who got into an identical golf buggy, then headed back. Frank said he had some ambiguous-sounding business to attend to, so would I mind meeting him in a few hours. He subtly suggested I change into some smarter clothes to go to dinner. Then I arranged to meet him back at his at six-thirty.

It was approaching four o'clock and I didn't really have time to go home so decided to mosey around the plaza area for a bit. School had finished so the place was busy with well-dressed full-time mothers and Filipina maids walking around with gaggles of blond-haired children with too much energy and international school transatlantic accents. I went for a contemplative solo ale in McSorley's pub and considered the evening ahead.

Frank was a pleasant – albeit slightly strange – man and he seemed to trust me. We had been to a driving range together, and he had paraded around naked twice, so surely that had consolidated our friendship? I just needed to keep spending time with him and when the time was right, I could try to find out more details about his operation.

CHAPTER TWENTY-THREE

Sophie called and I told her my plans for the evening. She had a habit of ringing me with little to say if she was waiting for someone or if she was bored. At least three times a week she rang and asked what I'd had for lunch. I don't see the information as being phone-call-worthy and occasionally told utterly pointless lies about what I had eaten just to make things a bit more interesting – a cheap adrenaline rush. For example, I might tell her that I'd had a McDonalds when in fact, I'd had a Subway. Maybe it was unconscious lying practice for the bigger picture. I had already lied to her several times about my whereabouts and was becoming quite skilled in the art of telling untruths.

On this occasion, I didn't have to lie, telling her that I was at Discovery Bay and would be staying out for dinner with friends, simply withholding some information (namely that I was searching for a cocaine king-pin.) She coolly assured me that this was no problem and we arranged to meet up the following night. I finished off my ale and went in search of some trousers and shoes to wear for the evening dinner. The only option was a sports shop but I managed to get some golf trousers which were a bit too tight but looked fairly trendy, and some plain black pumps. I deemed my slightly sweaty white polo shirt presentable so opted against buying a new T-shirt. I paid, using Dixon's float. The new clothes were indirectly related to the matter in hand after all. I still had a while to kill so decided to amble slowly along the beach and back before going to Frank's.

I approached the French windows which were open and rapped my knuckles on the glass. Frank swiftly arrived and welcomed me in.

"You look much better now," he complimented me, but I noticed he was wearing exactly the same clothes as before, which was both confusing and irritating. "Have a seat," he said, offering me a Corona with a freshly squeezed lime at the top. "We'll set off in ten."

Frank and I idly chattered over our beers, discussing his improving golf swing and speculating about the availability of the attractive receptionist at the golf club.

"Who are we meeting, then?" I asked.

"Just a few of my friends from DB. There should be about seven or eight of us. We meet up once or twice a week for dinner and drinks et cetera," he informed me.

It's unusual to say "et cetera" so I wondered what it meant in this context. We got back on to the golf buggy and made the embarrassingly short trip to the Marina Club. It was a modern, white building with large shiny windows and plastic-looking, Corinthian Columns framing the entrance. There were a couple of statues of dolphins, mermaids and other aquatic-related things scattered around. To the left of the main entrance you could see all the sparkling white yachts bobbing around in the orange, sun-stained water. I was considering the value of the largest of the splendours, when Marcus strolled over smoking a thin cigar and wearing an outfit not dissimilar to my own last-minute effort. He had a red cashmir jumper slung over his broad shoulders.

"Glad you could make it, Tiger Woods," this is how Marcus greeted me, and we went inside the club.

There were no problems getting me in. Marcus flashed his Tom Cruise-esque smile to the well-dressed, male receptionist and I signed my name on a piece of paper, using a fancy new signature. We walked upstairs to the restaurant called the Anchorage. Marcus's movement would be better described as gliding, a slow but assured movement emphasizing his charisma. Frank, on the other hand, was definitely more of a stumbler. He also had an issue with his flip-flops, as one of them came off and it took him at least ten seconds too long to get it back on. The two men were an unlikely pair of friends. With me, a much younger man wearing badly-fitting golf clothes, people were probably wondering what on earth we were doing with each other.

The restaurant held about one hundred people and was three quarters full with a buzz of chatter and the pleasant aroma of well-cooked, garlicky food.

"This way," beckoned Marcus and led us to a circular table, where two couples were sitting down. The four people stood up on our arrival and much handshaking and cheek-kissing ensued over the next few minutes. My arrival seemed to have caused a bit of a stir. The men – Kevin, a short but muscular late-thirties-looking pilot, who was wearing a suspect denim jacket and Richard, a sharp-suited white-haired man of retirement age – greeted me with warmth and a barrage of questions.

"How do you know Frank?"

"How long have you been in Hong Kong?"

"Marcus said you're some golf player?"

Cue laughter.

After this, I was introduced to Marcia, Richard's much younger-looking, oriental – probably Thai – wife and Kevin's "partner", Elaine – an attractive blond who looked not a whole lot older than myself and was wearing too much perfume.

The ladies subjected me to a similar level of questioning while the two men joked with Frank and Marcus. After the buzz of the introductions had died down, I took my seat inbetween Marcia and Rob which gave me a picturesque window view of the yachts and the sun setting over Peng Chau Island.

"Where's Vicky?" asked Kevin to nobody in particular.

"She's on her way," replied Frank, waving his I-phone and pointing to it, which apparently proved this information.

"Let's order some vino then," Richard said, in a well-spoken, methodical southern-english accent which resembled that of a university lecturer.

While supping my expensive-tasting merlot, I got into conversation with Kevin who was from Belfast. He told me he was a pilot with Cathay Pacific and had been in Hong Kong for two years now. He was friendly and easy to talk to, even if he did talk a bit too much about the technicalities of flying a plane. I asked him one question.

"How much does the autopilot do these days?" to which I was given the history of Boeing aircraft mechanisms over the last twenty-five years. Fortunately, the tirade was interrupted when people put their drinks down, and stood up to greet the new arrival.

I got up, turned round and was astonished.

"Vicky" was the only Vicky that I knew in Hong Kong – my miserable, depressive colleague at work. I was aware that Hong Kong was a small place with a tight-knit, expatriate community, but this latest coincidence totally caught me off guard. It seemed as though someone was taking the piss. Unsurprisingly this was the first time I'd seen Vicky outside of work and she looked a different person. She was wearing a long black dress, had had her hair blow-dried, and was wearing make-up. If I hadn't known her, I might have even, nearly, said she looked glamorous. She was almost unrecognizable, when compared with the downtrodden, old-blouse-and-black-trouser-wearing misery that I saw on a daily basis.

"Alright, Vicky," I managed. "This is a surprise!"

"It certainly is," she responded while clearly thinking, "What the fuck are you doing with my friends?"

"What? You two know each other?" Frank said, his bloodshot eyes lighting up.

"You bloody love a chance meeting don't you Troy?" he said. Then, after remembering the nature of our own chance meeting, stopped talking.

We told the group about our work and how we knew each other. Given that we didn't like each other, it was suitably awkward. To my surprise, Vicky painted a totally false picture of our relationship and put on a façade that we were good friends. I wondered why she was doing this. Her entire demeanor was totally different to what I knew. She was lively, bubbly, made a few jokes and was clearly well liked by the rest of the group.

After she had done the kiss cheek rounds (I did notice I was not included in this rigmarole – it would have been too much), Vicky took her place on the spare seat next to Frank at the opposite side of the table. I might have imagined it but thought that she flashed a grin at me.

Over the exquisite, French-style dinner, the mood was jovial. Wine and conversation were freely flowing as we talked about varying topics ranging from summer holiday plans, the slow walking pace of Hong Kong locals, the book that Richard was in the process of writing (I'd discovered he had been a newspaper journalist and had moved to Hong Kong to semi-retire and enjoy the life with his yoga-teaching younger wife), and Leeds United's promotion hopes for the following season. The only low point was when Kevin repeated everything he'd told me previously about plane engines to the whole table, which incurred follow up questions and a wide-scale debate about the merits of auto pilot. It was a very pleasant evening; the group was funny, friendly and interesting and I'd been made to feel extremely welcome. Even Vicky and I were bouncing off each other at one point, when talking about Leroy, the tubby student at our school.

My only regret was that I'd made the mistake of ordering the cheapest item for each course, which I regretted when Marcus fronted the entire bill with minimal fuss. By the time we had left the meal, I felt as though I'd known these people for much longer than a few hours. We stood outside the Club while Marcus dished out his thin Henry Winterman cigars to the men and the ladies standing chatting. As neither Vicky nor I were smoking, we took the opportunity to stand aside and talk about what had happened.

"I honestly can't believe it," she said, smiling. It suited her.

"I know. So do you live out here, then?" I asked her.

"Yes. I've been in Discovery Bay for six years now. I love it out here."

"It seems like a good group you've got," I replied.

"Yes, they're great. I met Marcus's wife Sheila many years ago. She used to work at our place before she had the kids," Vicky continued, her tone chirpy.

We continued to chat, still not breaching the taboo of our struggling relationship at work, until Frank, who had drunk considerably more wine than anyone else, called out, "Right, let's go back to Richard's for a few more!" to the delight of the intoxicated crowd.

With merriment we headed to the golf buggies, of which there were three between the six of us. I was fortunate to secure a ride with Richard and his wife. I found Richard to be very captivating, and in regard to my general safety as a passenger, he was considerably more sober than either Frank or Marcus. Frank was now singing 'Wonderwall' and becoming annoyed that nobody was joining in with him. I feared that if I'd been on his buggy, I would have been expected to do the backing harmonies. Meanwhile Marcus' smoothness had been momentarily knocked as he mistook someone else's golf cart for his own, got angry that it wasn't starting, then – too proud to laugh at himself – pretended that it hadn't happened.

Richard discussed his feelings about Discovery Bay as we buzzed along, telling me that, while it was a good place to retire, he also found the place to be totally ridiculous – "A purpose-built nonsense." My first impressions were that Marcia and he had got together recently so I was surprised – and a bit disappointed in myself for being so presumptuous – when she told me that they had been married for twenty years. They had met in London when she was performing in a play in the West End. Also, she wasn't from Thailand, but Croydon – her dad was Indonesian.

After I'd given a slightly glamorized brief history of my own life-story (the Leeds United Youth team lie recurring), which I can tell in less than ten minutes (no-one wants a longer biography) and we had wound our way further up the steep road, we pulled up outside a large spanish-style villa. Richard parked the vehicle. Then we walked through some hostile-looking electric gates and into a vast courtyard, complete with a ten by ten metre swimming-pool, which beautifully illuminated the courtyard amidst the black night sky.

Lantau Island is one of the few places in Hong Kong where you can see the stars in the sky, as there isn't as much light pollution. Everyone likes a swimming-pool at night – there is something unerringly romantic about it. (That said, I had recently fulfilled a long-standing ambition by having sex with Sophie in a swimming-pool and the reality hadn't been great. Practically speaking, the water didn't help things and after splashing and fumbling with little enjoyment, we abandoned it after ten minutes.)

The pool was surrounded by six deckchairs with comfy sponge mattresses – the type that you get only in hotels with four stars or above – and a large wooden dining-table.

"Welcome to my humble abode!" Richard said.

The comment didn't really work properly, when the abode in question clearly wasn't humble at all. It was a beautiful two-story effort with stunning views of Disneyland and right over to the twinkling lights of Hong Kong Island. The other two carts pulled up shortly after us and I was relieved to discover that Frank hadn't driven off the road and clattered down the hillside.

"It's a beautiful evening, so let's sit out," Marcia said.

"I'm not working tomorrow so let's get the champers out," Marcus happily demanded, gesticulating to Richard. He was apparently over his embarrassing mix-up at the Marina club now. The six of us sat down at the wooden table and there was a moment or two of awkward silence as we awaited Richard's return from the kitchen.

An I-pod with speakers emerged and a Motown Compilation was playing slightly too loud for the speakers to deal with, causing fuzzing and distorted bass. Richard and Marcia returned with champagne and glasses and we went about the enjoyable fuss of cork-popping – Richard carried out the standard gag of pretending to aim the cork at Frank – and filling up the glasses. It seemed like a special occasion but in reality, it was just a Wednesday evening in June. I considered whether this was a regular occurrence for these people. If it was, there was apparently little to fear about getting older. We sat drinking and talking for half an hour before the evening took an unexpected turn.

"Right, who's in?" Frank addressed the table.

I initially thought he meant going for a swim but his intentions were clarified when he pulled out a huge bag of his cocaine, poured it on to the table and proceeded to cut it up into generous lines. I monitored the reaction of the other people, trying to gauge their feelings. I assumed that Frank might just be drunk and on a self-annihilation mission, uncaring about how he was perceived by the others. Subsequently I was shocked to see that everyone excitedly agreed then took it in turns to bend down and snort the powder; everyone, including Vicky. I felt ridiculously uncomfortable seeing my colleague taking class-A drugs.

"Come on mate, get involved!" Marcus said, snorting his share greedily.

Peer pressure is something I've always struggled with. From the days of being urged to attempt a back-flip from the top diving-board at Barnsley Metrodome, aged nine, I've always had difficulty in saying no. In this case, "no" didn't even cross my mind and I joined in with the rest of the party.

From this point onwards, the night became hazy. It's funny how cocaine seems significantly to enhance your sharpness and coherence at the time, but the next morning you don't remember a thing. Champagne continued to appear and Frank happily distributed his drugs. By eleven, everyone was drunk and wired, talking loudly over each other, but in their own minds, having brilliant conversations. Despite my best intentions, the drug had taken over and I started to ramble furiously on to Vicky.

"I can't believe you're like this! Why do you never speak to me at work?" I asked her.

"Why do you think I'm not the chirpiest at work, Troy?" she asked me, apparently expecting me to know the answer.

"Because you think I'm a twat?" I half joked, forgetting that people don't really laugh when they're on cocaine; it is serious fun.

"Of course not," she replied. "It has more to do with my lifestyle choices than my opinions about you," she continued.

So there it was. One of my questions had been answered. "Why are some people so miserable all the time?" – Because they are constantly hung over and coming down from cocaine binges – obviously.

After dancing to 'Sexual Healing' twice (Richard had put it on repeat and thought no-one had noticed) I took a seat next to

Frank who had been consistently snorting cocaine for the past two hours, seemingly without stopping.

"So is this a regular Wednesday night?" I asked him when his face returned to a horizontal position.

"Not just Wednesdays. When we fancy it really," Frank replied sounding surprisingly coherent.

"This lot in Discovery Bay love a good party. Obviously I do too, but it's bloody good for business as well. I can make my money here throughout the week then at weekends, I sell it to the young whippersnappers like you in Wan Chai and Lan Kwai Fong."

"Is there really that much demand in Discovery Bay?" I asked, intrigued.

"Take a look around you. This is only one group that I knock around with. There're loads of others who buy it off me too." He lowered his voice. "I give these guys mate's rates but the amount that they get through means I still make a killing."

I looked around at the crowd we were with. Elaine and Kevin were in a tight embrace, grinning and kissing each other. Richard was standing precariously on a chair, clumsily dancing, Vicky and Marcia were locked in an intense yet nonsensical conversation and Marcus was stripping off, ready to bomb into the swimming-pool.

"I had no idea that there was such a scene for it out here," I said, after politely turning down a now naked Marcus's invitation to join him in the pool.

"Well you do now," Frank continued. "We older folk have got to enjoy ourselves now and then, you know. Besides, there are a lot of people here with more money than they know what to do with, so the powder is a good way to stop the money burning a hole in their pockets. These guys are nothing compared to some people I sell it to. There's a whole bunch of "ladies of leisure" who drop their kids off at school then spend the day taking cocaine. Sure enough they do Pilates, play tennis and go to cookery classes, but most of the time they are wired."

As Frank continued to explain this middle / upper class cocaine use, it became more understandable that there was a wide-scale subculture active in Discovery Bay. Cocaine is an expensive drug, and the people who live here can afford it. Add to that, high-pressure jobs where people need an escape from the reality of work, or at the other extreme, retirees and housewives with lots of money and time on their hands. It all made perfect, logical sense.

I'd been totally naïve to it and cocaine was clearly much more prevalent than I'd previously thought. I had been looking at the scene through blinkers, assuming that it was only something that young, party-going people / dickheads did at weekends, but this was only one segment of Frank's custom.

I was heading towards another planet by now, but strained to keep in touch with reality as I realized that right now, in this conversation, was a chance to find out some valuable information. Not for the first time, Frank was openly talking about his drug-dealing escapades and his tongue was loose. He didn't seem to care what he said.

"So, how much do you usually shift in a week?" I asked him.

"That depends. I usually make about twenty grand in Discovery Bay, if I'm lucky. I'll make a similar amount on Hong Kong Island at the weekends. It can be as little as five grand though, depending on if the bankers earn their commission."

I nodded thoughtfully then bit the bullet.

"How do you get hold of so much? Where does it come from Frank?"

CHAPTER TWENTY-FOUR

I opened my eyes and was met with glaring sunlight blinding me. It was boiling hot. I was dripping with sweat. My mouth felt like a furry desert, and even by my own standards, my breath was vile. I was desperate for water. My nose was crusted with dried snot and when I tried to breathe in, I became aware that both nostrils were completely blocked.

I felt something on my head and reached up to find that I was wearing a plastic, golden crown. Every bone in my body was aching, especially my weak back, which was in agony. I was completely disorientated. After a minute of squinting and groaning, I removed my crown, peeled my sodden T-shirt from the deck chair, sat up and started to take in the surroundings.

I noticed that there was a woman slumped on top of a man in an unlikely, drastically uncomfortable-looking position on the deckchair opposite me on the other side of the pool.

On further inspection I recognized the man as Kevin. He was lying on his back with one leg dangling off the chair and the other bent with his knee up towards his chest. The woman, Elaine, was flopped over him, her head hanging loosely with her wet hair flailing. I hadn't seen such a sight since a teenage house party. Next to the agile couple was Frank who was wide awake and smoking a cigar. If there was anything I wanted to do less right now, it was smoke a cigar.

Frank gave me a thumbs up to which I didn't respond. I gingerly stood up, trying to straighten my back out and getting some circulation moving round my aching limbs. Behind me were the remains of the previous evening – a horrendous detritus of broken glasses, empty bottles and stubbed out cigarettes. The I-pod was on the floor with a smashed screen.

I was startled by the sound of the front door opening as Marcus stepped out, two coffees in his hands, wearing a dressing-gown and looking almost fine.

"Morning! You lot got it wrong by sleeping out here. I bet you're boiling."

I was annoyed, yet impressed by his perkiness. I was a good while off being capable of conversation and grunted something that has never meant anything in any language.

"Here, have a coffee. It will perk you up mate," he offered sprightly.

"Water!" I spluttered.

Marcus went back into the house and returned with a litre bottle of cold Bon Aqua water. If my lips hadn't felt like they were stuck together, I could have kissed him. After glugging over half of the bottle in one, I managed to remember what words were and hoarsely asked.

"You have a good night?"

"I sure did. Feeling it a bit now, though. I don't think I'll be too good at golf this afternoon."

Marcus and I chatted for a while, discussing the night's events. We agreed that our last memory of the previous evening had been 'Sexual Healing' being played. I had no idea how I'd ended up on the deckchair. Marcus also had no answers to where the crown had come from or what it represented. After a five minute burst of decent conversation – the remnants of drugs and alcohol giving one last blast of euphoria and energy before spectacularly crashing – our communication dried up. Marcus stood in a deliberating silence for a few seconds then said.

"Right, it's time I left. Just going to go and get some clothes on, then I'm away. Don't want to stick around to be reminded of what I did last night."

I forced a laugh. Then my heart sank with alarming suddenness. Time...shit!

"What time is it?" I asked Marcus, heart pounding.

He took an awfully long time rolling up his dressing gown sleeve, getting his watch out and looking at it, frowning.

"It's just coming up to one o'clock. Why?"

"Fuck. I was supposed to be at work two hours ago."

"Ouch!" was Marcus's cool response.

I called over to Frank, who had remained quietly seated. He looked red-eyed and jaded.

"Can you give me a lift to the ferry pier?"

"Yeah, that's fine."

I grabbed my wallet which was under the table. Opening it, I was greeted by one screwed-up twenty dollar note and absolutely loads of almost worthless change. Why is there always loads of change in your wallet after a night's drinking? I found my phone on the table, then after a few seconds' looking, found the battery strewn on the floor. I stuck it in, turned it on, and discovered seventeen missed calls from work.

"I've got to go now. See you soon Marcus. Thank the others for a top night."

"See you later. Tell them that you had diarrhea. Nobody wants to ask follow-up questions to that," Marcus said, then headed back to the house to get changed. "Good luck!" he called back.

Frank had now stood up and said, "Come on, then. Let's go."

I was incapable of conversation on the journey. Hung over, in pain and horribly stressed out. I was staring at my phone's clock. If I made the one o'clock ferry and things went smoothly on the trains, I could be at work for my afternoon classes which ran from three until six. I had the journey to sober up and think up my excuses, which were going to have to be good.

"Thanks so much," I said to Frank as he dropped me off. "Great night. I just hope it hasn't cost me my job!"

"No problem," he said, then paused for a moment and asked, "Do you remember much from last night?"

"Not much after dinner to be honest. Why?"

"Just wondering," he replied. "Right, get out of here. I hope you can talk your way out of trouble."

I had made the semi-conscious decision that I wouldn't call my work. A broken phone was going to have to be part of my plan and in all honesty, I was too scared to call. The travel time was swift. With the final hooter sounding, I ran and managed to catch the one o'clock ferry then took the MTR to Wan Chai where I sprinted home and got changed. There was no time for a shower so I masked my odor with a generous mouthwash and by spraying aftershave all over myself and my clothes. I arrived outside work just after two-thirty. If it had been a different situation, I would have congratulated myself on my ruthless traveling speed. I took the lift upstairs, took a deep breath and headed in.

"Hi!" I said, with over-the-top friendliness, to a receptionist whom I didn't recognise. "Where's Kit?"

"He's out for lunch. He's been teaching your classes all morning," she said, without looking up.

I poured myself a coffee and sat down in the student waiting area, running through my story in my head one more time. Kit bounced in, finishing off a tuna baguette, then looked at me and his smile vanished.

"What happened?" he asked, coldly.

"I was really sick all night – diarrhea and vomiting. My phone has broken so I couldn't call in. Then because I was up all night, I fell asleep this morning. The alarm didn't go off because my phone was broken…." I was rambling spectacularly.

"Come with me," he said, heading to his office, which doubled up as a classroom if we were busy, and telling me to sit.

"Troy, I like you. You're a good teacher but I can't rely on you. This isn't the first time you've let me down."

"I know. I'm so sorry. It will never happen again," I said.

"And you smell of alcohol," he continued. This was the blow; unrecoverable.

"I don't, do I? Really?" I asked, trying to buy myself some time to think.

"I've spoken to the area manager, and we think it's best for all parties if you look for other employment."

"What?" I asked, devastated. "I've made one mistake. Come on!"

"You know that's not true Troy. I'm sorry. I suggest that you go home and go to bed. I will email you the termination of employment letter later."

"Oh, come on, Kit. For fuck's sake!" I was angry and upset but swearing was, in hindsight, unlikely to get me my job back.

"Go home, Troy," he said firmly, then stood up and left. I followed and walked out the door.

As is often the case with bad news, I didn't really believe that it had actually happened for the first few minutes. My knee-jerk reaction was inconsistent with the seriousness of the situation: "Excellent…I don't have to work this afternoon." I didn't initially appreciate that the reality was that I would never work at Super English again.

I went downstairs and got myself some slop masquerading as spaghetti bolognaise from a local café and tried to make sense of what had happened. Besides being sacked from my paper-round aged thirteen (which I could have little complaint about), I'd never received the boot before, so I was in uncharted territory.

After wolfing down my food – I hadn't realized how hungry I'd been – I suddenly felt a lump in my throat. At first I thought it was some of the alleged minced beef that had got stuck, so was surprised to notice that I was actually about to cry. How embarrassing. I thankfully managed to catch myself before the tears started but I was totally gutted.

I was way over my head with the police informant stuff and now I was jobless. The only good thing I could think about was Sophie. Then my heart sank again. I had to tell her I was jobless. No girls appreciate a jobless boyfriend. It's not something that they would proudly tell their friends. I'd estimate that most girls would love a jobless boyfriend at least thirty per cent less than an employed boyfriend. This percentage would increase over time, probably at a ratio of about two percent for each week spent without an income, until loathing starts and jobless man becomes single jobless man.

Everything had gone to shit.

After retaining at least some masculinity by not breaking down in the café, I realized that I had to pick up my rucksack – which was packed with spare shirts and teaching materials (a scruffy, barely used A4 pad) – from the staff room. Of course the staff room was right at the back of the building and the only way to get it was by walking past every single one of my now ex-colleagues and students who were in the building. Why wouldn't it be right at the back? Hell. I briefly considered leaving the bag but given that there were three shirts in it, I had to go back. Two shirts and I probably would have fled with my dignity intact.

I opted for the look at the floor, don't speak unless spoken to, routine but it didn't serve me well. Clearly the news hadn't been made public yet and staff and students alike acted as if everything was fine.

Aiden asked, "Do you still need the big room on Saturday?"

The not knowingly insulting but always offensive local teacher said, "Wow, heavy night? You look dreadful!" and two students asked if I could check some work they had written. I made some excuses and got to the staffroom. The only difference between this and a film was that there wasn't a muscular security-guard escorting me and my things were in a bag, not a cardboard box. With the sight of my bag and the fact that my class had been due to start five minutes ago, people seemed to gather what had happened. I upped the pace and walked past the staring eyes of people whom I had seen six days a week for the last eight months but would now probably never see again. It was tragic.

I bolted up the road to the MTR and got on the first train, which was actually going the opposite direction to my house. My head was muddled and my heart was still pounding from the walk of shame. It's not often in life where you literally have no idea what you should do next. I decided I would text Sophie and tell her the news. She would be at work but I couldn't deal with waiting until the evening. I simply said, "I was late for work so I've been sacked. Gutted!"

She swiftly replied, "What?" with no kisses.

The demise of her feelings for me had started already.

I went to Wong Tai Sin Temple without really thinking about what I was doing and sat in the park which was a pleasant antithesis of my current mood; fish ponds and flower arrangements. I had hoped that the calm of a temple would help me plan my next step but unfortunately a mainland Chinese tour group of twenty or so middle-aged folk, wearing matching, yellow T-shirts, arrived shortly after me, shouting, spitting and taking photos of every square inch of the park. I don't see the appeal of taking a photo standing next to a bin but some of the party clearly did. I sat down and resumed my now familiar head in hands pose.

Deep into my despairing thoughts I suddenly had a vivid flashback from the previous night's festivities and felt a surge of adrenaline. After everyone else had gone to bed or passed out, Frank and I had stayed up on the deckchairs talking. He had told me in-depth details about his drug-dealing and the cocaine-importing business. Despite my memory from the rest of the night being spectacularly fuzzy, I could remember what Frank had told me with a startling clarity:

"I work for a bloke called Nigel. He's a nasty piece of work but he's a genius."

I hadn't pushed him. He'd seemed happy to divulge, possessing an almost boastful demeanor while animatedly telling me the story.

"He started out with a legit company importing wine from Chile to the UK. After a few years, he got to know some locals and decided that cocaine would be a more lucrative market. He started off small just sneaking a few grams from Bolivia to the UK. Obviously the demand was high, so he started shifting bigger amounts. A few years ago he moved to Hong Kong. Cocaine in Asia is a rapidly emerging market and he figured he could make more doing it over here. Also, there is a growing demand for wine in Asia so it works on both levels. Hong Kong is perfect because it's the gateway to China."

"Does he still use the wine company as cover?" I'd asked.

"Yeah, as far as I know. He just lines the crates with cocaine. The South American contacts were happy to change to Hong Kong because people pay a fortune for it in Asia. It's a shorter trip for them as well."

"How does he get it in without getting caught?"

"He has a boat coming in once a month. Never came close to being caught. He pays off some of the coast-guards, so it's easy."

"How many of you has he got working in Hong Kong?"

"I'd guess there's about twenty of us."

"And Nigel delivers the drugs for you to sell?"

"No, that's too risky. We go and pick it up from Sheng Shui, then we shift it and pay him his cut."

"Sheng Shui?"

"Yeah, it's where he keeps it – would be stupid to keep that much in his house. Shit, why am I telling you this? I need to get some sleep."

And that was it.

*

I sat down and raked through the information in my head. I'd discovered some crucial information. I knew the name of the top dog, and I knew that the cocaine was stored in Sheng Shui. I just needed to know whereabouts in Sheng Shui. Granted, not easy; but I had something to work with. It felt as though I was getting there.

It had been a long day of hangovers, sackings and revelations. After taking the MTR back to Wan Chai from Wong Tai Sin, I was exhausted. I couldn't face Sophie's questions so I went back to mine, turned off my phone and secured fourteen hours sleep which was just one hour short of my personal best.

I woke up at nine on Friday morning and made a strong cup of Yorkshire tea. I had no job but the investigation was going somewhere. I'd left England in search of excitement, and although my situation was far from ideal, I couldn't deny that it was exciting – really exciting. I called Liu to tell her what I had found out.

"Good work," she said after I told her all I remembered about Nigel and the importing business.

"We are nearly there. Do they have the cocaine in the container now?" she asked.

"I'm not sure. I guess so," I responded.

"It seems like Frank trusts you. You must be tactful so that you don't arouse suspicion but I think he will tell you more. Try to find out where the storage container is. Or find out details of the next shipment. You're doing well. It could all be over soon," she said.

I was thrilled by the news that it could soon be over. However, there was still some way to go, not to mention the moral implications of potentially getting Frank – a man who'd been nothing but nice to me – jailed for a long time. My next step was to figure out how I could get specific information from him. He had happily talked before, but he was out of his mind on drink and drugs. Even then, he'd still had the awareness to stop before telling me any totally incriminating information; and the next morning he'd seemed anxious as though he knew he'd said too much. It was going to be extremely difficult to tailor a situation whereby he would tell me even more.

I decided that I would leave it a few days before contacting Frank again. I couldn't rush this. Besides, I needed to act naturally and more importantly, devise a plan where he would tell me more. The plan would almost definitely involve plying him with alcohol but I wasn't sure what else.

CHAPTER TWENTY-FIVE

I needed to clear my mind from the informant work for a while and face the difficulties in my other, normal life – namely, unemployment and a cross girlfriend. Sophie was pissed off with me for not seeing her the previous night and in a foul mood when I went to her flat on Friday evening. It was fair enough. I'd stayed out all night on Wednesday, got sacked on Thursday and not spoken to her properly about anything. I arrived at hers, she brushed off my attempted hug and we sat down on her bed.

"What are you going to do?" she asked, showing little by way of sympathy.

"I'll get something soon. There's plenty of teaching jobs in Hong Kong," I said, acting casual.

"Well, start applying then!" she snapped.

Whereas I, like many men, procrastinate and like to postpone shit tasks for as long as possible, Sophie was keen to get them done straight away. Applying for jobs is right up at the top of the shit tasks list. It is demoralizing, repetitive and, usually, completely futile. I was going to start looking on Monday. I needed my weekend.

"I'm not doing it now. I'll start on Monday. Don't worry," I said.

"Fine," she said, then went quiet. When a girl says "fine" it's never fine.

After stewing for a while, Sophie drank a large glass of white wine (she didn't offer me one) and gradually started to perk up.

"Shit, it's the weekend. Let's not argue. Promise me you'll really try to get something next week, though?"

"Sure," I said, happy at this reprieve. I'd been expecting silent treatment for longer.

"Anna and Dom are going to Tai O tomorrow. Do you want to go with them?" Sophie asked.

The thought of a nice day out appealed. When doesn't it? According to Anna, Tai O was "sick." Although according to

Anna, pretty much everything can be described by an irritating streetwise adjective.

"Yeah that sounds excellent," I replied. "Can I invite Sander? He said he wanted to do something this weekend."

I hadn't seen him since the night at Red Bar a few weeks ago where he'd confessed to what I already knew. I'd (nearly) stopped thinking about his smooch with Sophie and maturely, I thought, it would prove to Sophie that I didn't hold a grudge. (Also, I wanted to continue to showcase just how happy Sophie and I were, to ensure that he didn't see it as acceptable to try it on with her again.)

Sophie and I watched a few episodes of *Breaking Bad* while she drained the bottle of wine.

She started to fall asleep on the sofa at ten, then managed to say, "Let's go to bed. I'm tired."

This was unfortunate, as after my fourteen-hour sleep, I couldn't have been more wide awake. However, keen to get out of the bad books, I pretended to be tired and went to bed with her. After four hours of staring at the ceiling, my mind whirring, I finally drifted off.

I was woken up at half eight by bright sunlight seeping through the windows and a faint smell of smoke. I saw Sophie standing at the window having her morning cigarette. How people can smoke before breakfast is beyond me. I did enjoy the sight of her quite phenomenal bum sticking out of the bottom of the curtains though.

"What time are we meeting them?" I asked her behind.

"Ten, at Tung Chung, then we'll get the bus to Tai O," came the reply from behind the curtains.

It was an hour-long bus ride to Tung Chung. Although everybody was going in the same direction, I was happy with the decision to meet there. Nobody is up for conversation first thing in the morning on transport; I'm a keen advocate of not talking when on public transport at any time. Sophie usually liked to talk all the time but showed that I wasn't totally in the clear yet by uncharacteristically putting her headphones in for the duration of the journey.

Tung Chung, situated near the new airport on Lantau Island, used to be a rural village but in recent years a "new town" had been built with huge residential skyscrapers cropping up all over the place to house Hong Kong's ever-growing population. It's also home to the Ngong Ping 360 – a glass-bottomed cable car ride up to the Big Buddha – one of Hong Kong's premier tourist sights and therefore always far too busy to be an enjoyable day out.

Sander and Dom were standing together by the fountain in Tung Chung town square. Sander was wearing aviator sunglasses and sporting a new fluff of chin hair, while Dom was wearing a Yankees baseball cap. Both of them were wearing short shorts, flip-flops and tight white wife-beater vests. I enjoyed the fact that Dom was considerably more muscular than Sander and looked much better in the attire.

"Morning kids," Sander said and came and gave Sophie a kiss on the cheek and a hug which went on for approximately four seconds too long, then shook my hand firmly.

"Hey man, how you doing?"

Dom greeted us with a much more appropriately-lengthed hug of my girlfriend, and unasked, began to tell me about his three pointer in the dying seconds which won his team a vital play-off game. Anna arrived five minutes later and greeted us with a tirade about a taxi driver who tried to rip her off this morning.

"No way was I going to pay twenty-five dollars for that. It's twenty dollars absolute maximum!"

We wrestled through the crowds which were assembling to see the Buddha, and got the bus to Tai O. I was surprised to see a bunch of Chinese tourists wearing ponchos; it seemed a questionable choice, given that the sky was blue and there looked to be zero chance of rain in the near future. The ride to Tai O took forty-five minutes and the mood was good by the time we arrived there.

Tai O is a beautiful little fishing village where you can amble through market stalls and sit in quaint little cafés overlooking houses on stilts in the water – the sort of place that girls love and take way too many photos of and men like but get bored of within an hour. The only problem was the overriding smell of preserved meat, which was hanging from many of the market stalls. We had breakfast, then went on a short boat-trip where a chubby Chinese lady told us that we were guaranteed to see some pink dolphins.

"Money back if you don't see any!" she beamed.

We didn't see any dolphins. Nor did we see the chubby lady again.

In the afternoon we took a walk to a "natural infinity pool" that Anna had read about in *Lonely Planet* or some such guide. It took about an hour and I found myself strolling with Sander for the duration.

"So what you been up to, man?" He asked.

"Not much, mate. I lost my job, so been keeping a low profile."

"What? What happened man?"

I told him the story, minus the drugs / informant work, and he seemed satisfied.

"You want me to try to get you a job at my place? I bet I can sort you out," he said confidently. The reality was there was no chance whatsoever that he could get me a job. I had no relevant experience or qualifications. However, I did admire Sander's confidence, and it was nice of him to offer help. My resentment for him had substantially disappeared now and I was starting to remember what it was like being friends with him.

He told a few stories about a recent "nutcase" Japanese girl he had been seeing. This was probably the fifth different girl he'd referred to as a nutcase and I wondered if maybe it wasn't mere coincidence. Were these girls nutcases before they met him? It seemed that his definition of a "nutcase" was a girl who wanted to see him more than once a week. I wasn't sure if I agreed with him on this but nodded and made the appropriate noises to her "fucking crazy" behaviour of wanting to introduce him to her friends.

To Anna, and *Lonely Planet*'s credit, the pool was exceptional. After scrambling through a few bushes to get there, which added to the adventure, we arrived at a dark blue lagoon with a waterfall which you could climb up. We spent the rest of the afternoon at the pool, lazing around, and the men daring each other to jump off rocks into the probably-not-deep-enough-to-be-safe pool. Dom had packed some beers in his bag which we drank despite them being as hot as the sun. I wasn't sure if Sophie was just doing it as we were with other people, but she seemed to be happy with me and we were getting along perfectly again. In fact, everyone was getting along well; I even spent a good forty minutes talking to Anna and didn't find myself wishing that she would be quiet.

An excellent day out with people I liked (and Anna) was exactly what I'd needed. Thoughts of warehouses, drugs, police officers and job applications were temporarily forgotten and I thoroughly enjoyed the pleasant distraction. In the evening we headed to the Stoep, a South African Barbeque restaurant on the nearby Peng Chau beach. The feel-good mood was threatened briefly when Anna loudly complained to the staff that she had ordered medium rare beef not well-done, but other than that it was a fitting end to the day. After dinner, Sander, Anna and Sophie went for a cigarette, leaving me and Dom sitting at the table.

"What a day," Dom said. "Best day out I've had in ages."

"Yep, I agree. Superb!"

After sitting in happy silence for a minute, Dom turned and said in a quieter voice.

"So, what's the latest with the police stuff?"

"Not good mate. I've got somewhere but I haven't found out exactly what they need yet."

"What have you got?"

"I know the names of some of the guys involved and I know that the drugs are shipped from Bolivia, or Chile, to Hong Kong. They keep the drugs in a warehouse in Sheng Shui," I replied.

"That's better than nothing. How did you get all that?" he asked.

"One of the dealers opened up to me when he was trolleyed. Still, it's been horribly stressful and I've been in a few dodgy situations. Cost me my job as well," I told him. "It's not enough, though. The police need to know when the next delivery is so they can catch them."

"Don't get angry," Dom said, suddenly, the mood thickening.

"About what?" I asked him, confused.

Well, I told a few of the basketball guys about your predicament."

"What? You fucking idiot. I thought I could trust you!"

"I know. I'm sorry. I'm shit with secrets. And it's such a good story."

"Jesus, Dom, you could have totally fucked me!"

"Well, here's the thing," he said. "One of the guys at basketball happens to know quite a lot about cocaine-dealing in Hong Kong."

"Go on," I said, angry, but interested now.

"When he first moved out here, he got involved in a bit of dealing. He was in loads of debt and needed to pay it off. Anyway, he got in over his head and started working with some dangerous guys," Dom continued.

"And?"

"I think he can help you out. He only stopped doing it recently so he might be able to tell you some stuff."

"How do we know it's the same guys?"

"He told me he was working for the biggest cocaine operation in Hong Kong, and that it was run by English guys. Isn't that what you're after?"

"Why would he help me?" I asked.

"Because they robbed him when he said he wanted out; they threatened him and took thousands of dollars off him. He risked everything for months and ended up with less money than when he started."

"When can I meet him?"

CHAPTER TWENTY-SIX

The next day Sophie and I did very little. It was enjoyable to have a lazy day that hadn't been influenced by being hung over. True to her word, Sophie didn't nag me about job searching, saying that so long as I started looking on Monday, it was fine. We ate burnt eggy bread, drank copious amounts of tea, played cards and watched two bad romantic comedies, then did the Sunday Skype home palaver. The only low ebb was lying to my parents and saying that work was "going well." Despite the nature of my secretive lifestyle, I still don't like lying and I wasn't very convincing. For a moment I thought my mum had seen through me as she asked more follow-up questions than usual. I skillfully changed the topic by complimenting her blouse and asking where it was from.

It was a pleasant day of nothingness which completed an enjoyable weekend that I hadn't really deserved. I couldn't relax too much though. The next week was going to be important. Dom had texted me saying that his friend, Cody (which I thought was a girl's name) was free on Thursday afternoon. Fortunately Dom's school had broken up for the summer so he was able to come as well.

I decided that I would meet Cody and see what he knew before contacting Frank. Despite a week to think about it, the best idea I had was to go to a pub with Frank all day and try to ask him subtly where the warehouse was – not exactly a watertight plan. I called Dixon and said, with deliberate ambiguity, that I might be on to something and would be in touch on Thursday night, and he seemed satisfied.

Monday and Tuesday were spent worrying, playing FIFA and half-applying for jobs. On the basis that I wouldn't be lumbered with prison time and a career-ruining criminal record, I bid to broaden my horizons. I didn't apply only for teaching jobs. I also sent ("quick apply") applications to marketing jobs, PR jobs (what does a PR man do?) and a number of other highly ambitious and unrealistic positions ranging from "Experienced Lab Assistant" to "Project Manager" for an architecture company. I hadn't looked through the specification for a large number of them so the chances were that a lot of them were after Chinese speakers. Still, I tricked myself that I'd put in a good shift and all I'd have to do was wait for the job to come. If nothing came from the sweep, I would start doing proper applications to places and spend hours thinking up the perfect answer to, "When have you faced challenges in your career and how did you overcome them?"

I did also manage to get up to division five on Seasons mode of FIFA, which was a further confidence-boost and a sign of my productivity. By Tuesday night, I had sore thumbs and square eyes.

On Wednesday I met up with Carmella who was in a particularly good mood as she was flying back to the Philippines for a long weekend to go to a friend's wedding. I treated her to lunch in a local café where the food was cheap and unhealthy, then gave her a hug before she left. Her excitement was touching.

With Thursday came the end of my latest reprieve and a return to my unpaid, high-pressure work as a police informant. We arranged to meet Cody at the food court in a shopping plaza in Causeway Bay. Dom and I had already finished a chicken wings sharing platter when a tall, lean, mixed race man in his early thirties came over and sat with us. I realized that I'd met him once before, at Christmas. He looked different now though. He had braided his hair and was wearing jogging bottoms and a ridiculously baggy, white T-shirt vest.

"Yo," he said, giving Dom a complex handshake which must have been previously rehearsed, before offering his hand to – thankfully – give me a simple, standard shake.

"So, Dom tells me you're in a bit of shit?" he started. He was American.

He sat and listened intently as I told him everything. A bit of a gamble telling a near stranger about my story but I trusted Dom's judgment even if I now knew I couldn't trust his ability to keep a secret. Cody was cool, bordering on cold. It was a serious discussion but he seemed like the sort of man who took every discussion seriously. He didn't smile once and scowled when he spoke, in a deep, monotone voice.

"I think I can help you out. Those fuckers took all my money. I'd happily see them get caught."

"What do you know about the shipping procedure, then?" I asked him.

"You free now, yeah?" Cody asked. "Let's go to Sheng Shui and I'll show you where I used to meet them to pick up."

This matched Frank's story of Sheng Shui and was extremely promising. I looked over to Dom, who had ordered and nearly finished a second sharing platter to himself, and he nodded. Given the situation, the hassle of changing trains multiple times on the MTR didn't appeal, so we clambered into a taxi outside and asked the young driver to take us to the back end of Sheng Shui. Not a usual tourist destination. As it was a Thursday afternoon, we flew straight through the Cross Harbour tunnel (I'd spent entire Sunday afternoons stuck in traffic there), and arrived at Sheng Shui within half an hour. The mood was tense in the taxi. Cody had been looking at his phone the whole time and Dom seemed nervous. He also stank of fried chicken.

By the time we got out of the taxi, the weather had taken a turn and the sky was overcast, full of threatening, dark clouds. Sheng Shui, in the farthest of the New Territories, touching upon China, is not as developed as much of Hong Kong, with the skyscrapers sporadically situated in clusters, and spaces in between that resemble countryside. We got out of the taxi by the side of a quiet slip-road.

"This way," Cody instructed as we careened along the side of the road, which was lacking a pavement. We waded through some thick, damp bracken, which scratched at my shins, as cars flew past, centimetres away from us. We continued the uncomfortable walk for a long, ten minutes before Cody reassured us that we were nearly there. Despite his serious nature, he seemed to be enjoying his leading role in the adventure.

"There it is!" Cody pointed to an isolated, square hut that was set back a few metres away from the road. It definitely didn't qualify as a warehouse. It was the size of a garden shed, with splintered wood and a musty scent coming from the damp.

"How do you know it's in there?" I asked him.

"Why would I lie?" he said. "I came down here three or four times to pick up my packages from Nigel."

"So are you saying that it's full of drugs right now?" I asked him.

"I don't know about now. They might be waiting for a new shipment."

"How often do they get shipments?"

"I don't know how it works. Shit. All I know is that I came here, picked up cocaine, and left. And it was definitely in that warehouse."

Does this man know what a warehouse is? I wondered.

I glanced at Dom who was looking uneasy.

"What now?" he asked me.

"Good question."

We stood in silence as I tried to make a mental note of where the shed was so I could direct the Hong Kong Police here. If what Cody had said was true, then this was where the police needed to be.

I decided that when I told Dixon about the shed, the police should be able to take it from there. Surely if he found a container full of drugs, that would be enough? Or did they need to catch people red-handed to make the arrests? I tried to rack my brain for episodes of *CSI* and *The Wire* but couldn't remember how things worked – I doubted that the Hong Kong police would operate exactly the same way as McNulty and Co. did in a fictional TV show, but was hoping for some kind of reference point. There must be fingerprints or something to link it to Nigel's syndicate. Surely after directing the police to this location, I would have done my part of the deal and would be free to go?

After I instructed him, Dom took a couple of pictures of the shed on his phone. I thought that our work here was almost done and was about to suggest leaving when Dom suddenly looked startled and half whispered, half shouted.

"Shit! Someone's coming!"

"That's Nigel," Cody said. "We need to get the fuck outta here."

The three of us scurried and hid behind a thick, thorny bush that was adjacent to the potentially drug-filled shed. I peeked out of our cover as a black car gently pulled up at the side of the road, ten metres away and a man got out. He was walking with purpose straight towards us.

Unlike Frank and Browny, Nigel actually looked like a criminal. As he got closer, I was surprised by the sheer size of the man. He looked to be in his fifties and was tall and extremely well built, more muscle than fat. He had slicked-back black hair with a couple of strands flopping loosely on to his forehead, menacing eyes and a crooked nose. He was wearing a leather jacket and dark-blue jeans.

I could hear my heart beating and backed up against a thick-trunked tree, deftly hiding amongst the leaves, I maneuvered into an uncomfortable position where from the far corner of my right eye, I could see Nigel who was now approaching the shed. He had got his phone out and appeared to be sending a text.

Dom, who now looked terrified, and Cody were aggressively gesticulating that I get down and hide, but I had to see what happened next.

Nigel put his phone back in his pocket, then took out a packet of Marlboro' Reds and for the next three, terrifying minutes, I crouched and watched as he calmly smoked a badly-timed cigarette. My heart was beating at twice its normal rate. When in compromising situations and / or extremely scared, the adrenaline pumping through me seems to heighten my senses. My eyesight sharpens and I can hear and differentiate between many background noises that I normally wouldn't even notice. It had started raining. – The first heavy drops on the tree I was leaning on seemed magnified in sound, sending small vibrations through my already-shaking body.

The two huge, athletic men whom I was with looked even more scared than I did. Cody was gritting his teeth so hard that I could see his temples pulsating and Dom looked close to tears. In fact, on second glance, he was actually crying; for god's sake.

Nigel finally finished his cigarette and flicked it on to the newly damp floor, immediately extinguishing it. He put his hands deep inside his leather jacket. Irrationally fearing that he was going to whip out a pistol, I was relieved when he pulled out a set of keys and proceeded to twist them in the heavy-duty padlock which was holding the container shut.

It took an age for Nigel to unfasten the locks, and I watched, through half an eye, in growing anticipation, as the damp, splintered, door eventually thudded open. After hearing what Frank, Browny, and now Cody had said, I was expecting to see a container full to the brim of wooden wine crates that were presumably laced with cocaine. The initial sight was somewhat a disappointment. The container looked to be empty, minus a couple of redundant wooden deck boards.

Nigel disappeared inside and I heard some shuffling about. To my relief, I soon discovered that the container wasn't totally barren. He swiftly returned carrying a solitary crate of wine, then unfazed by the increased volume of the rain, casually placed the crate on the floor and laboured in slowly shutting the door and intricately locking the padlock.

Dom and Cody couldn't see what was going on so I turned and exaggeratedly put my finger to my lips which was probably unnecessary – they were unlikely to start chatting.

Nigel bent down to pick up the crate when I heard a phone ring. For a split second I thought it was my own which would have rumbled us from our spot. Fortunately, I recognized the ring tone as an I-phone default tune which ruled me out. It was Nigel's. He reached into his suit jacket pocket again and pulled out the phone.

"Yeah?" he answered. Pause.

"I've just picked up the last lot now," he said impatiently. "The new delivery is arriving at Pak Mai pier next Tuesday night so I'm going to need you there. Tell that reprobate Frank to make sure he's here on time as well."

That was it.

I felt my already pounding heart up its intensity a notch, but now with elation as well as fear. After all my tribulations, I finally had the information I needed to be free. There was a new delivery arriving at Pak Mai next Tuesday evening. All I had to do was tell the police and everything would be resolved.

I watched as Nigel hung up without saying goodbye. Then his phone started to ring again. I watched on, hoping to eavesdrop on some more information.

I realized that it wasn't his phone.

It was Dom's.

And Nigel had heard.

CHAPTER TWENTY-SEVEN

I looked at Dom and did the thing where you shout at someone without making any noise – wide eyes, scowling and teeth clenching. He mouthed "Shit!" then with shaking hands, fumbled around and finally turned his phone off about five seconds after it had started to ring. I edged my face back towards its previous location and got a clear view of Nigel, who was now soaked. I imagined his smell – stale smoke and damp leather. Having clearly heard the ringing phone, he was visibly confused.

Like a footballer when the ball has spun up in the air and they're not sure where, he was looking around trying to gauge where the sound had come from. If I wasn't terrified, I would have thought he looked fairly stupid, with his head jittering about as his eyes darted around aimlessly.

I looked to Cody who was pointing for us to run. It wasn't an unreasonable idea but I wanted to wait a minute. Besides, if we ran, we might draw even more attention to ourselves and / or get lost in the Sheng Shui woodland.

After a few seconds Nigel stopped looking around and he ran his hand calmly through his wet, black hair. He was still making no effort to cover himself from the rain. I suppose rain isn't much of an issue for a hardened criminal; he wouldn't have suited an umbrella. I was praying that he would simply turn and walk away but of course he didn't. He put his head down and started strutting at pace, directly towards us.

We were fucked.

He was going to find us and we would have a lot of explaining to do…especially given the fact that he knew Cody.

As I was mentally preparing what spiel I could feed Nigel as to why I was hiding behind a bush, spying on him, Dom looked at me and Cody and said.

"Stay here."

Unsure as to what his plan was, I watched in astonishment as Dom wiped a tear stain from his left cheek, took a deep breath, stood up and casually strolled out from our hiding place and right into the path of a dangerous drug baron.

"Who the fuck are you?" Nigel asked him, accusingly.

"Alright, mate. Shit day isn't it?" Dom replied in his Birmingham drawl. I noticed that his voice wavered slightly as he spoke but I was hoping that it wasn't enough for Nigel to notice.

"You didn't answer me," Nigel snapped back, making it quite clear that he did not want to partake in a conversation about the inclement weather.

"My name's Callum," Dom replied." I was walking my dog then it ran off into the bloody woods. You've not seen it have you, golden retriever?" His tone was more controlled now. He sounded more convincing.

"I haven't seen your dog, no. What are you doing walking a dog round here?" Nigel asked.

"Ah, y'know what it's like," Dom replied.

Nigel didn't accept this filler of a non-answer.

"No I don't. What's it like? You tell me?"

I could tell that Dom was panicking. Although he was a relatively bright man, Dom was the sort of man where you could almost visualize the cogs of his brain whirring. A lot of the time, I could predict what he was going to say long before he said it. I could see that the cogs were struggling here. They were slowing down, grinding to a halt.

"I just mean, it's hard to walk a dog on Hong Kong Island isn't it? So I like to take Troy out here."

Why has he used my name for the dog's name? Is Troy a convincing dog's name? Fortunately Nigel seemed to have believed Dom and I watched as the thick atmosphere seemed to settle, when Nigel relaxed and started to ask questions about the fictional dog. Silently breathing a huge collective sigh of relief, Cody and I watched as Dom and Nigel turned the other way and walked off, like old friends taking a stroll together, away from our hiding place. Dom had saved us. What brilliant intuition.

Cody and I sat in silence for the next five minutes, awaiting Dom's return. After ten long minutes, now soaking wet and starting to get severe cramp due to my ungainly crouching position, I decided that the coast was clear to stand up and have a look around. The rain was easing up and I was starting to worry what had happened with Dom. Had Nigel clocked that he was full of shit? What would he do to him?

Concerned about my friend's safety, I decided to call him. It took a while until someone picked up. It wasn't Dom. It was Nigel. Fuck.

"Who's this?" he quizzed in his husky South London accent. I was shocked to be talking to him.

Thinking quickly, I managed to think up a fake name. If I'd said "Troy," he would quite probably have had concerns about the legitimacy of a talking dog.

"It's Carl (great code name). Is Callum there? I've found his dog."

To my relief, Nigel handed the phone back to Dom, who shakily replied.

"Hi Carl. Where are you?"

"I'm on the bus. I couldn't find you and he was getting soaked so needed to get him home."

"Nice one. I'll just meet you at home then," Dom / Callum replied, sounding more natural in his role of potentially gay, dog-walker.

With that I hung up. Ten minutes later, Dom returned to our hiding place, ashen-faced and looking frazzled.

"He's gone. Fucking hell, that was intense."

"What did he say?" Cody asked.

"He's a horrible bastard. He clearly didn't believe me about the dog. He knew something was up. He kept asking me questions. I thought he was gonna do me in. When he grabbed my phone, I thought I was fucked."

"He bought it though?" Cody questioned him, worried.

"Yes. Great shout with Carl. Got him off my case," Dom replied, a smile forming.

"You might have just saved everything, Dom," I said, feeling an insurmountable level of relief.

Cody, who had stayed quiet didn't seem like the hugging type so I didn't embrace Dom, even though I had a strong urge to do so. We waited for five more minutes until Nigel was definitely away and then left.

After returning home, I called Dixon and told him everything that I had got – the storage container, the shipments and the plans for Tuesday night. He was full of praise and pleased with my work. We arranged that I would go to the police station on Monday when I would go over everything one more time and he would finalize the plans for the raid.

I was nearly there.

CHAPTER TWENTY-EIGHT

In one way or another, my ordeal was going to be over on Tuesday. Well, this part of my ordeal anyway. If things went pear-shaped, a whole new ordeal involving court cases and prison sentences would begin. Given the circumstances, I felt relatively calm and at ease. I'd been stressed, guilty and worried for so long now that I think my body and mind had endured enough and wanted a break. In the four days that had passed after the Sheung Shui adventure, I was surprised that I'd been able to get on with daily tasks without constantly fretting. I'd accepted the situation for what it was.

I decided to surprise Sophie on the Saturday night, booking us a table at a La Faucon, a swanky French restaurant in Soho that was strictly in the "special occasions only" category and which I could afford only because I still had over a thousand dollars left of the cash Dixon had given me. I'd been something of a rubbish boyfriend of late and wanted to start making it up to her. As I'd had these erratic emotions since the start of our relationship and I was currently unemployed, I was fully aware she deserved to be treated better.

This was going to start with Saturday night. Next week, I would tell her everything, which would subsequently explain all of my odd behaviour, sleepless nights and lies. I expected her to be shocked by the secret life I'd been leading but I thought that she would understand. I quietly fancied her to be impressed by my story and enjoy going out with such an exciting man although that was probably getting ahead of myself.

I wore my smart suit which hadn't seen the light of day since I'd met Sander and Kris in Armani Bar all that time ago. I'd told Sophie to put on her best frock and meet me at Spicy Fingers. She thought that we were simply going for a couple of happy-hour beers before returning to our usual Saturday night excitement of fast food and box- sets, so I was looking forward to playing my trump card and revealing that we were going to her favourite restaurant. I admired that Sophie had been so supportive of me. I think she was of the opinion that my stresses were down to losing my job, which was partially true but not quite the full story. When I thought of how good she had been, I felt satisfying warmness at the prospect of a romantic evening together.

I arrived at the pub at ten to eight and got a couple of stingily-sized glasses of wine in, ready for her arrival. At ten past eight, she still hadn't arrived so I'd succumbed to temptation and finished off my drink. At twenty-five past she finally arrived, wearing a new green dress that in truth, didn't particularly suit her. She was wearing full make-up and had straightened her hair though, so was looking pretty, despite the oversized emerald number.

"Hey," she said, giving me a short hug and a peck on the cheek. "Sorry I'm late. I couldn't decide what to wear."

I was sure that she had at least ten dresses that would have looked better, but resisted saying that she had made the wrong decision, opting for "no worries," before handing her the lukewarm glass of Pinot that I had been holding for half an hour. I noticed that she didn't say anything about my suit which was a tad demoralizing. I hadn't planned any special way to announce my surprise booking at the restaurant, so grinning stupidly, simply said.

"I've booked us into somewhere nice at nine."

"Where?" she asked.

"Your favourite restaurant," I replied, pleased with myself.

"Oh, Troy, that's so sweet but I've already eaten. Can we rebook it for another time?"

Shit. Why had I not just told her before?

"Yeah, no problem," I said, failing to hide my sizeable disappointment. "We'll do it next week. I'll just get some food from here then and we can have a few drinks?"

"Yep, sounds good. I'm sorry," she said, but it didn't sound sincere. She seemed distracted.

"You had a good day then?" I managed to ask, feeling slightly annoyed with her, despite not having rational reason to blame her. – It is perfectly acceptable behaviour to eat dinner before eight o'clock on a Saturday.

"Yeah, it was fine. Nothing special," she said.

I noticed that she had nearly finished her glass of wine.

"What did you do?" I asked.

"I went out for the early-bird dinner at that new Italian restaurant," she said.

"Ah, OK." I wondered why she hadn't mentioned this before. "Who did you go with?"

She took a long glug, emphatically finishing off her wine and then gestured to the waitress to top her glass up. Sensing that all was not right, I asked the waitress to make it two.

Sophie was looking down and started to massage her forehead, moving her thumb and forefinger from the temples, slowly meeting in the centre.

"Is everything OK?" I asked.

"I went with Sander," she said quietly.

"Ah, OK. How's he doing? I might ask him to come out now that our meal is off. Who else went?" I asked, not overly irritated that I hadn't been invited, as my assumption was that it was the banker-financial crowd.

"Nobody else was there."

That was weird. They weren't particularly good friends. I was confused.

"I don't understand," I said after a pause.

"I went with Sander. I've been seeing him a lot recently," she said. The head massaging had ceased now and she was looking me in the eye.

"You've been acting so weird, Troy. It hasn't been working with us and Sander has been so supportive. I stayed at his last night. I didn't mean it to happen."

Suddenly I felt my heart start racing, I felt light-headed. I felt sick.

"What the fuck?"

"I'm sorry Troy. We are over." Then, she said the same words again. "I didn't mean it to happen."

I was devastated, crestfallen. This was considerably worse than the first time a girlfriend had admitted to sleeping with another man. No man should ever have to say that, should he? I loved Sophie and she'd been sleeping with my friend. I just couldn't believe how horrific this was. Feeling a more intense anger than I've ever known, I was on the verge of screaming obscenities at Sophie. I even considered an *Eastenders*-esque throwing of my drink in her face. Happily, I did neither, and rather than causing a scene, I actually managed to keep a degree of face by looking at her and calmly saying.

"Fuck you, Sophie! I never want to see you again."

This cool façade was dented when, upon standing up, I smacked my knee-cap against the stool next to me. It really hurt. I limped off, a broken man. Sophie stayed seated, and my clumsy exit meant that I stayed long enough to see that she had started to cry.

I hadn't thought even Sander would stoop so low as to get with a friend's girlfriend. Is that not just an unwritten rule of something that no man should ever do, ever? It's right at the bottom of the barrel of horrendous moral conduct. What a shocking, backstabbing excuse for a man. I hated him.

I was devastated by Sophie's betrayal, but I felt as though it was Sander's fault. I reckoned that he had instigated it. I knew what a sleaze-bag he was. Well, I thought I did. I hadn't thought he was this bad. He had outdone even himself. I was beyond angry with him, I was raging. I've never actually been raging before so this was a new emotion to me and I felt quite excited with all the adrenaline pumping through my system.

All that time ago, when Imogen had told me the news, I was gutted, but was aware that we were on a downward spiral. So although the nature of the breakup was horrible, I had some idea that we were on our last legs and were on the verge of splitting up. Our relationship was comparable to the lifecycle of a piece of chewing-gum and the flavour had completely vanished. On that occasion, I'd bought a bottle of Southern Comfort and sat on a park bench drinking alone. I didn't need to do it. I had wanted to do the classic broken man in a film and go to an empty, dingy pub and keep asking the barman to top up my glass until I passed out on the bar, but the truth was I couldn't afford it. I had only twenty quid in the world, so the park bench self-annihilation was the practical option. It had solved little. I wasn't going to drink my pains away yet. First of all I was going to Sander's apartment.

I seldom went to Sander's. We did most of our lounging around, pre drinking and FIFA-playing at my abode, which was odd as his place was twice the size and much nicer. It was only a ten-minute walk away from the bar, situated on Hennessy Road. The walk did nothing to calm me down and only intensified my anger. I arrived at his, and knowing his door code buzzed myself in and took the plush, air-conditioned lift up to his twentieth floor apartment.

I could hear an abrasive, Euro-dance remix of 'We Found Love' by Rihanna playing so it was clear that he was at home. It hadn't crossed my mind that he wouldn't be in, so this was a relief. I hadn't got a plan B. His melodic bell ring seemed inappropriate so I rattled angrily on door and waited for him to answer.

The volume of the music was turned down and I heard him shout out.

"Hold on, I'm just getting dressed."

I waited for a minute until the door handle unturned and Sander opened it, clad in a towel wrapped around his waist. Since when did a towel constitute being dressed?

"Hey man, what's up?" he greeted in his usual confident tone, oblivious to any anger on my part.

I have punched somebody once. When I was thirteen, I got into a scrap with a small scrawny kid, who had deliberately kicked my shin during football training. I had landed what I thought was a relatively clean punch to his jaw and been pleased with myself. Unfortunately, the hardened, durable young thug barely flinched. He simply looked at me and struck back with a fierce left uppercut which sent me sprawling to the floor. A teacher came and ended the scrap, but in high school rules, he had won. It went round the school that he'd "battered" me which I thought was an injustice, but that was that.

Here I was, some thirteen years later, and ready to punch a man again. I had to get this one right. I stared at Sander, didn't say anything and launched a solid right hook into his smarmy, arrogant, tanned jaw. He stumbled back into his flat, holding his face. It was a good one. I turned and left without explanation. Unusually for Hong Kong, the lift was waiting for me on cue and I left thinking that it couldn't have gone any better.

As satisfying as the punch had been, I still had to come to terms with the fact that I had lost my girlfriend and one of my best friends. I couldn't think that there would be a time at any point in the future where I would want to see them again.

After the drama of the punch, I decided that I could now go and nurse a drink and mull over my next move. I cut through a ginnel (a word for "alley", used in Yorkshire and nowhere else in the world) and on to Wan Chai Road which was home to Champs Sports Bar. I headed down the steps into the suitably dingy, near empty, silent pub and ordered myself a whisky on the rocks. As the barman was a non-English-speaking Chinese man, we didn't build up the camaraderie that I had hoped for in the situation. Sadly, there was no, "I've seen that look before – is it money or women?" from my middle-aged, overweight host.

197

I sunk three drinks quickly and started to fall into a depression. How could people that you care about betray you so badly? It was beyond me. I thought about my Hong Kong situation as a whole. I had lost my job, I had been fucked over by two people that I trusted the most and I was facing a judgement day on Tuesday.

I weighed up the predicament I was in and decided that I wasn't bothered about Nigel who was clearly a nasty, money-grabbing crook but I felt fairly dreadful about Frank. He was just a middle-aged man enjoying a second youth. Admitted, he was dealing and taking drugs to enjoy this lifestyle but he wasn't a bad man; he didn't want to hurt anyone.

Thinking about Frank, my mind drew a parallel with my current situation. I had done nothing to hurt Sander or Sophie but they had royally fucked me over for their own benefit. If I couldn't trust my girlfriend and friends then who could I trust? In general I like most people but based on my current situation, I'd come to an angry, sweeping conclusion that everyone is selfish. The night's events had made me see this and I sunk my second whisky feeling that I'd lost faith in everything and everyone.

Now it was time to think about myself. So what if I was betraying Frank? I needed to be selfish. I had a right to be selfish. With the whisky playing a pivotal role in my fuddled thought process, I came to a conclusion; I was going to complete my informant work, get them all arrested and then leave Hong Kong. I needed to leave. I needed to start again. Again.

CHAPTER TWENTY-NINE

I celebrated my decision to leave Hong Kong by staying in Champs for a further six whiskies, in the process befriending a red-scarf-wearing Moroccan man who was also drinking alone and watching a replay of a Liverpool game from over two years ago. He thought that it was live and was shouting at the screen and cheering when they scored.

As a result, I woke up on Sunday with a cloudy head and a dry mouth. I instantly remembered the events of the previous day and felt another wave of depression sweep through my aching body. Determined not to get stuck in a rut, I called Dom and invited myself to his flat.

He had just woken up and said "OK" but it was the kind of "OK" where I could tell he'd prefer it if I didn't come. Unwilling to take this on board, I plodded to his flat to find his front door open and Dom sat on his sofa, in some questionably tight boxers, devouring a huge bowl of at least three different kinds of cereal

"Alright, mate," he greeted without energy, not taking his eyes away from his spoon which was balancing at least three different kinds of cereal with a precarious amount of milk, "How's things?"

"Pretty shit," I said, then proceeded to tell him the whole story with Sander and Sophie. It was good to get it out although it made it seem more real.

He listened intently while still eating, then after I finished, simply said.

"What a bitch. What a wanker."

This was the response that I'd been hoping for.

He then took me by surprise and embraced me in a clumsy hug which was awkward but heartwarming. He seemed genuinely angry with Sander and told me that he would never speak to him again. Although the two of them were friends, they rarely got in touch without my being there, so I didn't think Dom would miss him too much. I appreciated the loyalty and the two of us sat and bad-mouthed our Danish ex-friend for a good twenty minutes, until finally my anger died down when I found myself laughing at Dom's stirringly accurate impression of Sander's sleazy dancing.

"Fuck everyone," was Dom's conclusion to the affair, which supported my current way of thinking. I told him about my decision for the upcoming Tuesday night drugs-bust and he was relieved to know that I was going to go through with it.

"You have to get yourself out of this mate. You don't owe anything to Nigel and that lot. In my opinion, they deserve to get caught," he said.

We spent the rest of the morning and early afternoon ambling around in Wan Chai, having two coffees, some sickly Taiwanese Popcorn chicken and placing two losing bets on outside horses at the Jockey Club. Dom was a good pal and spending the day with him cheered me up no end. There was one thing I didn't tell him though; the fact that I was planning to leave Hong Kong.

Sander tried to call me three times on Sunday evening but I wasn't interested in talking to him and enjoyed symbolically deleting his number. Sophie hadn't got in touch and I was happy for it to stay that way. I couldn't face speaking to my parents on Skype so made a transparent excuse about having a sore throat. As far as they knew, I had a job and a girlfriend. I wasn't in the mood to tell them about my rapid downfall.

On Monday morning I awoke at nine-thirty to a call on my phone. Assuming it to be Sander, I didn't pick up but it rang three more times in quick succession until finally I succumbed. If it was Sander I could tell him that I never wanted to see him again which might give a satisfying closure to the whole thing.

"Hello," I answered warily.

I was surprised at the voice on the other end. It was Kit, my former manager.

"Hi Troy! How are you?" he asked, without awkwardness. Was this a social call?

"I'm alright. What's up?" I responded, confused.

"Are you free today?"

"Well, I'm hardly swamped with work," I replied, managing to get a slight chuckle.

"Can you come to the school? I need to show you something," he said.

"I suppose. What's this about?"

"You'll see. Just come in at any time today."

I had no clue what was going on. Had I left something at work on the day of my unceremonious departure? Did I need to sign some mundane tax forms or something? I showered, brushed my teeth and put on some jeans and a T-shirt.

My mind was spinning on the familiar MTR ride. I was a bag of nerves before heading into my old straying ground. It had been nearly a month since I'd been sacked and I hadn't seen any of my colleagues or students since then. My downfall must have been a hot topic of conversation around the school so I was unsure how I was going to be greeted.

Kit met me at reception.

"Hi, you look a lot better than last time I saw you!" he said. I thought the jokey tone of this comment was a bit off, but managed a fake smile.

"That wasn't my best day," I replied.

As it was still early, the school was fortunately very quiet with only one receptionist working and two students, whom I didn't recognize, sitting at the computers, wearing headsets and looking confused. Only one classroom was in action and I could make out Aiden's camp, Australian accent asking his students about their favourite holiday destinations.

"Come with me," Kit said and we headed off towards his office-come-classroom. "I need to show you something."

I sat down and Kit opened his drawer and pulled out a sheet of A4 paper.

"Take a look at this," he said, and handed it to me.

I was stunned.

At the top of the paper was the heading (ironically in broken English) saying, "Petition for get teacher Troy back in Super English."

I looked down and saw that one hundred and twenty-two students had signed the form.

"When did this happen?" I asked Kit.

"About a week after you err…. stopped working here, the students started to ask where you were. Eventually we told them that you had left. Somehow, they found out that it wasn't your decision and Marian started this petition to get you your job back. She has been on a mission this past week."

"So what does this mean?" I asked.

"Well I've spoken with the top managers and we have agreed to offer you another chance, if you are willing to take it?"

"Really?"

"Yes. You can take a couple of days to think about it but the job is yours to resume as of next Monday if you want it?"

I told Kit that I needed to think about it and I would give him an answer later in the week. He said he understood and I thanked him for the reprieve. This changed things.

CHAPTER THIRTY

I weighed up the rapid turn of events over the last two days. In basic terms, I'd swapped having a girlfriend for having a job. Not an ideal trade-off but at least I hadn't lost everything. The school petition was extremely poignant and it gave me a feeling of warmth that so many people had made an effort to try to get me my job back. I'd been of the opinion that I was an average teacher and had no clue that I was so highly regarded. It was a shock.

After returning home, I found my mind in conflict once again. Yesterday, I'd been certain that I was going to report everything that I knew to the police, leaving Nigel and the others to be dealt with, most probably in life-ruining punishments.

Now however, my anger-fuelled, generalized opinion that everyone was selfish had been challenged profoundly. Over a hundred people had shown me that much. My decision to leave Hong Kong was also under question. The local people had shown me that I was in fact contributing something and making a positive impact on them – maybe it wasn't time to leave yet?

The unfortunate issue was, that in order to get my job back, I had to get out of the police dilemma; teaching from the inside of a prison cell wouldn't be practical. I tried to watch a film at home in an attempt to clear my head. Unfortunately, I picked *Oblivion* with Tom Cruise, which only succeeded in further befuddling my confused mind. Full of nerves and anxiety, I tossed and turned for the majority of the night and must have got up to go to the toilet twelve times. I hadn't drunk much water so I was surprised and annoyed at the frequency of my trips.

I arose, stuck to my sweaty bed-sheets, at twelve, paced around the flat agitatedly not knowing what to do with myself for a couple of hours, had a coffee, put on some combat shorts and a long sleeved white T-shirt and headed to the police station; hopefully for the last time.

"Afternoon," Dixon and Liu greeted me in unison. "We have a busy day ahead."

"Everything is in place," Dixon said after taking a sip of Chinese tea from an oversized flask.

"What's the plan, then?"

"The three of us will go to Pak Mai," Liu said. "Dixon knows a spot where we can look out without being seen. We will wait until something happens. I need you to identify the criminals then when the time is right, we will call the back-up and make the bust."

I hadn't envisaged being so heavily involved. I thought I had done my part in the bargain by giving the tip-off.

"OK. I don't want to be seen when you make the arrests though," I said. "I don't want them to know about my involvement."

"Yes, I understand," Dixon replied. "You will not be there when the arrest takes place. You can leave once you have identified the men. A colleague will drive you away from the scene so there is no danger that they will see you."

Dixon's phone rang and he left the room and stood just outside to take it. He seemed very calm about the situation. He was a high-ranking experienced police officer who had probably done this kind of thing many times before. His relaxed manner was not infectious though. I was scared and stressed and Liu was visibly tense.

"Let's go," Dixon said.

We walked outside into the congested car park where Dixon slightly embarrassed himself by trying to use the electronic locking device on his keys too early so it didn't work. After giving up with technology and manually unlocking the doors of an unmarked police car – a white Toyota which had seen better days – he got in the driving seat. Liu took the passenger seat and I sat uncomfortably in the back, my legs cramped behind Dixon's seat, which, in spite of his short legs, was as far back as it could go. Dixon started the car up and we set off to Hong Kong's far outskirts.

Dixon and Liu chattered animatedly in Cantonese in the front as I sat feeling like a spare part. We got caught in traffic at the cross-harbour tunnel, and it took half an hour to get to Kowloon-side. I was quietly disappointed that Dixon didn't pull out a portable siren and put it on the roof of the car. The roads freed up after that and we buzzed past innumerable skyscrapers, shopping malls and residential housing before getting on to the motorway. After nearly an hour, and fast approaching the border with

Shenzhen, Dixon took a sharp left down a winding side-road where he skillfully negotiated the narrowness and sharp turns for a further fifteen minutes before abruptly stopping the car by the side of the road, seemingly in the proverbial middle of nowhere.

"We are here," he said.

Dixon led us up a steep hill via a well-worn path and heavy overgrowth. I could feel mosquitoes biting at my flip-flop-clad feet. Why are the bastards so keen on ankles? After an uncomfortable and sweaty twenty-minute trek, the path cleared and we found ourselves at the top of a modest-sized hill with a beautiful sea view that, for once in Hong Kong, was not obstructed by massive buildings. In the far distance, I could just make out the silhouettes of some cranes which I assumed to be aiding to the construction of Shenzhen's latest skyscrapers. The hill we were on sloped gently down towards a narrow road which was approximately two hundred metres away – although I'm poor at judging distances, to the point where I've long been in denial about definitely requiring glasses.

Beyond the road was a vast, grubby pebble-beach which was scattered with pools of water shimmering in the fading afternoon sunlight. It was by no means an idyllic beach and I doubted that anybody would ever choose to visit. Even the Filipinas, who spend their Sundays having their picnics huddled underneath motorway flyovers, would concede that this was not a pleasant beach. Dixon called me to stand closer to him, then pointed to a rickety old pier which was jutting out of the pebbles and into the gentle waves of the navy blue sea.

"That's Pak Mai waterfront," he said. "According to what you heard, that is where the ship will drop off their drugs."

The deserted pier made a logical choice for Nigel's operations. There was no sign of civilization and even now, in the late afternoon, there were no cars on the roads and nobody nearby. Furthermore, it was so close to the Shenzhen border that it would be convenient to shift the drugs into the mainland from here. After taking in my surroundings, the enormity of the next few hours began to dawn on me. Everything was going to come to a head. Dixon advised me to sit down as we were likely to be here for "a while."

Waiting for any action to ensue was both nerve-shredding and arduous. For the first hour we sat patiently, barely talking, staring at the shimmering water. Liu and Dixon spoke intermittently, laughing a few times, probably at my expense, but then drifting back into comfortable silence. At five o'clock, Liu seemed to become restless and stood up to stretch her legs. Dixon followed her lead and a few minutes later, started to perform some impressively flexible, homoerotic tai chi manœuvres. I remained seated as this went on. We were waiting on a high-profile criminal drug-bust and my associates were acting like they should be in a lycra-clad eighties fitness video. There were some things that I would never quite get in Hong Kong.

Fortunately, the stretching and thrusting ceased and the police officers sat back down near me in time to witness the start of a quite stunning sunset. The entire sky was lit a brilliant firey orange as the sun began its steady descent. The white puffy clouds turned varying shades of red, yellow and then dark purple, creating shapes of anything your imagination wanted. (I'm a believer that cloud shapes, like dreams, are something that you should enjoy yourself, and it is boring and unnecessary to explain in detail how you can see a snake with a dog's head breathing fire. Keep it to yourself.) That said, this was the best sunset I'd ever seen, certainly in Hong Kong and possibly anywhere. The sight kept me transfixed in a hypnotic state for its duration until the sun finally vanished beyond the horizon and the sky gradually turned a shade of dark treacle as nightfall set in. My inappropriately-timed, sunset-influenced tranquility was cut short by Dixon suddenly standing upright and staring intently at the sea.

He said something quietly yet aggressively in Cantonese, then for my sake, "I think that's it."

At first I thought he was simply stating that the sunset was over, which didn't really need saying. However, as I followed his gaze, I noticed the tiny silhouette of a boat on the horizon. It hadn't occurred to me that this was the first boat we had seen. I felt a shot of adrenaline and pondered two key questions. "Is this the ship full of drugs?" and "How far away is the horizon?" I considered asking the latter to Dixon but didn't want to appear dim. Is a man supposed to know how far away the horizon is? Is it one of those things – like the first three digits of Pi – that a man is expected to know?

The police officers were talking, sounding both excited and angry at the same time. It's difficult to tell if Chinese people are arguing with each other or not. We watched intently as the boat gradually got closer and became clearer.

To use a cliché, it was now or never. If I was going to tip off Frank about the police, I had to do it now. The boat was fast approaching and I assumed that Nigel, Frank and anyone else involved would soon be at the pier waiting to pick up the goods. With Dixon and Liu continuing to shout at / talk amiably to each other, I reached into my pocket and snuck out my newly-acquired, secondhand, Motorola phone. I'd keyed in Frank's number in anticipation of this situation right now. Being a different phone and sim-card, anything I sent them could not be traced back to me. I figured that all I had to do was send a simple anonymous text saying, "Tell Nigel to abort the shipment. The police know."

Surely that was all the information that was needed?

Dixon had stopped talking now and was in the process of taking his own phone out, presumably to call for backup. He had his back turned and Liu was staring at the emerging ship. The pair of them were oblivious to my existence. I scrolled down to Frank's number and the empty screen as my mind weighed up the dilemma for the seven thousandth time. I started to type. It was an old phone so no predictive text. With my phone held inconspicuously by my right hip I started to punch in the letters. "Tell Ni…."

I was interrupted as Liu suddenly turned round and stared straight at me.

"They are coming," she said and pointed to a black people-carrier that was winding round a corner trailed by a small red car.

The vehicles lacked a sense of urgency and appeared to be moving at the pace of a funeral procession. The cars ambled towards the pier which was now barely visible in the evening's darkness. Dixon turned and looked while moving his phone up to his left ear.

"OK. Lie down," Dixon instructed me.

On descending to my lying position, I skillfully slipped the phone which was midway through the message back into my pocket just in time before Liu looked straight at me again and nodded. I wasn't sure what she meant by the nod. Did she want me to do something? Had she seen the phone?

Juxtaposed with the slow pace of the lumbering cars, the boat was hurtling through the water now, chopping through the sea, leaving a frothy white v-shaped trail in its wake. As it got closer, I could make out a diminutive, dark grey speed-boat with three men on board.

As the cars finally meandered around a final corner and began to slow to a halt close to the pier, Dixon, who was positioned in a plank position, hung up the phone and looked at me.

"OK. Backup is waiting and they can be there in three minutes. We just need you to identify the men; then we can move in.

"Take this," he said and, seemingly pulling them out from nowhere, handed me a small pair of binoculars. My mind continuing its strange habit of wondering wildly in critical situations, I found myself thinking about *Robin Hood Prince of Thieves* and the scene where Morgan Freeman uses a telescope. Surely telescopes weren't invented in that time? I peered through the cylinders and the size of the cars multiplied fourfold. I could make out that the people-carrier was navy-blue in colour and Nigel was behind the wheel. My heartbeat accelerating rapidly, I focused on the red Ford Fiesta behind and recognized Frank as the driver.

The cars parked up and Nigel got out of the car and stretched his arms. He was dressed more casually tonight, wearing a pair of jeans and a striped rugby shirt. Frank had now clambered out of the Ford which looked too small for him. It wasn't an appropriate car for a large middle-aged man. He was wearing his usual uniform of combat shorts and a baby-blue polo-neck. He walked and stood slightly further away from Nigel than you would stand from a friend. The two men simultaneously pulled out packs of cigarettes and Nigel offered his associate a lighter before sparking his own. They left the cars behind and headed on to the beach and towards the pier.

The boat was hurtling towards the pier and would be there before they finished their cigarettes. Liu's and Dixon's attention was on me now, so as a result, the decision had been made for me – I wasn't going to text Frank. I was selling him high and dry; he was going to be arrested imminently and it was because of me.

"That's them," I said, identifying Nigel and Frank.

Immediately Dixon called his colleagues and told them the information.

It was done.

CHAPTER THIRTY-ONE

After a prompt phone-call, Dixon put his hand on my shoulder, looked me sincerely in the eye and nodded his head.

"Thank you," he said. "My colleagues will be here soon. Your work is done now. Liu will drive you back."

"I want to stay," I said. I had to see what happened next.

I stared at Frank, feeling deeply sorry; but then watched with an astonished curiosity as he stuck his hand deep into his shorts' oversized pockets and pulled out his phone. He stared intently at it for a few seconds then tentatively walked over and handed it to Nigel. Nigel flicked his half-burnt cigarette to the floor and looked at the message before staring to the sky and placing his hands on his head. What did the message say? Had my phone brushed against my pockets and sent him the barely coherent, half-message?

Nigel proceeded to pull out his own phone, punch a number in and make a call. He stopped walking towards the pier.

Dixon who was also staring through binoculars and Liu, who had to make do with the naked eye, were staring at the scene unfolding, their eyes flashing from the beach to the boat. What on earth was happening?

Dixon pulled out his phone again and spoke hurriedly to the backup.

I stared at the boat which was now fast approaching the pier, then saw that the captain, whose face I couldn't make out clearly yet as he was wearing an unseasonal woolly hat, was talking on his phone.

I looked back at Nigel. They must be talking to each other? What message had Frank received?

Perplexed, I watched as the boat abruptly stopped about twenty metres from the pier. I hadn't noticed its motor sounding before, but an eerie silence fell as it ground to a halt. I watched as the captain frantically stood up from his chair, and walked to the back of the boat.

"What's going on?" Dixon asked angrily.

The three of us watched as the hat-wearing boat captain called his partners to the back of the boat and they all disappeared out of our sight.

In addition to my straining eyes, my senses were further heightened when I heard the high-pitched wailing of police sirens. I looked back up to the road where three police cars were now flying towards the pier. Nigel and Frank stopped walking towards the pier and started to walk with urgency back towards the road. Something was up.

"What the hell is happening?" Dixon asked again, rhetorically.

The captain and his pals came back into view from the back of the boat. They were wearing high visibility life jackets. In astonishing scenes, I looked on as two of the men jumped into the sea and started to swim away from the boat, clumsily thrashing but making good ground as the incoming waves helped their cause. The third man was pouring a clear liquid all over the boat from what looked like an oversized watering-can.

Back on the beach, Nigel was splashing through the shallow puddles and sprinting away from the scene with Frank struggling to keep up. They had become visibly aware of the three police cars that were closing in on them and must have known that there was little chance of escape.

In the sea, two of the smugglers had quickly swum a good distance away from the boat and were nearly at the pier. The third man had finished emptying the liquid and I watched as he pulled out a lighter and in one dexterous movement, jumped into the water while throwing the light back onto the boat. A fluorescent, yellow glint appeared gradually at first before vicious orange flames lashed through the entire boat as it went up in flames with dark clouds of thick, black smoke rising from the carnage.

"No!" exclaimed Dixon, disbelievingly. "How did they know?"

The police cars screeched to a standstill, parking at ugly angles in the middle of the road and blocking in Nigel and Frank's cars. Resigned, the two men realized that there was no point in sprinting, and gradually slowed to a halt. With the glow of the burning vessel illuminating the night sky, two policemen got out of their cars and proceeded to handcuff Nigel and Frank, who offered no resistance.

Dixon began shouting incoherently in Cantonese, while Liu remained silent, simply staring; crestfallen at the night's events. In the aftermath we saw the swimming drug smugglers greeted by police officers at the pier and also handcuffed. Within five minutes, it was all over. Nigel and Frank were arrested and taken away in the police cars. They had got the right men but they hadn't got any evidence.

"We have nothing," he said dejectedly. "They will walk away."

In the Honda civic on the way back, the mood was tense. Dixon was devastated and Liu was silent. They had been so close to getting their men, but had simply watched as it all – to use an unavoidable cliché – had gone up in flames. I was baffled by the entire proceedings and couldn't get my head around what had happened. I checked my phone and my message hadn't gone through to Frank, so who had sent him the tip off? Who knew?

I sat in an awkward silence that was sporadically punctured by Chinese swear words, "Aiya!"s and exasperated groans.

"What now?" I finally asked.

"We have a long night ahead. We will be questioning the men and trying to get a confession which won't come," Liu responded. Then after some deliberation, she said, "You can go home."

"Sorry?" I asked, struggling to hide my excitement. "I can go?"

"Yes, you did all that we asked," Dixon said. "We will take you home and then we won't see each other again. Do not tell anybody about any of this."

"But you haven't got the cocaine?" I stupidly asked, seemingly determined not to get out of this mess.

"But nobody else does. The cocaine is gone. We won't get the arrests, but we have stopped millions of dollars of drugs from entering Hong Kong," Liu said. "In fact much more, I doubt these men will be stupid enough to try anything else now."

This was all true. I suddenly began to feel a euphoric wave sweep over my body. I was free. The whole barely believable tale couldn't have had a better conclusion. I had done my job and it was probable that Frank would walk free.

*

We arrived back on Jaffe Road at ten p.m. and all three of us got out of the car. Liu took me by surprise and embraced me and I smelt her vanilla hair shampoo for the last time. After waiting patiently, Dixon came over and, for the first time, gave me a firm, solid handshake. He meant it.

"Thank you, Troy," he said, looking into my eyes. "Now, please stay out of trouble."

I watched the two police officers get back into the car and drive off in the opposite direction from my apartment, signaling the end of my role as a police informant

CHAPTER THIRTY-TWO

It was over. Well, nearly. I rang Dom and told him the whole story. This was a story that didn't need exaggerating. He sounded truly, momentously relieved and was delighted with the successful outcome. I could tell that he was pleased with himself for his role, which was entirely justified. If it hadn't been for him, I wouldn't have got out of the whole mess. I told him how he'd saved me and thanked him profusely, to the point where he had to cut me off as I was becoming maudlin.

"So, who sent the message then?" he asked.

"I honestly have no idea, mate. Whoever it was picked their moment. The timing was unbelievable."

"It really was. You don't need to know though, do you? It doesn't matter. Forget about the whole thing. Well, don't do that, because it's an incredible story and I'll probably never hear a better one in my life!" he said.

We bid farewell and arranged to meet for fajitas and beer later in the week. We agreed that we needed to find a new local pub as Spicy Fingers had been irreversibly tainted. Whatever else had happened in Hong Kong, I'd made a fantastic friend in Dom.

Feeling happy and deliriously tired, I went to bed. How on earth have things worked out this well? I thought, before the racking of my brain to the unanswered question was ousted by my need to sleep and I drifted into a deep, dreamless slumber.

I awoke early on Wednesday morning and was initially in a thoroughly jubilant mood. Despite the minor snag of my girlfriend leaving me for my friend, it had been a remarkable few days. I had my job back, I'd assisted the police in stopping a boat-load of drugs from getting into Hong Kong and incredibly, improbably, I was free. However, not letting me rest on my laurels, was a constant nagging at the back of my mind. Who sent the text? What did it say?

Just as I was pouring a bowl of cornflakes, I was startled to receive a text message. It was from Frank.

"Just to let you know, I'm leaving Hong Kong so don't try to get in touch with me. All the best."

Rather recklessly, I decided that I would call Frank. Although extremely bland, his message was friendly so I was almost certain that he had no idea of my police involvement and I was intrigued as to what had happened.

"Alright," he answered groggily.

"Hi, I just got your message. I'm surprised you're going. I thought you loved Hong Kong?"

"Yeah, I've had enough of it mate. Things got a bit much for me, it's not a healthy lifestyle."

"What do you mean?" I asked with a skillful ignorance.

"Well, I got into a bit of shit last night."

"Really?"

"Yeah, really…" He paused, probably considering whether or not to tell me the story. "I got arrested."

"What?"

"Don't worry. It's alright. They couldn't charge me with anything."

"Jesus, Frank. What happened?"

"Well, long story short; we were trying to get some coke in but the police knew about it and were waiting for us," he said. "Fortunately we got rid of the drugs just in time."

"So they couldn't charge you?"

"Nope, they've got no evidence, so we're free. It was a bloody close shave though. And we lost a few quid in the process," he said seeming oddly casual about it. "That's that for me now. No more drug shenanigans."

"How did you know that the police were coming?"

"One of the bosses saved us, he texted me saying to abort the deal."

"Nigel, the guy you told me about?" I asked, just to evidence that I had no idea what had happened.

"No, he got arrested with me. It was the top Chinese guy that we work with. He shifted our coke to the Triads."

"How did he know that the police were after you?"

"Well, here's the fucked up bit. He said he'd been worried that the police were on his case for a while and he'd been telling us to be extra careful with this delivery. Anyway, yesterday, he found some wires in his house. He found one of them in the fucking *Guinness Book of Records* apparently; ridiculous! He reckons that the police must have snuck into his flat when he was out and bugged him."

Frank continued. "He rightly assumed that if the police had managed to bug him, they'd be all over us."

"Fucking hell, that's lucky," I said.

"Tell me about it! Thank god he texted me just in time. If he'd been five minutes later, we'd all have been fucked."

So it was Raymond. My instinct had been right all along; he was involved with the Triads. He'd been incredibly fortunate that the lead the police had chased was for a legitimate deal. How had he got away with it? A warm feeling of comfort swept through my body, filling in the final holes of worry. If he thought the police had bugged him, he couldn't have suspected me.

I hid any signs of emotion at the revelation and Frank and I continued to talk amiably. He told me that he was, "done with Hong Kong for good." The arrest had shaken him up badly and he said he had reassessed his life when sitting in the cell overnight. He told me that his involvement with drugs was over and he was going to drastically change his lifestyle.

"Are you going back to England then?" I asked.

"Don't be stupid. No, I'm moving to Thailand. I decided this morning after getting out of the cells. I know some lads who run a bar in Pattaya so they'll put me up until I sort myself out."

This didn't sound like much of a lifestyle change at all. We made conjectural plans to meet up before he left but deep down I knew that I was never going to see him again.

Feeling overjoyed and delighting in not having tense, negative feelings coursing through my whole body, I put the kettle on and sat down on the sofa, exhaling exaggeratedly to add to my overwhelming feeling of well-being. I'd come full circle. I'd ended up in exactly the same position as I was in before setting off to the chemist to buy my hay-fever tablets on that March afternoon. What a ride it had been.

So many of the people that had shaped my last year were no longer going to be part of my life; Sander, Kris, Anna, Frank, Dixon, Liu, Browny, Raymond, Cody, Nigel. Sophie. It's funny how people that have such a huge impact on your life appear to mean so much to you, then suddenly they are gone and will become nothing more than a mixed bag of memories. They will get on with their lives, I will get on with mine and I will soon be completely irrelevant to them – a man whom they used to know. This chapter of my life was over. Done.

I was abruptly snapped out of my thoughts (and startled to hear the sound of a key rattling in my front door). My heart started to pound as the handle turned. Was it Raymond? Had he pieced it together and realized that it was me that had bugged him? Even worse, had Nigel found out what I'd done? Had he sent someone to kill me?

The door flew open, and thankfully, there was no gun-wielding gangster letting himself in to my flat.

"Carmella, it's lovely to see you," I said, and genuinely meant it. It really was.

"Hello Mr Troy!" beamed my smiling Filipino friend, then threw her arms around my neck and gave me a long, heartfelt hug.

"You've arrived at a good time. I've just put the kettle on. Do you want a coffee?"

"That would be lovely."

We chatted about her trip for a while. She told me that she had a fantastic time at the wedding.

After finishing her coffee with an exaggerated slurp, she said. "You know you've been here for almost a year."

"You've got to be kidding me!" I replied, shocked. I'd completely lost track of time. "Really?"

"Yep, it will be exactly one year next week," she said and started to grin. "When are you going back to England? It must be soon?"

"Do you know what, Carmella? I'm not sure I'm going back yet. I think I might do another year after all."

She walked over, with her grin turning into high-pitched laughter and her hand held out in expectation. After a second of confused deliberation, I reached into my trouser pocket, took out my wallet and handed her a crumpled twenty-dollar note.

**We are interested to know how you enjoyed reading
Andrew Carter's *Bright Lights and White Nights*.**

Write to our email address, giving us a few sentences which you
are willing for us to publish,
describing your response to this book.
If your comments are chosen to be included
in our E-Newsletter or website,
we will select another title published by Proverse
and send you a complimentary copy.
Please include your name, email address and mailing address
when you write to us, and state whether or not we may cut or edit
your comments for publication.
We will use your initials to attribute your comments.

**Find out more about
Our authors
Our books
Our events
And the international Proverse Prize**

Visit our website
<http://www.proversepublishing.com>

Visit our distributor's website
<www.chineseupress.com>

Follow us on Twitter
Follow news and conversation: <twitter.com/Proversebooks>
OR
Copy and paste the following to your browser window and follow the
instructions:
https://twitter.com/#!/ProverseBooks

Request our free E-Newsletter
Send your request to info@proversepublishing.com.

Ebooks
Most of our titles are available also as Ebooks.